**"YOU PROMISED!" HIS VOICE SOUNDED
WOUNDED AND
A LITTLE DESPERATE.**

"Promised?" Ginger said in angry confusion.

"Remember? You always kept your promises, Ginger."

"We're not children anymore!"

Devin's eyes were firm and intense as he looked at her, but his face was pale. "No, we're adults. All the more reason why promises should be kept."

"You tricked me," she objected weakly.

"I didn't trick you. *I* was serious. You've always wanted to bolt from uncertainties. You haven't changed much in that respect. Why don't you try facing it—facing me? I expect you to keep your word and see me."

"For how long?" she asked bitterly.

"For as long as it takes."

All Our Tomorrows

**Books by
Lori Herter**

No Time for Love
Too Close for Comfort
To Have and to Hold
All Our Tomorrows
Private Screenings

All Our Tomorrows

Lori Herter

SPEAKING VOLUMES, LLC
NAPLES, FLORIDA
2017

All Our Tomorrows

ISBN 978-1-62815-675-1

CHAPTER ONE

Ginger looked out her kitchen window as she stood at the sink sipping her morning orange juice. The sky was cloudless. The slowly rising sun flooded the hay fields of the small farm she loved to gaze at, which was visible to the distant left. Below, in the rose garden immaculately kept by her landlady, buds of varying shades—yellows, pinks, and reds—were breaking forth into glorious bloom.

Ginger Cowan had always been happy to have been born and raised on Whidbey Island, but on beautiful spring days such as this she felt especially blessed. Though Seattle and the mainland were only thirty miles away by ferry, the bustle of the large city had little effect on the quiet, small-town pace of Langley. And that was the way Ginger liked it.

She would walk to the shop again today, she decided. It took a little longer than driving, but she knew she needed the exercise. After all, she would be thirty years old in less than two years. If she didn't lose her extra fifteen pounds now, she might never.

She glanced at her watch. It was a little after nine and about time to leave. She usually opened the shop at nine thirty, though if she didn't open until ten it didn't make much difference. Still, she ought to maintain some discipline in her easygoing little world. Sometimes she thought her life had become too easy.

As she rinsed out her empty glass in the sink, the phone rang.

"Hi, it's Val," responded a clear, bright voice when she answered. Ginger smiled as she heard the wailing cry of one of her sister's three young children in the background.

"How is everyone?" Ginger asked.

Her sister groaned. "Well, everyone was nice and quiet half a minute ago." Val's voice faded as she apparently turned her face from the receiver to yell, "Brian, stop that! You and your brother go help Lisa find the finger paints."

In a few seconds everything was quiet and Val was back on the line. "That should give us about three minutes of peace. Gee, Ginger, isn't it dull in that quiet attic of yours? Wouldn't you like to borrow some kids to liven things up?"

"I'd love to, so long as it's only for a weekend," Ginger joked.

"Sometimes I think you were smart never to marry again! Ginger, the reason I called is—I heard some news via the Coupeville grapevine that I thought you'd want to know." Val was referring to the town on the northern half of the island where they had both grown up and where Val and her family still lived.

"Oh?" Ginger sounded nonchalant, but in fact she was holding her breath, bracing herself just a bit. There was something in her sister's tone of voice.

"Grace Smith—you know, whose farm borders the MacPhersons'—was in our antique shop the other day. She told Mom she heard from Bob MacPherson that—Devin is moving back to Seattle." Val's voice had grown hesitant. "His firm is transferring him back to their Seattle branch, and Devin's going to be made a partner."

"Oh." Ginger's hands shook slightly as she took in the news. Her voice grew waspish and flippant. "He must be disappointed. He probably was hoping for New York City!"

"No. They say he asked to be transferred from Chicago back to Seattle." There was a momentary hush over the phone as neither sister said anything.

"That's odd." It was the only response Ginger could think of while sustaining the shock of the news.

"Mom was kind of upset about it," Val continued. "You know how she is, always dwelling on how he ruined your life. I told her it's not going to matter. He'll be living and working in Seattle. He'll probably only come to the island occasionally to see his family. There's no reason why you should ever have to meet him, living there in Langley as you do. And if we happen to run into him sometime when he's in Coupeville, well, so what? We've been ignoring the MacPhersons at church all these years anyway. It won't make much difference."

Ginger sensed that her sister was trying to ease her mind.

"Sure," Ginger said, managing to regain some composure. "Let him come. What Devin MacPherson does is of no consequence to me. I'm sure he's forgotten me, and I never think of him anymore. Really. I'll be fine."

There was an earnest, calm quality in Ginger's tone that made her sound perfectly in control. Val could not see Ginger's trembling fingertips or the shaken look in her widened brown eyes.

"I know you will be. I wasn't so sure when you saw him at his mother's funeral . . ." Val said.

"Oh, well, funerals are always upsetting," Ginger said with a nervous little laugh. "And that was six months ago. I haven't given it a thought since. Anyway, Val, like you say, I probably won't run into him."

"Even so, I think you can handle it," Val agreed. "Oh, one more thing . . ."

"What?"

"Well, like you, he's never remarried. Maybe he'll try to—you know, get back with you again. You and he were so close once."

"Oh, don't be silly! If he decided he could do without me eight years ago, I don't see why he'd come back for me now. He's probably used to a different type of woman altogether—the type he left me for." Ginger noticed that her voice was growing bitter, and she tempered herself. "No, Val," she said, trying to put some self-mocking humor into her tone, "he's not going to come knocking at my door."

"Well, you never know—" Val began, and then there came the sound of screaming children drowning her voice. "Oh! Sorry, but I've got to go before they get paint all over everything. Will you be coming to see us this weekend?"

"Saturday morning!" Ginger responded. She feigned her usual enthusiasm for such visits. "I'll leave the shop closed all weekend."

"Aunt Ginger's coming!" she heard Val tell the kids, and then came a loud, high-pitched cheer. "We'll see you then!" Val said, laughing as she hung up.

Carefully Ginger hung up her own phone. She stood silently for a moment, staring out the window at a distant stand of fir trees that bordered the farm. She mustn't be alarmed, she told herself. Val was right; there was little chance she and Devin would ever see each other. She had no idea why he had decided to move back to Washington, and she was certain it had nothing to do with her. It was just the idea of his living in the area again. She had grown comfortable with him being two thousand miles away in Chicago.

11

She glanced nervously at her watch as she walked to her small bedroom to check her appearance in the dresser mirror. After touching up her medium-length dark blond hair, whose loosely curled locks casually framed her face, and applying a little pink-tinted lip gloss to her mouth, she grabbed her purse and left.

She walked down the back-stairs entry to her attic apartment. Stepping down the outside steps onto the gravel driveway, she saw her gray-haired landlady watering the garden with a hose.

"Good morning, Mrs. Poole! Pretty day, isn't it?"

"Yes, indeed!" Mrs. Poole replied with a smile. She was a widow who loved gardening, and she and Ginger had gotten on well over the years.

Ginger grinned and gave a wave as she continued down the driveway. As she walked out onto Third Street, she glanced back at the neat wood-frame house, painted yellow, that had been her home since she moved to Langley six years ago. It was an adorable little place, and she felt lucky to have found it.

After graduating from college, she had borrowed money from her parents, who owned an antique shop in Coupeville, to set up a shop of her own specializing in kitchen and dining room items imported from all over the world. She had chosen to move to Langley for several reasons. For one, it was located on the southern half of the sixty-mile-long island and was much closer to Clinton, where the Mukilteo ferry from the mainland docked. Its location was better for business from visitors from Seattle. Also, Langley was a small, turn-of-the-century town, not unlike Coupeville, but modernizing at a faster pace than her hometown.

But the main reason she had moved from Coupeville was to get away from the talk, the pitying looks of some of her neighbors, and the despairing remarks of her mother, whose character naturally tended toward the hysterical and pessimistic.

Almost eight years ago quiet, conservative Ginger Cowan had suddenly become a prime subject of gossip in Coupeville. She soon felt stifled in a town where everyone knew her humiliation. She found it hard to walk about town or attend the church she had gone to all her life without one or two of her neighbors or some relative eagerly showering her with sympathy, giving advice, and declaring their astonishment that Devin, that fine young man, could have behaved in such a despicable way. So she left, first to finish college out of state and then to settle permanently in Langley.

Now for the past six years she had led a peaceful life in Mrs. Poole's sunny little attic apartment. Her fledgling business had soon prospered, and her parents' loan had been repaid. She belonged only to herself now, and she was content.

As she gazed up the road with its comfortable homes and rural setting, she recalled how very careful she had been six years ago about deciding where to spend her life. She had been certain she wanted to stay on Whidbey, the long, narrow, crooked island lying in Puget Sound like an irregular stepping stone between the mainland and the Olympic Peninsula. Her roots were there. And she loved the island's rolling farmland, its thick forests and quaint towns, its many beaches and agreeable climate. She simply wouldn't live anywhere else.

But Whidbey Island also had many haunted places for her, places with unusual, romantic names and painful memories of Devin. There was Cranberry Lake at the northern tip of the island, where in their youth she and Devin had gone swimming a thousand times; and the bridge at Deception Pass, where they had first talked of marriage when she was only seventeen. And Double Bluff Beach, his favorite place, where he'd always said he would buy or build a house someday. Double Bluff Beach, she thought with dour amusement now, was located on Useless Bay. How appropriate.

Langley was one of the few places on the island that didn't harbor any memories she would do better to forget. Now she knew most people in town, was recognized as a clever businesswoman, and was quite well liked.

She turned down Anthes Avenue, which went gradually downhill to cross Second and then First Street. First Street, where her shop was located, bordered the beach and the cold, blue waters of Saratoga Passage. Across the passage she could see the dark green forests of Whidbey's smaller sister island, Camano.

As she came to Second Street she turned at the sound of someone calling her name. She smiled when she saw Marla Rosetti walking toward her, apparently coming from the real estate office where she worked as an agent. Tall and slim, with shoulder-length dark hair, she was a graceful image as she hurried her steps to meet Ginger.

"Hi! I'll walk with you a little way. I'm passing out our maps again. Want some for your shop?"

"Sure," Ginger said. "The tourists often ask for them." She took a wad of the rectangular printed maps of Whidbey Island which a local brokers' association had printed for its multiple-listing-service members to distribute.

"Free for lunch today?" Marla asked.

"Yes. In fact I'd like to meet you. I got a phone call from my sister . . ." Ginger left off uneasily.

"Something wrong?" Marla asked with immediate concern.

"Well . . . my ex-husband is moving to Seattle. Val heard about it from neighbors in Coupeville."

"Moving to Seattle," Marla repeated, appearing a trifle perplexed. "That's upsetting?" Her fine features took on a sober expression. "Has he threatened you or something?"

Ginger found herself feeling a little foolish. "No, no, of course not. It's just . . . why don't we wait and talk about it over lunch. We'll have more time then."

"Of course," Marla said, glancing at Ginger's tense smile.

They were in the business area of town now, which was basically confined to the two long blocks of First and Second streets between Anthes and another street called Cascade. The area immediately surrounding was residential, gradually becoming mixed with patches of farm, meadow, or forest further out. It was like a postage-stamp town; one could leisurely walk past all Langley's small businesses in a quarter of an hour.

Ginger's skirt and loose gauze blouse blew in the light morning breeze as they walked past small shops and offices and the chamber of commerce. Marla was chatting about a house she had just sold. She interrupted herself as they came to a stop at First Street, where Anthes Avenue ended.

"Whoops, I meant to drop some of these off at the chamber," she said, indicating her maps. "I'll have to backtrack. Usual time and place for lunch?" Ginger nodded. "Good. And don't look so worried, Ginger! We'll talk more later."

"Thanks, Marla," Ginger said with appreciation. She liked talking things over with Marla. It always made her see situations more clearly.

They had met by chance about four years before at the local beauty parlor, shortly after Marla had moved to the island. Ginger had been drawn to Marla's air of confidence and her svelte good looks, and she struck up a conversation as they sat for a few minutes in the waiting area. They had an immediate rapport. The friendship quickly grew and continued over the years, even though Ginger

14

sometimes felt herself a little out of her depth with Marla. Marla had such a quick mind. Nevertheless, she looked upon Marla as her best friend.

Ginger crossed First and turned right, passing the old totem pole standing near the wood staircase that led down to the beach. A few doors down, in a small wood frame building with large windows, was Ginger's Spice, the name she had given her shop when it opened.

After unlocking the door and fixing it to stay open with a doorstop, she walked by carefully arranged merchandise to her small private office at the back. She put away her purse and the maps and looked out the window for a moment at the sand beach below and the view of Camano Island. This was such a beautiful place to live and work, she thought moodily. Why had Devin been so bent on leaving the island?

Devin. She had hardly thought of him for months. And now, after Val's news, she was finding it difficult to think of anything else. Really, it would be much easier to forget the past if her family didn't keep reminding her of it.

How they all worried about her—her parents, aunts, and cousins back in Coupeville! Was she all right living all alone? Hadn't she met some nice man to marry yet? Didn't she want a family of her own? Only Val seemed to understand that her sister was perfectly happy as she was.

But even Val was still protective of Ginger when it came to Devin. Val had been the one who had found her that day in Seattle, much too soundly asleep in her bed, a bottle of sleeping pills on the night table. It was the morning after Devin had left for Chicago for good. Val had rushed her to the hospital, then was relieved to learn her sister had taken only a few of the pills. Providentially, Ginger had cried herself to sleep before deciding whether to swallow the rest of the bottle. She had never told Val that, but she knew Val suspected the truth even though Ginger always denied having had thoughts of suicide.

Val had told her parents, of course, and Ginger was put under lock and key in Coupeville for a while. It was then that she had decided she had to leave and had convinced her parents that the best thing for her was to finish college—in Oregon.

It was a wise decision. College business courses had given her the training with which she became self-sufficient.

15

She heard customers talking in the shop and went out to assist them. It turned out to be an unusually busy morning, but even so there was not quite enough distraction to keep her mind from wandering continually to Val's phone call.

As lunchtime approached Ginger grew more and more jittery. She was eager to talk to Marla. Marla was the only person who could laugh her out of her fretful mood.

"The idea of his living nearby makes me nervous. I don't want to run into him again," Ginger said as she poured herself more tea.

They were sitting at their usual front window booth in a small restaurant on Second Street. The real estate office where Marla worked was across the street, and her Out to Lunch note could be seen taped to the door.

Marla shrugged. "My former husband lives in Seattle, and it doesn't bother me any. In fact, when I was still living there, we used to work around the block from each other for a while. I'd run into him occasionally. It was no big deal," Marla said, opening the cellophane on the crackers that came with her chef's salad.

"I know, I'm—just being silly, I guess." There was a lost look in Ginger's beige-brown eyes. "He's been off in Chicago for so long, I don't know how to handle his being nearby."

"What is there to handle, for Pete's sake?"

Ginger felt a little bewildered. "I don't know. My own nerves, I suppose. If I should run into him—his family still lives near Coupeville—I'd want to be able to take the situation with composure. Besides, my family's always worried about me where he's concerned."

"Why?" Marla asked. Her discerning dark brown eyes were slightly troubled as she noted Ginger's averted gaze. "They don't think you should have ended the marriage?"

"No, they think I did the right thing. They just hold a lot of bitter feelings toward D-Devin." Ginger reddened a bit. Now she couldn't even pronounce his name without stuttering. Marla must think her a fool.

Her attractive friend eyed her almost suspiciously. "Why don't you tell me the whole story, Ginger. I'm willing to listen. Don't spare any gory details, either!"

Ginger laughed. One of the things she liked about Marla was her rather irreverent sense of humor. "All right," she replied, imitating Marla's tone, "get ready for an earful!"

"Really!" Marla exclaimed with a throaty little chuckle.

"It all started when I was five years old," Ginger began half-facetiously. "Devin was eight, and he rambunctiously ran into me in the church play area one Sunday morning and knocked me down. I started to cry, and he came back to see if I was all right. I had a skinned knee, so he brought me to my mother and apologized. Devin was a well-mannered young man even at age eight," she said a trifle sarcastically. "He always made a good impression on the grown-ups because he was so polite. I was impressed, too. As I grew older I developed a crush on him."

"He lived nearby?" Marla asked.

Ginger nodded. "On his family's farm, just outside Coupeville. I lived in Coupeville, above our antiques store, but we went to the same schools and attended the same church. Besides that, his mother liked antiques and often came to our store. She'd bring Devin and his older brother, Bob, along when they were still young. So our families knew each other pretty well, too. When I started high school we began dating—under my mother's strict supervision, of course. I was only fourteen."

Ginger looked nostalgic and rueful. "He was the only boyfriend I ever had. We grew very close in the next few years. He was a friend and companion besides being someone to date. We'd spend hours talking, confiding in each other. I've—I've never been that close to anyone else . . ." Ginger's voice trailed off.

"Did you sleep with him?"

The question broke Ginger's trance. She stared numbly at her friend for a fraction of a second. One thing dependable about Marla —she was direct! "No," Ginger replied with a slightly embarrassed smile. "I was brought up in a proper, old-fashioned, church-every-Sunday way. Although when Devin and I were older we had gotten beyond the necking stage. Maybe I was what you'd call a technical virgin."

Marla laughed. "Didn't he want to make love to you?" she asked curiously.

"Well, he was always so gentlemanly and polite, you see," Ginger replied, her tone ironic. "I was afraid to, and he never pressed the issue."

Marla nodded. "Actually, that was kind of nice."

17

"I used to think so," Ginger agreed sardonically. "I used to think he was wonderful! Everyone did. He was handsome and intelligent —he won scholarships for college because of his outstanding grades —diligent and hardworking, had a sense of responsibility . . . or so it seemed. He was the type every mother prays her daughter will marry. And I was lucky enough to marry him! So no, I didn't sleep with him until our wedding night. And then I wished I hadn't," she finished bitterly.

Marla's dark eyes widened in astonishment. "What a thing to say! Was he that bad a lover?"

"I—no—I don't know." Ginger's face sobered and paled a little. "The way he touched me—it was like I could have been any woman. He had changed toward me. I guessed then that . . ."

She paused. "I got a little ahead of my story. Devin was three years ahead of me in school, so I was still in high school when he started college in Seattle. For the first two years he lived at home and commuted. Things didn't change too much for us. We still saw each other a lot. His last two years he lived on campus in Seattle, and I saw less of him.

"I could sense him gradually changing. He was studying to be a CPA, and he began to talk about moving to Seattle to work. He said there wasn't enough opportunity on Whidbey Island. I liked living where I was, and his talk of moving bothered me. Still, I didn't want to stand in his way if it was better for his career. I was only seventeen, but we were already planning on marrying one day. And there were other little changes. He had worn glasses for a long time, and then suddenly he got contact lenses. He began wearing more expensive clothes and got a different haircut. He lost his small-town look. Sometimes I felt him growing away from me, but yet it didn't seem that his feelings toward me had changed. He still liked to talk with me, be with me . . . touch me . . ."

Ginger paused for a moment. She felt unexpected tears starting in her eyes, and she quickly quelled them. How stupid she was, she chastised herself. To still want to cry about it after all these years! Her eyes hardened and her voice toughened.

"Well, to make a long story short: He graduated from college and passed the CPA exam first try. He took a job with a large accounting firm in Seattle. We set a wedding date. His firm was headquartered in Chicago, and they sent him there to attend training seminars for a month. It was the month just before we were to be married. After he had been away a few days, he called me one night and said he really liked Chicago and the business opportunities there. Would I be willing to move there with him after we were married?

"I've never been to Chicago, but I've always had the impression it's a big, dirty, industrial city. I said no. The next week when he called, our conversation was difficult; he seemed distant and uneasy. Then, two weeks before we were to be married, he called again. He said: 'I have something that's difficult for me to tell you, Ginger.' " She imitated his words sarcastically, the hurt still showing in her voice. " 'I've met someone attending the training classes here, a local girl. I don't know how to say this, but . . .'

"He proceeded to tell me he found himself very attracted to this—girl. He said he was confused about his feelings and didn't know if he should go through with our wedding when he could find himself so drawn to someone else. He said he still cared for me, didn't want to hurt me, et cetera, et cetera; but he wanted to do what was best for us both. And he pointed out how young we both were: me, barely twenty, and he, twenty-three. I didn't think it was so young at the time, but now I look back on it, he was probably right about that.

"Anyway, I got pretty hysterical. Actually, I was shocked senseless. He had always been so devoted to me all those years. I had never worried about him meeting other women. And everything was set for the wedding. My dress and the bridesmaids' dresses were ready, the flowers were ordered, invitations had already been sent. It was a wedding everyone had been waiting for for years—his family and mine—and most of Coupeville, too."

"How terrible!" Marla said.

"Yes, and I was immature enough then to worry more about the humiliation of canceling the wedding than the fact that I might be losing him," Ginger said ruefully. "I felt so sure of him because of our long relationship that I thought once he was back home and with me he would quickly forget this passing fancy. I cried and pleaded with him over the phone. He tried to calm me down and said he would call again. I spent a horrible night and day waiting. Finally he phoned again and said he would marry me as planned."

Ginger interrupted herself with a weary sigh. "So we got married at our old Coupeville church," she continued, "with half the town present. We went to Lake Louise in Canada for our honeymoon. It's a beautiful place, but I would never go back again. When he made love to me—had sex with me would be describing it more accurately—I sensed something was still terribly wrong. I asked him, 'Did you have an affair with that girl in Chicago?' "

Ginger paused and swallowed. She had to drum up the stamina from somewhere to finish this disgusting tale. "He finally admitted he had. That was something I had never guessed he would do. I never thought he would be unfaithful. Never! But I could tell when we were in bed that something had come between us. He must have been thinking of her, wishing he were with her instead of me. That was why he was so—mechanical about it. He said he didn't tell me because he didn't want to hurt me. Thoughtful, wasn't he?" Ginger's voice had a bitter quality now.

"I don't know why he even went through with the wedding. For appearance's sake, I suppose. We tried living together in Seattle for a month, but it didn't work. I felt he had betrayed me. Everything we had—that pure, lovely relationship we had had—was gone. He broke it—by picking up with some easy girl who flirted with him in Chicago! There was nothing left for us. So he went back to Chicago where he wanted to be. His firm thought he had so much potential, they willingly transferred him there at his request. I went back to Coupeville and—well, you know the rest."

Marla shook her head sympathetically. "I'm sorry, Ginger. That must have been awful to live through. I've often sensed that you're leery of getting involved with a man. I can see why now."

Ginger chuckled grimly. "If someone like Devin could be untrue, any man could—probably would be! A woman is less likely to get hurt going it alone. You had a bad marriage. Don't you think the same?"

Marla was thoughtful for a moment. "I think I see men realistically now. Knights on white horses they aren't. My husband had a roving eye, but I don't think he was unfaithful. He was just unstable and couldn't even stay at one job for more than a few months. So yes, I decided I'd feel more secure going it alone. In a way, I do agree."

"Didn't you miss him, though?" Ginger asked.

Marla shrugged. "It passes." She watched Ginger lower her gaze. "Doesn't it? Are you still carrying a torch for Devin?"

As Ginger raised her eyes again, they flashed. "Are you joking? All these years I've been glad that he's been two thousand miles away! I wish he'd stay there!"

Marla stared at her, her dark eyes still and discerning. "You may not want him back, but—you still love him, don't you?"

Ginger was startled and rather horrified by the conclusion Marla had come to. "Not in the least! Why do you say that?"

"Because you're so afraid to see him. If you didn't care, it wouldn't matter to you where he was."

"No," Ginger said with a little laugh. "No! It's just that my family, especially my mother, will get upset at his being nearby. They've never forgotten what he did. And—well—I'd just as soon not see him, that's all. But I'm not still in love with him. I don't care about him! I told my sister that just this morning. He doesn't mean a thing to me."

"If you protest any more, you'll have me convinced," Marla said, smiling to herself.

Ginger looked at her in puzzlement. It wasn't like Marla not to take her at her word. And she was telling the truth!

"Well, I wouldn't worry about it too much," Marla said. "Ex-husbands sometimes pop up like bad pennies, but they can get lost as easily, too. Just concentrate on your own life and don't worry about him. Or your family, either. You're all probably upset for nothing."

"I know. You're absolutely right," Ginger agreed. She felt better now, having talked it out and gotten Marla's down-to-earth reactions. Marla always had so much common sense! Ginger wished she were more like her. Instead she sometimes feared she took after her mother, getting alarmed at every little thing.

"Sorry, what did you say? My mind wandered off," Ginger apologized, realizing Marla was talking.

Marla's eyes glinted with amusement. "I said I had dinner with Jack Whiting last night."

Ginger stared at her, speechless for a moment. She was aware of a slightly sinking feeling. "Jack?" she finally said with surprise. "Oh."

Marla studied her reaction for a half-second, then continued, unflustered. "I went to his gallery yesterday on my lunch hour to see if he had any paintings I liked. I've been wanting one to put over my fireplace. I told him what I was looking for, and we got to talking. I bought a painting—one of his own works, as it turned out—and when he was helping me put it in my car, he asked me to have dinner."

"Jack's a wonderful artist. What's the painting like?" Ginger asked with nervous interest.

As she listened to Marla describe the seascape she had bought, her mind was busy. She wondered if Marla remembered her mentioning in the past that she had gone out with Jack, too. She had been dating him casually since he had opened his art gallery in Langley about two years ago. She didn't talk about it much, but she was sure she must have mentioned him to Marla once or twice.

Ginger wasn't jealous. In fact, she might have been dating Jack much more frequently had she shown more interest in him in the beginning, had she not avoided his amiable passes. Now they were more like friends who enjoyed each other's company from time to time.

What worried her was what Marla's view of the situation would be. They had never found themselves dating the same man before. Would she view Ginger as competition? Would this get in the way of their friendship?

"So . . . how was the date?" Ginger asked with a smile when Marla had finished.

"Fine. I didn't know he could talk so much!" Marla said, chuckling.

"Yes, that's how he's gotten to know literally everyone in town since he moved here. He's—taken me out now and then . . . I think I've mentioned . . ." Ginger said with hesitation.

"I know," Marla said, still amused. "I remember you telling me after one date that he spent half the evening talking about other women he sees. He did the same thing last night! I had a hard time keeping myself from laughing sometimes. Really, I've never been out with a man who in the course of the evening gave me a list of everyone else he dates or has dated!"

Ginger began to laugh, too. "Was it that bad?" she asked with surprise.

Marla waved her hand, laughter still in her voice. "Oh, no. He doesn't mean to flaunt it. He's just an active, vibrant person with a lot of things going on in his life, and he likes to talk about it all. But it took me a little while to get used to it. He's kind of a character!"

"Yes, he is," Ginger agreed, relaxed now that they were laughing over the matter. "But fun to be around. Will you go out with him again?"

Marla shrugged. "Why not? It would be worth it just for the fun of comparing notes with you afterward!"

Ginger started laughing again. Discussing men with Marla was always amusing. "Marla!" she said, pretending to chide. "Is that nice?"

"Whoever said I was nice?" Marla retorted.

CHAPTER TWO

After lunch Ginger went back to her shop. It was a slow afternoon, compared to the flurry of customers she had had that morning. She got out a dust cloth and began going over some of the merchandise displayed in the window and inside the shop.

It was a job she was used to. From childhood on she had helped out in the family antiques shop, dusting and polishing. It was one of the reasons she had decided against opening an antiques store of her own—she thought modern merchandise would be easier to keep clean.

As she dusted her imported china pieces and silver servers, the wooden bowls and cutting boards, the cutlery and kitchen gadgets, she tried diligently to keep her mind from wandering to Devin. She knew from the grapevine gossip her family kept her apprised of that Devin had apparently become very successful, making an unusually fast rise to the higher echelons of his firm. No one had ever heard anything more of the young woman he had had his affair with.

No doubt it had only been his first affair, Ginger had long ago decided. He had probably found some flaw in her and had gone on to other women. He had become so disdainful toward the end, Ginger remembered now as she carefully polished a crystal fruit bowl. Nothing seemed quite good enough for him anymore. Whidbey Island was nothing to him, just a rural place with no opportunity for a rising young businessman. Even Seattle wasn't big enough or important enough, once he had seen Chicago. My, how he must have wanted to make his mark on the world, she thought bitterly, placing the bowl carefully on the shelf again.

When she was young she used to excuse his growing restlessness to be somewhere bigger and better. Because he had been such an outstanding student, she told herself that it was natural and right for him to want to achieve a certain status in life. It didn't occur to her then that he might want to discard her, too, because she wouldn't fit into his new life-style. She was just a small-town girl, nice enough and sweet enough, but not adequately chic and sophisticated to be an asset to him.

He had never actually said that, but she had guessed it. Ginger's confidence in herself, in her own attractiveness, had never been the same after that. Somehow she hadn't been good enough; why or how she had never been quite sure. But since he had betrayed her sexually, she assumed that she must not have been appealing enough physically to hold him. Their wedding night had been proof of that. When he made love to her that cold, miserable night in Lake Louise, it had been a humiliating experience. Her kisses and the loving warmth of her body apparently weren't enough to make him forget what he had found in another woman's arms.

So she wasn't sexy, she told herself now as she tossed away the used, dirty dust cloth. She didn't need a man in her life anyway. And she had no desire for marriage. Her one month of married life had been enough to sour her on the idea forever. The tense atmosphere, the sense of betrayal, the quiet, expressionless indifference of the man who had once loved her . . .

"I'm getting transferred to Chicago, Ginger. It's settled," he had told her one day after coming home from work to their apartment in Seattle. "You're welcome to come with me if you want."

The words echoed through her mind now. His tone had been calm and detached, as though it didn't matter to him what she answered. It was the manner he had used with her in the weeks after their ill-fated honeymoon: patient, yet indifferent. It was as though he had no emotions. He went on making his plans for his future as though he had already forgotten everything that had come between them and everything they had once been to each other. She felt as though she were someone who was just around, like a roommate he had lived with for a while but hadn't gotten to know too well. He had invited her to come with him as if out of good manners.

"I won't go to Chicago! You know that!" Her voice had been hoarse with emotion as she said the words.

He didn't answer.

"How can you expect me to move to the city where that—that woman is? How can you even ask it?"

Still he said nothing. The man she used to confide everything to,

25

who used to talk to her by the hour, said nothing. He was leafing through some business papers as if he didn't hear.

"This is the end of our marriage, Devin. The end of everything!"

He had slowly put down the papers at that, but he was still silent. He didn't look at her.

After watching him for a moment she had said, "It *is* all over, isn't it? It's been over since—since before we even took our vows. We shouldn't have gone through with the ceremony. You shouldn't have let my hysterics influence you so much. But that's all right." Her voice was quiet and defeated. "I'll remember it as your last kindness to me."

Kindness! she thought with rancor now. No, whatever it was she had needed to keep his love, she had certainly lacked it! And what would he think if he saw her today?

Dismally she sat down on the stool behind the cash register and absently fingered the edge of the tunic blouse that draped to her hips. She began assessing herself ruthlessly: a little too plump—with her fifteen extra pounds she might as well have had three kids like her sister, she thought, sighing; blond hair that was never quite blond enough to be striking; a pleasant but nondescript face; eyes that stayed round and innocent no matter what kind of makeup she tried using.

"How's it going, Ginger?"

She turned her head swiftly toward the open front door. "Hello, Jack! How are you?" she asked, startled.

"Fine!" he said with a broad smile, showing a row of large, even teeth beneath a wide, blond mustache. "But you look a little down. Would a light dinner and a movie cheer you up?"

She smiled and found herself feeling comforted by his amiable invitation. "Tonight?"

"Right now, if you're ready. It's almost five fifteen." He leaned his tall, rangy body against the doorframe. The sunlight from outside back-lighted his blond hair. The lines around his mouth and blue eyes betrayed his thirty-eight years, but the sense of physical energy he exuded and his lively, cheerful personality always made him seem younger.

Ginger often marveled at the way he seemed to dance through life, like Fred Astaire in an old movie. But she always knew she was Ginger Cowan, not the glamorous Ginger Rogers who so gracefully kept pace with Astaire. An evening with Jack's quick mind and

26

effusive personality tended to exhaust her. But she enjoyed his company, as long as it was in small doses.

"Five fifteen already?" she said with surprise and glanced at her watch. She was a little annoyed at having spent a whole afternoon raking up memories of the past. "Let's go! I'm sick of this place!"

Jack laughed in his hearty way. "You love this shop!"

She didn't deny it. Having started the shop from scratch and nurtured it into a successful business, it had become like her child and was, indeed, the very center of her life—as Devin had once been.

She emphatically pushed Devin from her mind once more as she hurried to her office to get her handbag. She locked the shop, and they left.

The movie theater was across the street and several doors down. When they reached it they found the feature about to start, so they decided to see the movie first and eat afterward. It was a comedy, and Ginger enjoyed it. Her spirits were lifted a bit as they went around the corner to a little restaurant that specialized in quiche and sandwiches.

As they sat at a small table, Jack talked at length about his gallery, about a talented woman artist he had had dinner with in Seattle, and then he mentioned Marla's having bought a painting. "You and she are friends, aren't you?" he asked, gesturing one hand toward her. Jack always talked with his hands.

"Yes. We meet for lunch a lot. She's really been a good friend to me."

"I enjoyed getting to know her," Jack went on. "We had dinner together that evening."

Ginger smiled. She had been waiting for him to mention it. She was beginning to wonder if there was an unmarried woman in a fifty-mile radius of Seattle that he hadn't had dinner with.

And yet he never quite spoke of them as dates. They were more like casual dinners with a friend—like her evening with him tonight. From his easy attitude it was impossible to tell if he was romantically involved with anyone.

"She mentioned it and said she had a nice time," Ginger told him. "Marla's a lively person, isn't she? Much more so than I am!" She realized she sounded like she was asking for a compliment and immediately wished she hadn't said that.

He tilted his head and looked at her with curiosity. "You are rather quiet, but interesting in your own way," he said with a smile. "You're an enigma! A pretty lady who runs her own business and lives alone in an attic." He was looking at her as if she were the subject of one of his haunting portraits. "You gaze about you with those quiet, warm, little-girl eyes, wanting to trust but a little wary, sometimes a little sad, but always—I don't know—complacent, as if your world were complete."

"Maybe it is."

"I hope it is, Ginger, for your sake. Sometimes I get an odd feeling with you . . ." he said, then trailed off as if searching for words.

"What?" Ginger was growing uneasy, but she wanted him to finish.

"As if you had cloistered yourself, purposely shut yourself off from the outside world."

"How can I be shut off when I'm in business?" Ginger argued. "I even went to Europe last year!"

"But your mental attitude isn't world oriented. I have the impression your mind is—stopped in time somewhere." He noted Ginger's troubled eyes and said, "Well, don't pay any attention to me. We artists always get carried away romanticizing."

He *was* getting carried away, she thought. She smiled and purposely changed the subject. "How would you describe Marla?"

He leaned back in his chair. "Marla. Well . . ." An appreciative look came into his eyes. "Quick, mysterious—a touch of fire in the eyes—"

Ginger leaned back in her own chair and listened. Marla may be in for a surprise, she thought with hidden amusement.

At her shop two days later Ginger got a phone call from Marla. "How about lunch?" she asked, slightly and uncharacteristically breathless.

"Sure," Ginger replied. "Anything wrong?"

"No . . . no, no. Usual time and place? See you then," she said and hung up.

A couple of hours later Ginger sat across from her friend at their favorite table. After they had ordered, Ginger said with a grin, "I think Jack may be interested in you! He took me out to dinner the other night, and I distinctly got that impression."

"That's nice. Ginger, I have some news for you. Now"—she

reached across the table to touch Ginger's hand—"it's nothing to get alarmed about."

Ginger immediately grew anxious. "What?"

"We have an ad in the Seattle papers for a house we're selling on Double Bluff Beach. It first appeared in this morning's paper. I got a call soon after I got to work from—a man named Devin MacPherson. He's interested in looking at the house. Now it's perfectly possible that two people could have the same name . . ."

Ginger was pale. "No. It must be Devin." She swallowed, for she could hardly speak. "When we were young he always said he'd like to have a house there." She put a trembling hand to her forehead and shook her head. "He's in Seattle already! I thought—I thought it would be awhile. It must have been old news when my sister heard it!"

"Now, Ginger," Marla said in a stern voice. "It doesn't mean you're going to see him. Keep your head!"

"I know. You're right. It was just the shock," she said, trying to compose herself. "I wonder why he'd want to live on Double Bluff Beach after all this time? It's not very convenient if he's working in Seattle."

"He said he was interested in it for weekends, although a lot of people do commute to Seattle."

"How—what did he sound like?" Ginger asked, her eyes stark, her breath arrested.

"Well, I don't know, Ginger. He was just a voice over the phone. Low and courteous, self-assured. He sounded nice enough."

Ginger nodded, understanding how ridiculous her question had been. "He's coming to look at the house?"

"Saturday morning."

"Will you be the one to show it to him?"

"Yes."

Ginger put her hand over her mouth and felt as if she couldn't breathe for a moment.

"Ginger, relax!" Marla admonished her. "Look at what an ideal situation it is. I can give you a full report on him, and you won't have to see him at all."

Ginger was breathing again, but unevenly. "You won't tell him—you won't mention me—"

"Of course not. There's no reason to mention I even know you!"

"He might ask if you know me. I suppose he may have heard I live in Langley," Ginger said apprehensively.

"If he asks, I'll just say I've met you. How's that?"

"I guess that's okay. I'm sorry to be so silly about this. I never expected that he'd want to buy a house on the island, or that he'd wind up talking to *you*. Maybe this island *is* too small." Her thoughts flew. "He's coming this Saturday! I was supposed to visit my family in Coupeville this Saturday!"

"So what? Go and visit them."

"But if he's going to be on the island, he might decide to go up to Coupeville, too. I'd better stay here."

"But he'll be coming here to our real estate office to meet me," Marla pointed out.

"Well, I'll just stay home, that's all."

"Ginger, that's ridiculous! You can't hide yourself away every time he comes around. Go to Coupeville and see your family. Even if he goes there, he won't look you up. Not if he knows how your family dislikes him. Maybe he doesn't want to see you, either!"

"Yes, you're right," Ginger said quietly, cowed by Marla's common sense. "Sometimes I'm afraid I'm just like my mother. You're absolutely right; I have to learn to live with this. I'll go to Coupeville."

Coupeville was busy with weekend visitors wandering through its numerous antiques stores on Front Street that Saturday. But her sister's house on the outskirts of town, where the family was gathered, was peaceful. Val's children were playing ball outside with their father and grandfather after lunch. The women were finishing up the dishes in the kitchen.

"We have a lot of leftovers," Val commented, putting plastic-wrapped food into her refrigerator. Val was a year younger than Ginger and about twenty pounds heavier. Though she had lost her figure, her easy manner and pleasant facial features hadn't changed much since her marriage to a local man seven years before. In appearance she resembled Ginger a bit, but she had inherited darker hair from her mother. In personality she took after her father and was usually calm and reflective, characteristics Ginger often wished she had inherited.

"It's no wonder we have leftovers," Martha Cowan said as she wiped the counter clean. "Virginia hardly ate a thing."

Ginger's eyebrows constricted in irritation as she loaded the last dish into the dishwasher. She hated the way her mother still called her Virginia, when everyone else had been calling her Ginger since childhood.

Martha had named her girls Valerie and Virginia because she liked the sound of the syllables on her tongue, and she would not give the names up. She had wanted a large family but had given birth to only two children. Her daughters had always thought this was fortunate. Martha, now in her fifties, had worn herself into ill health worrying about the two she had.

"I'm trying to lose weight," Ginger said. It was true, but the real reason she hadn't eaten much was because she felt almost sick with nerves knowing Devin was somewhere on the island.

"Lose weight!" her mother exclaimed. "You're just starting to look healthy! It's those loose blouses you always wear that make you look heavy." She settled her own portly body into a chair at the kitchen table and looked up at her eldest daughter. "You used to be so thin when you were a teenager," she said, shaking her gray head. "I'd take you to the doctor just to see if you were all right."

"And he always told you I was perfectly healthy," Ginger reminded her with a tolerant smile.

"Well, doctors don't know everything. What do you want to lose weight for? You look good! I'm glad to know you're eating enough, living alone like you do."

"You're always saying I should get married, Mom. Men like slender women," Ginger pointed out.

"Ha! You'd be surprised. Just because Devin used to like you when you were skinny doesn't mean all men would. And *he* certainly wasn't worth having! He has a lot of nerve showing his face in Coupeville! They say he visited his family here last Wednesday!"

A shudder ran through Ginger. She hadn't heard that.

"He has a perfect right to come here, Mom," Val said. She gave Ginger a quick glance. "I'll finish up. Why don't you sit down. Want some lemonade?" she asked gently.

"Uhm . . . okay. Thanks." Ginger smiled weakly and sat down, nervously toying with the drape of the cotton-print overblouse she was wearing over her blue jeans. She knew Val had detected her shock.

"Lemonade, Mom?" Val asked as she took a pitcher out of the refrigerator.

31

"No, thanks. I'm going to lie down in a minute. I hardly got any sleep last night." Martha shook her head disconsolately. Her brown eyes, permanently squinted from worry, carried a tragic expression as she looked at Ginger. "When I think of what he did to you—to all of us! When we welcomed him and accepted him like one of the family all those years! He was like a son to me—"

"Don't think about it, Mom," Ginger begged her, more for her own sake than her mother's.

Val set a tall glass of lemonade in front of Ginger. Nervously she took a sip.

"Well, I can't help it! All this news of his coming back! What if he tries to see you, Virginia?" Martha's voice was rising with impatient anxiety.

"He probably won't," Ginger said as persuasively as she could. She felt her own anxiousness escalating in response to her mother's.

"Oh, I wouldn't put it past him! Not after what he did, taking up with that woman when he was about to marry you!"

"Well, what if I do run into him?" Ginger said with a heavy sigh, feeling at the end of her tether. "I'll just say hello and good-bye and walk away."

"Oh, don't you believe it! He's a dangerous man, Virginia!" her mother said with emphasis. "He had your heart once and he won't have forgotten it. He might try to use you like he used that girl in Chicago. They say he never married her, you know. He could try to win you back, Virginia, use you, and then leave you like he did before! I'm warning you, he's dangerous! I'm certain of it! And if he hurts you again, I just don't know what I'll do. It'll be the death of me, I'm sure!"

"Mom, you're getting yourself all upset again over nothing," Val said. "You know the doctor said it's not good for you. Remember your blood pressure."

"What do doctors know?" Martha replied with a wave of her hand. "Remember," she said, addressing herself to Ginger again, "how you reacted when you saw him at his mother's funeral? Why you went, I'll never know. I told you not to!"

Ginger pushed the loose curls off her forehead with a tremulous hand. She was trying to keep her composure. "Mrs. MacPherson was always very kind to me. I used to admire her; she was such a lady. I—I just felt I ought to go."

"Yes, she was kind, poor thing," Martha agreed sadly. "Never

32

meant for the farm life her husband gave her. They say she never forgave Devin for the way he behaved. He learned her good manners, but not her sense of right and wrong! I felt very sorry when she died. But it was foolish of you to have gone to that funeral. It was a good thing Valerie decided to go with you. Otherwise you might have fainted dead away with no one to help you!"

"You're exaggerating, Mother!" Ginger said testily. "I just felt a little dizzy, that's all, so we left early."

"But it was after you saw *him*! Valerie told me; she saw how it was," Martha said, nodding toward Val. Val silently looked at the floor. "You see how he still affects you? You have to stay away from him." She shook her finger at Ginger. "I believe you still love him, in spite of everything! Heaven knows why! That's why you've never remarried, why all you think about is your shop, why you never dress up. You're still wishing for him!"

"I am not!" Ginger said with a tensed jaw.

"Mom, please, why don't you go lie down for a while?" Val said soothingly. "You said you were tired. We can talk more later." Val was at her mother's chair, urging her out of it.

"Well, all right," her mother complied. "I do feel my pressure's up. No, you don't need to come with me," she said, waving Val away. "Stay and talk some sense to your sister!"

Val sat down at the table with Ginger. Both visibly relaxed when their mother had left the room to go upstairs.

"Sorry about that, Ginger. She's getting worse as she gets older. I was reading a magazine article by a psychologist the other day. I think Mom has what he called catastrophic expectations. She figures out all the worst possible things that could happen and then spends all her energy worrying how and when they will happen."

Ginger nodded numbly. "Maybe her expectations aren't so wrong. My friend Marla—you know, the real estate agent—is showing Devin a house today on Double Bluff Beach."

Val's eyes studied Ginger speculatively. "He always used to say—"

"That he would buy a house there; I know." Ginger's shoulders were slumped as if with fatigue, and her voice had a weak finality to it. "It's beginning to seem inevitable that I'll meet him sometime. I can feel it in my bones."

She looked up suddenly at Val. "And it's not true that I still love him! I don't know why everyone jumps to that conclusion. I just

33

don't want to get weak-kneed like I did at the funeral. I don't know why that happened. I really thought I could handle it. All those years had gone by. I didn't think it would bother me in the least to see him." Her light brown eyes were transfixed momentarily as she envisioned the scene in her mind . . .

They had purposely come at the last minute that day six months ago. Ginger didn't want to be noticed. She and Val had sat together at the back of the room.

The casket was centered in front of the seating arrangement, surrounded by flowers. The fragrance of the elaborate bouquets was all about them. Ginger could just barely see the pale, refined profile of the dead woman's face.

Something had drawn her eyes to the right of the casket, and suddenly she was looking across the room into Devin's eyes. He was speaking and shaking hands with someone else, but he was looking at her. His face was the same: handsome, warm brown hair, luminous green eyes, and the characteristic expression he'd always had that indicated patience, intelligence, trustworthiness. In spite of what he had done, he hadn't lost that steadfast aspect in his countenance that automatically won confidence in his character.

She had stared at him, riveted, for a long moment, then tore her gaze away. A violent tremor ran through her nervous system; she felt for an instant as if all the nerve endings in her body would explode.

But it passed. She sat for a while, breathing unevenly, the sounds of voices around her unreal in her ears. When she had dared to look back, she found Devin had seated himself at the front as the service was about to begin. She heard the minister's voice.

After a little while the heavy odor of the flowers began to make her feel nauseous, and soon points of lights began breaking before her eyes. There was a queer feeling in her head. She turned to Val, who was watching her closely. Val had quietly helped her out of the room, apparently without anyone noticing.

Ginger shook her head, bringing herself back to the present. "I didn't think it would bother me," she repeated, rubbing her forehead.

"The room was kind of stuffy. Maybe that was all it was," Val said.

"You think so?" Ginger looked at her sister. "Maybe." Her glance fell to the Formica tabletop. "It better not happen again. I

34

don't want him to think that he still has any hold on my emotions, because he hasn't. It's all just nerves, that's all. I want to show him that I didn't need him, that I made it all right on my own."

"Well, you did!" Val said in a positive voice.

Ginger's tone was quiet. "Yes . . . I did."

A number of miles away the Mukilteo ferry was leaving its dock near Clinton, beginning another seventeen-minute crossing to the mainland. A man leaned against the ship's railing as he watched the dock and the heavily forested island gradually recede. His brown hair whipped about his forehead in the wind, but he appeared not to notice. His green eyes, behind dark-rimmed glasses, had a distant, pensive quality as he gazed at Whidbey Island.

It was a good house, he was thinking. Almost the image of the beach house he had built in his head over the years. He would have made an offer today, but the real estate woman had a sharp mind and he knew he'd better have his wits about him before dealing with her. It was his second visit to the island since coming back, but he still felt that odd sensation of the ground seeming to vibrate beneath him when he set foot on it.

With a brusk, masculine movement he brushed the windblown hair off his forehead. Had he been foolish to come back, he wondered. His superiors at the Chicago office had certainly thought so. He had hassled with them for the last six months before they finally gave in and allowed him to be transferred back to Seattle.

They couldn't understand his reasons. He had eagerly and diligently climbed their ladder, and when he neared the top, had found there was nothing waiting there for him of any real value. What he wanted now could not be acquired through money or position. Perhaps it could not be acquired at all anymore. But he had only himself to blame for that.

His eyes blurred and burned. The wind was so sharp today. What was he standing out here for? He ought to go inside, he told himself.

He gazed without really seeing at the clouds slowly moving over the island's treetops. How would she react, he was wondering. Was he staking too much on the fact that she had come to the funeral? She had disappeared without even speaking to him, but he still could not forget her wide, stark eyes when she had looked at him across the room. There had been nothing encouraging in her stare. Why had it given him hope that there might be a chance? Was he a fool to think she might still forgive him?

He wondered what she would have said to him if he had seen her today. What would *he* have said, was a better question. His hand went to his stomach as the gnawing feeling he had been having lately came back. Perhaps she had changed, he thought uneasily as he took a half-used roll of antacid tablets from his pocket. She must have changed. He had! Maybe their personalities would no longer blend they way they used to.

Yet her shop reflected the gentle, careful, feminine character she had had years ago. He smiled slightly as he chewed the minted tablet, remembering the attractive window display of teapots and bone china cups and saucers over a draped lace tablecloth. It was certainly her work. He remembered watching her do such an arrangement in her parents' antiques store when she was only ten or eleven. Even then she had had a unique flair for it.

And he liked the clever name of her shop: Ginger's Spice. A low sound of appreciative humor came from his throat. Ginger. He had given her that nickname when she was still a little girl. It had a warm, piquant sound; warm as her eyes were when she used to look at him. Would she ever look at him that way again?

His face sobered. He would find out soon enough. If only she had been there today, he might know now! He wouldn't have to go through the process of building up his nerve again, like he had this morning. After giving himself a long pep talk, he had finally approached her shop, only to find it locked and a Closed sign hanging in the window. Closed, in big black letters. He could see it before his eyes even now, like an omen.

He walked along the side of the vessel and saw it was approaching the mainland. It was time to go below and get into his car, to drive, after they had docked, back to his condominium in Seattle. Before going down he glanced again at the distant island that had been his home long ago. You can never go back, the saying went. And yet he was. He had to.

CHAPTER THREE

Ginger had planned to spend Saturday night at her sister's house, but she asked Val to make some excuse to the family and left that afternoon. She didn't want to go through any more conversations with her mother. Also she was hoping Marla would be home so she could find out what had happened when she met Devin. When she called that evening, however, Marla wasn't there.

The loud ringing of the phone woke her late Sunday morning. Ginger had been wide awake most of the night and had finally dozed off toward morning. She was still groggy as she lifted the receiver to her ear.

"Want to come over for brunch?" Marla asked.

"Okay," Ginger said, blinking the sleep from her eyes. "Did you see him?"

"Yes. Come on over and I'll tell you about it."

Ginger showered and dressed as quickly as her jittery hands allowed, then drove to Marla's small frame house up the hill on First Street.

Casually dressed in slacks and a T-shirt, Marla smiled as she let Ginger in. "I've got everything ready to make an omelet. That sound okay?"

"Sure," Ginger replied, not really hungry. She was about to ask about Devin, but Marla spoke first.

"You look great in that top, Ginger! Is it new?" she asked, leading her into the kitchen. It was a small room, cleverly decorated in rustic reds and browns.

"It was my sister's. She has some knit tops and sweaters she can't wear anymore because she gained weight. She insisted on giving them to me when I left yesterday," she said with a sigh. "My family doesn't seem to like my taste in clothes." Ginger self-consciously adjusted the V neckline, which showed a glimpse of cleavage on her high, full bosom. The yellow knit material clung to her warm, graceful contours and narrowed to her surprisingly small waist. "Don't I look kind of—showy in it?"

"I hadn't realized you had all that to show!" Marla said with amusement as she heated butter in a pan. "Why don't you wear things like that more often?"

"I used to," Ginger explained. "But when I gained weight, my figure changed, and I noticed men started looking at me different-ly."

"Of course men will look. Enjoy it!" Marla said with a smile.

"Enjoy it? The way a couple of them were staring at me one day in the store, I felt like they were going to ask how much I charged—for my services!"

Marla began laughing and almost burned her finger on the pan. "You're too sensitive!"

"Maybe, but I certainly didn't enjoy being looked over like mer-chandise in a window." Actually she didn't even like talking about it. "What about Devin?" she asked, quickly changing the subject.

"Well, Ginger," Marla said as she carefully turned the large omelet, "he's quite a man! I know he hurt you badly years ago, but I have to say, when you lost him you really lost something!"

Ginger was taken totally off balance. She hadn't expected a reac-tion like this from Marla. She sat down in a chair at the small kitchen table that was set for two. "Wh-what—how do you mean?"

"He's got everything most women would want: looks—he's very handsome, even with the glasses; money, apparently; intelligence; and a very nice—unusually pleasant!—personality. With all that, some women would be willing to take him even if he did play around behind their back."

Ginger sat stunned, unable to respond. Marla's words whirled in her head. "Glasses?" she said vacantly.

"Yes, tortoiseshell, like you'd expect an accountant to wear." She slipped half of the big omelet onto Ginger's plate and then served herself. "Oh, that's right, you said he wore contacts. Maybe he doesn't bother with them on weekends."

"Maybe," Ginger said absently. She stared at the food on her plate. What had she expected? That Marla would describe him as an ogre? Ginger had seen him herself six months ago. She knew he was still handsome. "Did he like the house?" she asked.

Marla swallowed a mouthful of food before answering. "He

seemed very interested. It's a wonderful house! I told him it would probably sell quickly. He said he needed a day or two and he'd let me know."

"Oh." Ginger had a forsaken look about her, as if all hope were lost.

"Eat your omelet. It'll get cold."

"Yes," Ginger replied, picking up her fork with rubbery fingers.

"Don't worry so much, Ginger. Double Bluff Beach is across the island. He probably won't be coming into Langley much."

"It's no more than ten miles away. Whidbey Island may be long, but it's not very wide! It's no use thinking I won't see him. I know I will eventually."

"Maybe it's a good thing," Marla said. "If you do see him, maybe you'll fall for him all over again."

"I certainly won't!" Ginger said crossly.

"Don't protest so much. You haven't forgotten him, that's obvious. Your mind probably won't be settled until you do see him and speak to him again."

Ginger did not reply. She kept her eyes on her plate and rather testily shoveled food into her mouth, trying to wash down the suddenly dry eggs with grapefruit juice.

"As I looked at him," Marla continued, "I could see you two together. It reminded me—did you ever hear the story of Abelard and Heloise?"

Ginger's brows came together in annoyance. She shook her head.

"I read it for a history class I took at college years ago," Marla continued, ignoring Ginger's lack of interest. "It happened in the twelfth century—a true story. Heloise was a girl of seventeen and Abelard was a famous teacher and philosopher several years older than she was. He was hired to instruct her at her home, and they quickly got involved in a full-fledged love affair. She had a child by him—"

Ginger's brows shot up.

"I knew you'd find it interesting!" Marla smiled and continued, "As I say, she had a child. Later they were secretly married, but her uncle, who had charge of her, had it in for Abelard because he had disgraced her. He sent men after Abelard and they castrated him."

Ginger put down her fork and leaned back in her chair. "Why are you telling me this?"

"You'll see in a minute! After that happened Abelard advised

39

Heloise to join a convent. She became a nun and later an abbess. He also took vows and became a priest. Ten or twelve years went by. He wrote a letter to a friend telling his life story and about his relationship with Heloise. Somehow she got hold of this letter and read it. After that she wrote Abelard a heartrending letter saying that she still loved him, still grieved over having lost him, asking why he had so totally forsaken her? She wrote that if an emperor had offered to make her his wife, she would have rather been Abelard's whore! She begged him to write to her and comfort her so she could have the strength to carry out her vows to the church. He answered the letter and they corresponded until he died. To this day their bones are buried together somewhere in France."

Deeply moved, though she didn't wish to be, Ginger looked away, feeling tears starting in her eyes.

"I remember wondering when I first read her letter to him how anyone could feel so strongly about another person after a decade of separation," Marla said. She was in an unusually introspective mood. "It seemed to me like a fairy tale, yet they were real people, and their letters to each other still exist. I figured people must have been different in the twelfth century, because *I* certainly would never react that way. It was only when you began talking about Devin the other day that I realized some women can become that deeply attached to a man."

She paused and lowered her eyes as if in thought. Looking up at Ginger again, she said, "In a way it's wonderful to be capable of feeling such a strong, enduring emotion. The dangers may be greater, but so may the rewards. Someone like me just kind of skims the surface, but you really experience life! I think you ought to look forward to meeting Devin again. Maybe you should even seek him out."

Ginger shoved her half-eaten omelet away and threw down her napkin. "Are you crazy? What he did to me years ago nearly killed me. I don't want to have anything to do with him! And I don't care about your twelfth-century stories. I'm not still in love with him!"

Marla nodded slowly, taking in Ginger's protests. "Okay, if you say so." Her eyes gleamed mysteriously. "*I'll* be happy to take him if you don't want him!" She watched Ginger closely with steady eyes.

Ginger's mouth dropped open, but with uncharacteristic quickness she replied, "Be my guest!"

"You're sure?" Marla said as if only half-joking. "You don't have a single twinge of jealousy at that thought?"

"Actually, Marla, I would feel sorry for you!" Ginger said the words forthrightly and ignored the odd feeling in the pit of her stomach.

"Okay!" Marla said airily. "Like some more grapefruit juice?"

"No, thanks," Ginger replied in more subdued tones, remembering she was a guest.

"Shall we sit in the other room for a while?" Marla invited.

"Don't you have to go to work today?"

"Yes, but we can sit for a few minutes," Marla said, rising from the table.

Ginger followed her into the living room, which was done in a modern style in off-white and warm browns. As she sat down on the white sofa she noticed a large corrugated box near the door filled with decorative candle centerpieces. "What are those for?" she asked curiously.

"Housewarming gifts we give to people when they move into a house we've sold to them. I picked them up yesterday after work. I'll have to bring them down to the office today." Marla chuckled a little. "Jack wasn't too impressed with them. He doesn't like artificial flowers."

"You saw him again?"

"We went out last night, and I invited him up afterward," Marla explained.

"You must have come back late. I called a couple of times last night."

"So that was you!" Marla said with amusement as she sat in an easy chair across a small coffee table from Ginger. "Sorry, I couldn't answer. We were—preoccupied."

"That sounds interesting!" Ginger said with a smile, but she felt a little uneasy. What did that mean exactly, she was wondering. A kiss on the couch or . . . "You're getting to like each other, then?"

"Oh, maybe," Marla said with an easy shrug. "You know how it is—things just seemed to click, and we wound up in bed."

Ginger didn't know, and she was feeling peculiar. She hadn't realized Marla had such a casual attitude toward sex. She didn't seem to have any deep feelings for Jack Whiting, and wasn't it only their second date? Ginger felt she could never sleep with a man she wasn't in love with. Maybe she was too old-fashioned, but it distressed her to find that her friend apparently followed different guidelines.

Marla was studying Ginger's expression. "You and he weren't . . .?"

"No!" Ginger replied.

"I didn't think so," Marla said. "But you look a little surprised."

"I didn't realize things were moving so fast with you two. But as long as you're happy . . ." she chattered. "Is that his painting?" She pointed to the seascape above the fireplace, glad to have found a way to change the subject gracefully.

They discussed the painting and its suitability to Marla's living room decor, and then Ginger left. As she was driving the short distance home, she was still bewildered by the fact that Marla had actually started an affair with Jack. Just where does that leave me, she wondered. Should she go on seeing Jack, or was he Marla's property now? If she did keep dating him, would he expect the same as he got from Marla? He'd better not!

Oh, who cares, she almost muttered aloud as she shut her car door after stepping out onto Mrs. Poole's driveway. She had better things to worry about, she decided as she climbed the back steps. What Jack and Marla did together was really none of her business. What Devin did—or was about to do—was much more important to her at the moment.

Monday morning Ginger walked to work as usual. Throughout the day she schooled herself to keep her mind off Marla, Jack, and Devin. It seemed as though her world was going a little haywire around her, and she didn't want to think about it. She just wanted a normal day with normal, inconsequential problems. And the day was like that—until Marla called late in the afternoon.

"Ginger?" Marla's voice sounded as though she had hurried to call. "Devin just left. He's going to buy the house."

"Oh, no . . ." Ginger said. She sank onto the stool behind the cash register.

"That's not all. I watched out the window after he left here. He didn't go back to his car. He was walking toward First Street. You don't suppose he may be going to see you?"

A rush of acute apprehension swept through Ginger. She gripped the counter with her free hand. "No! You're sure?"

"Yes, I saw him take the shortcut at the drugstore."

"Maybe he was going to buy something . . ."

Ginger left off midsentence. The room had darkened slightly, and she knew without looking up that someone was in her open doorway. The phone still in her hand, she slowly gazed up to find herself looking into Devin's green eyes. She stared at him, standing stock still for a few seconds, seeing the broad shoulders and handsome face she had once known so well, and then an unreal calmness came over her like a cloak.

"I'll talk to you later," she said in an easy tone as though she were just finishing a friendly chat. With a strangely steady hand she put the phone back onto its cradle. She looked back at the man in her doorway. "Hello." Her voice was straightforward and clear, eerily devoid of emotion.

He stepped in then. "Hello, Ginger," he said in a warm, subdued tone. She hadn't heard his voice in eight years; the low, subtly modulated sound of it affected her like an old, haunting melody. He seemed slightly apologetic. "You're probably surprised to see me—"

"No, not too much," she said coolly. "I'd heard that you'd come back to the area." She didn't have time to analyze it, but her emotions were at a place they had never been before. Inwardly she was on the edge of panic; yet outwardly she was somehow distant and tranquil, as though nothing mattered. She felt as if she had become enclosed in glass. Everything about her was real, but she felt she couldn't touch her surroundings and they couldn't touch her.

"Oh, I don't doubt everyone in Coupeville is talking about it," he said with regretful humor. "You heard through your family, I suppose." Ginger made no comment. She began tying small price tags on some hand-crocheted doilies, the job she had been at when Marla phoned. "How *are* your parents and Val?"

"Fine, thank you," she replied politely.

He moved closer to the counter where she was sitting behind the cash register. She looked up as she felt him invade her space. For the first time she noticed what he was wearing: a gray pinstripe three-piece business suit of fine wool. He must have left work early and come directly to the island.

"And how are *you*?" he asked.

"Fine." As she watched him place his hands on the outer edge of the counter, she at last felt her nerves penetrate to her calm exterior. He seemed to have quietly shattered her invisible barrier.

She was beginning to feel unprotected. Her eyes subtly rose from his large, strong hands to his vested chest. Years ago he used to be lean and well proportioned. He still was, she guessed, by looking at the fit of his vest.

But there was a masculine assertiveness to his figure now; his chest seemed to have broadened and deepened, and beneath his suit coat she sensed his shoulders and arms to be more muscular and developed. He had been a good-looking boy and a handsome young man, but now in full maturity he was—

Ginger's mind rushed to block her thoughts. She lowered her eyes and studiously went back to her price tags, but her fingers had grown shaky.

"I've always wanted to thank you, Ginger," he said with hesitance, "for—coming to my mother's funeral. I—appreciated that you—took the trouble . . ."

She raised her eyes to his face with a startled look. "There's no need to thank me. I admired her. I wanted to come." Their eyes held each other's for a moment, and then Ginger looked down in confusion.

"She was always very fond of you," Devin said softly, his voice almost grave.

Her eyes flew to his again in unthinking reaction. She saw a green blur as he glanced away. Turning from the counter, he stepped toward the center of the room and began to look about her small store. He reached into his breast pocket to pull out a pair of thin-rimmed tortoiseshell glasses. Ginger was weak with relief that he had moved away from her again, yet she watched him put on the glasses with a kind of numb fascination. She studied his clean-chiseled profile and the smooth sheen of his well-cut dark brown hair as he gazed about the place, looking at the merchandise on her shelves along the walls and the long tables in the center of the room.

"You have a nice shop here," he said in complimentary tones. "You run it all by yourself?"

"Yes."

He smiled nostalgically and glanced at her. "It's hard to imagine you as a businesswoman."

"A lot of things are hard to imagine," she said with a trace of bitterness. Now that he was keeping his distance, she was feeling stronger, collecting her wits. She was beginning to resent his invasion of her life. Why had he come to her store? What did he want?

44

"I'd heard that you had a shop in Langley," he continued as if her sardonic tone hadn't registered. "I always wondered what it was like, how you were doing . . ."

So he had come out of curiosity? Ginger was hard put to believe it. Devin had never been the type who was curious about other people's affairs.

"Is your overhead high? Do you have a good profit margin?" he asked.

She almost felt like laughing. After eight years and all that had been between them, he was asking about her profit margin! She answered his questions, all the while conscious of what a farce this was turning into. With all her concern about his coming back, she hadn't expected their first encounter to be anything like this.

But he was turning now and walking back toward her. Her brief moments of sarcastic amusement dissolved as he approached. She grew nervous again.

He was smiling slightly. It was the polite, cordial smile she remembered him using with acquaintances or when meeting strangers. "I almost forgot to mention—I'm buying a house on Double Bluff Beach. You—may remember I always liked it there."

"Yes. Are you planning to live there?" she asked, her voice sounding weaker than she would have liked.

"I thought I'd use it on weekends, to get away from the city. I have a condominium in Seattle."

"I thought you liked the city," Ginger said quietly, sliding her brown eyes up to meet his. There was the hint of a taunt in her gaze.

His green eyes flickered, but he did not look away. "I used to. I still do, in some ways. But over the years I've come to miss what I had here on Whidbey Island." The lucid green of his eyes seemed to intensify as he said the last phrase. She felt her heart stop.

He looked away and changed the subject. "I'm working with the real estate agency on Second Street. The woman who showed me the house is Marla Rosetti. Do you know her?"

"Yes, I do," was all she said. He didn't have to know they were good friends. Her private life was her business, and the less he knew about it, the better she felt.

"She's been very nice and extremely helpful," Devin said.

"That's good." His politeness was growing tiresome. How long was he going to stand there and make pleasant small talk, she wondered. She looked at her watch and then eyed the sign that was hanging in her window. Maybe if she switched it around so it read Closed, he would take the hint and leave. It was getting late enough to close anyway. And she had had more than enough. Her nerves couldn't take much more.

"Ten to five," Devin muttered, looking at his own watch. "I didn't have much for lunch. I'm beginning to get hungry."

A fresh wave of apprehension came over Ginger. He was making no move to go; she could almost hear him asking her out to dinner next. She fidgeted nervously with the price tags, then gave up and began putting them back into the box she kept them in. She braced herself when she heard Devin's low voice again.

"Maybe we—"

"Hi, Ginger! About to close up yet?"

She looked up past Devin to find Jack Whiting walking into her shop. Her eyes brightened as if he were an answer to a prayer.

"Hi, Jack! Yes, I was thinking about it," she said breathlessly. "How are you?"

"Terrific, as always!" he said jovially. He glanced at Devin. "Sorry, I didn't mean to interrupt."

"That's all right," Devin responded good-naturedly. "I had just stopped in to say hello."

"You know Ginger?" Jack asked with interest, glancing at them both.

"Yes. We grew up together in Coupeville," Devin replied before Ginger could even open her mouth.

"So you're a native of the island, then! I'm not, but I live here now. I'm Jack Whiting," he said, extending his hand. "I own the art gallery down the street."

"Devin MacPherson. It's a pleasure to meet you," Devin said, firmly shaking Jack's hand. "I'm a CPA with . . ."

Oh, good grief! Ginger said to herself. You'd think they were at a business meeting making contacts! Devin, her one-time husband, shaking hands with a man she'd been dating for two years! She was beginning to get a headache.

"I was wondering if you wanted to go out for dinner," Jack said, turning to Ginger, "but maybe you have other plans."

"No, no other plans!" Ginger said with quick enthusiasm. "That would be fine, Jack."

"Oh," Jack said with some surprise. "Well, good. Are you ready now, or should I come back?"

46

"No, I'm ready now," Ginger said, digging the key to the door out of her purse. She had left her bag behind the counter today after coming back from lunch. She did not look directly at either man, but could sense the sudden tension in the atmosphere.

As if the pressure were too great on Jack's sensitive good nature, he said, "If you're free, why don't you join us, Devin?"

Ginger felt as though she were sinking into the floor.

"Thank you, but I have to get back to Seattle," Devin said with a gracious half-smile.

With monumental relief, key in hand, Ginger slung the long strap of her purse over her shoulder and walked around the counter. After turning the sign over to read Closed, she went out the door, and the two men followed her. She locked up, then made some work of putting her key back into her purse so she wouldn't have to look up as she said, "Well, it was nice seeing you again, Devin." Her tone carried intentional disinterest. "Hope you enjoy your new house."

She glanced up then. It came as a slight shock to find them both staring at her, the same subtle, absorbed glimmer in both sets of male eyes. She was instantly confused, and her color heightened as she realized what they were looking at. She was wearing another of her sister's knit tops over a navy A-line skirt. The top was white and had a high, round neckline. Though it was cut demurely, the way it clung to her curves was undeniably eye-catching. She had been partly hidden before, sitting behind the counter and her cash register. It hadn't occurred to her that she would be on display when she got up.

Her eyes grew cold and clearly annoyed. "Good-bye, Devin. Shall we go, Jack?"

The men muttered good-bye to one another, and Jack fell into step with her as she began to walk up the street. She did not turn to look at Devin again; she was thoroughly glad to be rid of him. Her heart was still beating at an unnatural pace from the whole encounter, and her nerves were severely taxed. And she was angry at the way both men had looked at her just now. Jack, her old friend, ogling her! And Devin in his immaculate business suit and glasses, overflowing with cordiality and good breeding, yet suddenly looking at her like he wanted to—

A wave of heat weakened her, and she put a shaky hand to her forehead. Her step faltered a bit.

"Are you all right?" Jack asked, taking her arm.

47

"Yes, I—I'm just a little nervous."

"Something to do with Devin? I sensed you were anxious to get away from him."

"Devin was once my husband," Ginger said. There was no use beating about the bush.

Jack looked at her in astonishment. "I see. I guess you did mention once that you were divorced. He seemed like a pleasant fellow. It upsets you to see him?"

"I haven't seen him in a long time," she said, not realizing she hadn't really answered his question.

"You still care for him?" Jack asked with quiet empathy.

"No!" She said the word so forthrightly, it seemed to startle Jack.

He smiled benignly. "I must have been mistaken. Why don't we forget it all and have a nice, quiet dinner. You look beautiful today, Ginger," he said, as if eager to change the subject.

Oh, be quiet! The words rose to her lips, but she managed not to say them.

Later that evening, home alone in her bedroom, Ginger was thinking over the day's events. Jack's dinner chatter was still playing in her ear. She had had a hard time concentrating. He kept talking about Marla, asking questions about her, almost as if he was hoping Ginger would tell him some confidences Marla might have shared with her about him. He had apparently learned what close friends they were.

Ginger's frazzled mind, gradually unwinding now, was ironing it all out. Jack must be falling for Marla, she realized. Poor Jack! She didn't think Marla had quite the same feelings for him, even if Marla did sleep with him. Ginger had obviously been needlessly concerned about her own position with Jack. That had all worked out without her even thinking about it. Jack and she would carry on their friendship just as before, though she would have to be careful not to betray Marla's confidences. She hoped she hadn't tonight; her mind had been so addled! Damn Devin! Why couldn't he have stayed in Chicago?

Feeling restless, she walked over to her dresser and absently picked up a recent snapshot of herself taken by her sister at a family gathering. As she looked at her figure in the picture, she wondered again if she would ever get used to her extra pounds. Until a few years ago she had always been very thin. Her self-image was still

48

that of a woman who could count her ribs just by looking in a full-length mirror. Her bosom had been of average size and her hips narrow. Now her hips were well rounded—too well, in her opinion —and her bosom had become quite prominent. She supposed that age and family heredity had finally caught up with her.

It was a shame, she thought with a sigh. Many women would envy her. Others who were too thin probably wished they could gain weight exactly the same way she had. When she was young, she used to wonder herself if she would ever develop more of a figure.

But now that she had one, Ginger was uncomfortable with it. To her own eye she looked plump, and with the reaction it brought from men, she felt more comfortable in the loose, flowing garments that her family and friends apparently thought looked dowdy. It was probable that Devin had once preferred someone who had no embarrassment about showing off her physical attributes—that was how Ginger had always imagined his Chicago woman to be—but she had no intention of appearing to be such a woman herself.

She wanted men to be friends with her, that was all. She didn't need physical contact. Her wedding-night experience had shown her that sex wasn't all it was cracked up to be. She didn't see that there was much to enjoy in the physical act, at least not for a woman. Perhaps his Chicago paramour had relished being used like a wind-up doll, but she hadn't. She had gotten more pleasure from Devin's restrained caresses before they were married. In those days he had been so caring and tender with her . . .

Oh, why think about that now, she asked herself with intense annoyance. She turned away from the dresser and sat down on her bed. Because she had seen him today, that was why. Maybe it was natural to remember old times, but she didn't have to dwell on them. If she was going to remember the past, let her remember that he had been untrue!

She sat still for a moment, a wistfulness creeping into her eyes. How could he have done it? She still didn't understand. She had trusted him so, and she had to admit that if she had met him for the first time today, she would trust him now. There was that certain something in his looks and manner that made one think: Here is a fine, reliable man! He seemed so considerate and sensitive—even more so, if that was possible, than he used to be. The way he had thanked her for coming to the funeral had taken her completely off guard. And yet this same man had once done something that was so callous, so insensitive, that it had badly stained all her previously positive views of love and marriage.

It was safer not to put faith in a man, she thought as she began to undress for bed. Beneath their tall, strong frames and low, reassuring voices beat hearts that were fickle and inconstant.

She slipped on her pajamas. Men and women were just different, she supposed. They had two different objectives in life: Women wanted love; men wanted sex. The two goals might overlap, but not enough for true harmony. Here was Jack getting possessive about Marla, probably because he enjoyed sleeping with her and wanted it to continue. She still couldn't fathom what Marla was thinking of. And Devin! Devin had once had her total love, but he threw it away when he found someone who excited him more sexually. Sex must be all men thought about. It had been obvious in the way they both looked at her today.

She took the decorative quilt off of her bed and let it tumble into a pile to one side. After getting under the covers, she turned off the light. With tired eyes she looked out into the darkness. She was glad she had spent all these years alone. Women really were better off that way. Thank heaven women had each other to rely on! She smiled, remembering how Marla had called to warn her about Devin's coming. Just what a friend ought to have done!

And thank goodness her encounter with Devin was over. If she had been rude to him, she was glad, even a little proud of herself. She had managed to handle the situation much better than she had expected. Jack couldn't have appeared at a more ideal moment. Devin wouldn't think she lacked for male attention. No, after her cool dismissal, Devin wouldn't be back. He wasn't stupid; he would know where he wasn't wanted.

Feeling secure with those thoughts, she turned over and went to sleep.

The light was still on in the bedroom of a condominium in Seattle. On the nightstand next to the bed, two large tablets were fizzing in a glass of water. Devin lay on the bed, reclining with his shoulders against the headboard. His hand lay limply across his stomach. His face was drawn and tired, his eyes bleak, his stomach distressed.

Earlier he had eaten half of a TV dinner, and his stomach had soon rebelled. He wondered if he ought to see a doctor. His condition had all the signs of an ulcer, or the start of one. But if he was

50

having digestion problems, he knew it was his own fault, a nervous reaction to the changes he was forcing into his life.

He had known when he walked into her shop that he might get kicked in the teeth. And he had been—subtly, but kicked nevertheless. When the other man took her arm as they walked away, that was the worst. The guy seemed nice enough, but he wished he could have punched him in the gut.

Did she love him? Were they still together now, at this moment?

Don't think about it or you'll get an ulcer for sure, Devin warned himself as he reached for the glass. Grimacing, he drank its contents.

He leaned back again and closed his eyes. She had grown so beautiful, so—womanly. But she had the same gentle voice, the same sweet eyes—only now there was such distance in them. She hardly looked at him at all. She didn't want to see him, that was plain; she didn't want him back in her life.

Well, she would have to adjust, because he was going to *be* back! Even if it made her detest him and wrecked his health, he was moving into her quiet little world, come what may!

CHAPTER FOUR

The next few days went smoothly for Ginger. In fact, she was feeling much better about herself than she had been lately. That she had dispatched Devin so easily the afternoon he appeared in her store gave her new confidence that she could handle any situation that might arise from his proximity. She also felt sure that if they ever met again, it would be only by accident.

She felt so carefree that she even drove up to Oak Harbor, the largest city on the island, and bought herself some new clothes. Having taken an honest look at her dwindling wardrobe, she had decided that perhaps her mother and sister were right. When her figure changed and her frail, willowy look disappeared, she had lost interest in clothes for a while. She hadn't bought much, and nothing expensive, because she kept hoping she would lose weight and could use her old wardrobe again.

It had finally come home to her that this was the way she was probably going to be from now on; in fact, if she wasn't careful she might grow as big as her sister. It was in the family. But Val's discarded sweaters were definitely not her style.

She came home with a few dresses and some soft feminine blouses that showed her shape demurely and much more tastefully than the inexpensive tunic tops she had been wearing lately. Some added pairs of shoes, pants, and skirts filled her closet.

She was wearing some of her new purchases—a mauve skirt and pale lavender silk blouse with a ruffled collar—the following Friday, the day Devin walked into her store once again. It was early afternoon. She was talking with some customers at the back of the shop when she saw him come in. Her nerves were immediately on edge. His return shattered her sense of security that she would no longer be bothered by him. But she felt no panic this time. She would deal with him.

She tried to prepare herself mentally, taking her time and finishing with the customers before turning to him. He waited patiently.

"Hello, Devin," she said politely but without enthusiasm.

"Hello!" He greeted her with a broad smile. "You look lovely today, Ginger."

She watched his eyes glide over her blouse, pausing for a lingering fraction of a second on her beckoning curves. Her eyes told him she knew exactly what he was admiring and she wasn't flattered. "Are you in town to see about your house?" He'd better have some good reason, she said to herself.

"Yes. I stopped to see Marla to discuss my bid on it, but she's out with another client. I thought I'd look in on you for a few minutes until she gets back."

He was still smiling, and Ginger had the impression that he didn't mind having time to kill.

"Well," she said, stepping back and gesturing toward the room full of merchandise, "feel free to look around. You'll have to excuse me; I have some bookkeeping to do." She began to walk away from him toward the back room, but immediately sensed him at her heels.

"Mind if I glance at your books? I'd be interested to see what methods you use."

Good thinking, Ginger, she said to herself morosely. Obviously it had been a poor ploy to get away from him. Intuition told her he'd be only too happy to give her free advice.

"My methods are a little sloppy," she said, feigning a chuckle at herself. "I'd be embarrassed to show them to a big-city CPA."

Why was she trying to invent nice excuses? Why didn't she just tell him her books were none of his business? Why didn't she tell him to go away? He was so sweet and polite she found it difficult to speak crossly to him.

Devin laughed lightly at her self-denigration. "I bet you're very careful and neat, the way you are with everything."

She paused and gazed up at him. "How do you know what I'm like?" she subtly challenged.

"You—used to be."

"What, eight years ago? People change."

"I don't think you have," he said softly, looking into her defiant eyes. They were near the open door to her small office, and the light from the back window was shining into his green eyes. It gave them

53

that bright, translucent, almost ethereal quality that had always filled her with admiration and awe when she was young.

She looked away, annoyed at the memory and at the coaxing intimacy and sureness in his voice. His comment that she hadn't changed chilled and angered her, as though he was intimating she could still feel the same about him as she used to. Her jaws clenched to repress a tide of resentment mixed with other emotions she had no time to examine.

She walked into her office, and Devin followed. Her feelings were too intense at the moment to think of any way to get rid of him. She took a ledger from the file cabinet and handed it to him. Whether he saw her business papers or not didn't really matter to her; she had no secrets. For the moment she was glad to have some way to keep him occupied while she collected her wits.

But that was difficult. Her heart was beginning to pound now as a thought reverberated in her head: Does he hope to recapture what we had together? Is that why he's here? And then the further question: Why? Why now?

She shook her head imperceptibly, trying to keep touch with reality. Why would he, indeed? Wasn't the idea a little ridiculous? After all the women he'd probably known, including the one he had left her for, why would he come back for her now? Maybe she was misreading him, trying to soothe her own still-injured ego.

As he inclined his head over the ledger he had opened on her desk, she studied him. She noted his earnest profile, its studiousness enhanced by his glasses; his beautifully tailored light gray business suit; his neatly knotted, conservative tie. He seemed to her a graceful portrait of dedication to propriety. His precise mind could look over her rows of figures and find any flaws; his refined manner and well-modulated voice could politely tell her exactly where she might have erred. He was everything a mature man with a well-trained, intelligent mind ought to be.

And yet beneath that fine exterior, *he* was the one who had erred against propriety! And having rejected her once, he certainly wasn't going to want her again. Not now, when he had reached such perfection, she thought with a sarcasm that hurt her own heart. How silly even to consider that he might still want her! She didn't want *him*, in any case!

He was slowly leafing through the ledger's green columnar pages. A smile gradually came over his face. "I'm impressed, Ginger! Very

54

well done. And this from the girl who used to dissolve into tears over her high-school algebra!"

Her brows drew together, and she turned away. He used to help her with her math homework years ago. An image came to her now of them sitting at her mother's old kitchen table with its well-used plastic tablecloth. Her books and papers would be spread over it, and he would go over what she didn't understand step by step. And yes, she had started crying out of frustration once or twice. Devin was quick with numbers, and it upset her that it seemed to come so slowly to her. But Devin would soothe her and patiently make her go through each problem until she understood it. And then he would kiss her.

Tears started in her eyes. She forced them back, telling herself she was stupid to let old memories sway her emotions so much. "Book-keeping for your own business is a lot different from algebra," she told him in a strained voice.

She heard him step toward her and soon felt him standing behind her shoulder. "Yes, it is," he agreed quietly. His masculine presence, his voice in her ear, the heat radiating from his body seemed to permeate her until she began to feel distracted, too warm, and a little light-headed.

Devin looked down at her softly curled hair and small shoulders. She was standing so still in front of him, it was as if she was afraid to turn around. Was being so near affecting her the same way it was him, he wondered. His heart was beginning to pound so hard he was worried that she would hear it. He wanted to put his arms around her, kiss her hair, but it was too soon. She might bolt. He was afraid even to touch her hand.

Well, say something, he told himself. The silence was becoming too prolonged.

"Ginger . . ." He reached momentarily to touch her arm, then put his hand in his pocket instead. "Why don't we have dinner tonight?" He was amazed to hear his voice sound so smooth.

His eyes flinched as she turned suddenly to face him, backing away. He braced himself; he could read the signals in her beautiful eyes, so resentful and wary.

"Why should we do that?" Her voice was cold as she stared at him.

She's gotten so direct, he thought. His brain stumbled for an answer. "Why not? Since I've moved to the area again, I thought— we could be friends. We were once."

"Yes, once. We were more than friends, Devin. But I'd rather not remember that. I don't feel there's any room or any need for friendship between us. I don't care to have dinner with you."

He watched her as she stood there in her high heels, crossing her arms over her soft blouse as she said the words. Her voice quavered slightly with anger. Outwardly Devin withstood her rebuff with composure, but he had to swallow as he felt his stomach react. Still, he had no intention of giving up without an argument. "How can there not be room for friendship? Everyone needs friends. *I* feel the need for your friendship."

He watched a kind of helpless alarm pass through her eyes. But her expression was steadfast, her voice hard as she replied, "Then why did you betray it eight years ago?"

Devin bowed his head, feeling as though she had punched him in his aching stomach. "I . . ." What could he say? "I never meant to hurt you, Ginger. I told you that."

"I never understood how you could have knowingly had an affair with another woman and thought that it wouldn't hurt me!" she flared at him.

He winced slightly. "I know you never understood. How could you? I didn't understand myself—" He stopped. There was no use trying to explain anything now. There wasn't time, and she wasn't in any sort of receptive mood, anyway. "Ginger, why must we let something that happened eight long years ago influence whether we have dinner together tonight? Can't we forget the past for one evening?"

Her voice and expression were tough as she answered him, but her lower lip was beginning to tremble. He realized he had pressed too far. "You've got it backward," she said. "I *have* forgotten the past. I just don't want to be reminded of it again! I'm well and whole and doing fine now, but I don't mind admitting it took some effort to get over what happened. Now that that's all past, I want to keep it in the past. I don't want your friendship, Devin. I have friends— friends whom I can trust! You'll have to forgive my bluntness, but I don't trust you! I don't know what you want or why you've come back here, but just do me a favor and leave me alone!"

Her voice broke on the last word, and she put a shaking hand to her lips momentarily. She stiffened her posture, but he sensed that her whole body was trembling as she tried to suppress her emotion.

The wound inflicted so many years ago had been opened. He had wanted with all his heart to avoid that. He would have put his arms around her to try to comfort her if he hadn't known how much she despised him.

He felt limp, spent. There was nothing more he could do. Looking up at her, he tried to think of something to say. Finally he just turned and quietly walked out, leaving her there. He would have given anything to be able to go back and soothe her. She had always been an emotionally intense person. Years ago he had learned how to talk to her, to reassure her. She would never let him do that now, he thought with pain.

As he walked to Second Street, he tried to breathe deep and calm his own emotions and burning stomach. He had to get his head together to discuss the house.

When he walked into the realtor's, Marla Rosetti was there. He sat near her desk and they discussed business for a while. As they finished their conversation about the house, Devin took a roll of antacid tablets from his pocket and put one in his mouth.

"You look a little tired today," Marla said. "Are you feeling all right?"

"Just a jumpy stomach," Devin said. Thoughtfully he eyed her left hand. He had noticed she wore no rings and assumed she was single or divorced, like Ginger. He wondered. "Do you live here in Langley?"

"Yes, I moved here about five years ago," Marla replied.

"I understand you know Ginger Cowan. Her shop is over on First—"

"Of course!" Marla said, her face brightening. "We've been great friends for years!"

"Have you?" Devin said, leaning pensively against the edge of her desk. He had hoped that was the case. He straightened his posture and smiled at Marla. She was looking at him expectantly, as if already receptive to whatever he might say next. "I'm—kind of at loose ends tonight," he began hesitantly. Marla's interested expression encouraged him to finish. "If you're not busy, would you like to have dinner with me?"

Marla smiled warmly. "As it happens, I'm at loose ends tonight, too. I'd love to!"

* * *

At Ginger's Spice on First Street, the shop's proprietor was sitting slumped over her desk in the small back office. A few tears were running down her cheeks, and in annoyance she brushed them away with fingertips that still trembled. At least she had managed not to cry in front of him.

Actually, all things considered, she had handled the encounter rather well, she told herself—especially since he had come so unexpectedly. She was glad she had been able to tell him so clearly what she thought of him. It had affected him, she was sure. He had looked hurt. He wouldn't dare come back again, not unless he was a masochist!

Yes, she had done well. So why was she crying now, she asked herself helplessly as she felt a new wave of emotion rising in her throat and tears welling in her eyes again. It was ridiculous to feel sorry for him. So he had looked crushed—good! It was only what he deserved. There was no reason at all why she should have gone to dinner with him. He had a lot of nerve even to ask her! If he was hurt it was his own fault. She was too kind-hearted, that was all!

She reached across her desk for a tissue and blew her nose. Resolutely she rose from her chair and went through the motions of tidying herself. What if a customer should find her like this? She was behaving foolishly—very foolishly.

The next day Ginger called Marla to ask if she would like to meet for lunch. She felt like talking over what had happened. It was nice to have someone to confide in.

They met at the usual place. To make conversation while they were waiting for the waitress to take their order, Ginger asked Marla if she was still seeing Jack.

"Yes, I still see him," Marla answered easily, but yet without revealing much. "By the way, Devin stopped in yesterday."

"I know! He dropped in on me while he was waiting for you to come back."

Marla nodded her head as if she knew that already. Her reaction surprised Ginger a little. Their conversation was temporarily interrupted as their usual waitress stopped to take their order. They exchanged a few pleasant words with her before she left.

"Is there some problem with the house he's buying?" Ginger asked, wanting to get back to the topic on her mind but for some reason feeling a need to be careful about how she approached it. She felt a little uneasy with Marla today and didn't know quite why. Marla seemed confident and composed but a trifle less open than usual, Ginger sensed.

"Not really. Devin and the seller have been making bids and counterbids. They'll settle on a figure soon."

"Oh." Ginger hesitated about saying anything more. She still felt strangely insecure.

After some silence between them Marla said, "What did Devin have to say to you?"

Ginger was glad she had asked, afraid Marla was losing interest in her problems. "He wants to be friends again. He even asked me out to dinner! I refused."

Marla nodded again. "He seemed a little distracted when he came to my office. He asked *me* to have dinner with him."

"He did?" The noise in the crowded restaurant seemed to fade away, and Ginger felt a sudden stillness all around her. She tried to smile as if she were amused. "Did you go?"

"Yes. He took me to a nice place in Oak Harbor."

Ginger's eyes widened, but she kept herself from showing her shock completely. "W-why?"

"Why did I go?" Marla said, her voice matter-of-fact. She shrugged. "I didn't have anything better to do last night. We've been working together with regard to the house, and I figured it was his way of thanking me for my help. You don't mind, do you? You said you had no interest in him."

"N-no, of course I don't. It was just a—a surprise." Marla's answer was strange; her whole attitude about Devin seemed different. Wasn't it unusual that a buyer would take his real estate agent to dinner to thank her for her help? Wouldn't her high commission on the sale be payment enough? Didn't Marla think it was odd? She wasn't acting as if she did. "What did you talk about?"

Marla took a long breath, as if she was slightly bored. "Oh . . . let's see. He talked about his job, we discussed the house some more, he talked about Coupeville . . ."

"Did he say anything about me?"

"Yes. He—talked about you and him growing up together," Marla replied a little stiffly.

"Did he mention that he had been to see me yesterday?"

"Yes."

"What did he say?" Ginger wondered why she was having to pump Marla for information. Marla had spoken so spontaneously about Devin before.

"That he stopped in to see you," Marla replied.

"That's all?"

"Well . . . we talked about so many things, Ginger, I can't remember everything he said."

Ginger stopped asking questions. It was clear Marla didn't want to give any thorough answers. She couldn't believe Marla didn't remember, knowing from experience what a good memory for detail she had.

Was she trying to spare her feelings? Had Devin said something vengeful about her Marla didn't want to repeat because it would upset her? But Marla was usually much more straightforward about things. She couldn't dispel the feeling that her friend was camouflaging something.

What *was* that something? Had she and Devin . . .? No. Marla was involved with Jack. She wouldn't have affairs with two men at once. Would she? Suddenly the thought of Marla and Devin together made her feel ill.

She was letting her thoughts run away again, she chided herself. Marla wouldn't do *that*. Even if she did say once that she found Devin attractive, she wouldn't do that. She hadn't given any indication that their evening had consisted of anything other than conversation at a restaurant. Oh, what do I care? If Marla's stupid enough to want him, she can have him, she thought with anger.

"Something wrong? You seem upset," Marla said.

Ginger looked up at her friend. There was a subtle distance in Marla's eyes today that she had never seen there before.

"Nothing's wrong." Do you really care, Ginger wanted to ask.

Maybe she was being unfair. Perhaps Marla *had* grown bored constantly listening to her talk about Devin. Maybe she had even been bored when she was out with *him*. Was she so tired of the whole subject she didn't even want to discuss it?

Ginger didn't know what to think. They made idle conversation after that; it wasn't one of their usual stimulating and enjoyable lunches at all. Ginger went back to her shop confused and depressed.

Over the next week Ginger heard nothing more of Devin, and she

60

avoided Marla. She was surprised when Marla called early in the week asking if she wanted to meet for lunch. Ginger found some excuse not to go. Somehow she preferred to be alone, fearing she would be uncomfortable with Marla again.

On Friday Marla called once more and was so warm and enthusiastic over the phone that Ginger couldn't resist her invitation for lunch. As she walked to Second Street, Ginger hoped their friendship would resume its former easiness. She decided not to speak of Devin at all.

As she approached the small restaurant she saw through the large front window that Marla was already at their usual booth. With a smile Ginger opened the door and walked in. She greeted Marla and sat down opposite her.

"That's a beautiful dress, Ginger!" Marla said, her dark eyes eagerly noting the intricate tailoring of the shoulder and sleeves. It was one of Ginger's new dresses, a peach-color crepe with small, soft pleats sewn into the shoulder seam and at the cuffs.

"Thank you. It was a little more than I wanted to spend, but I couldn't resist."

"It's gorgeous on you! Well, how are things at the shop?" Marla asked. She listened with unusual interest as Ginger described the contents of a shipment of bone china tea sets she had just received from England.

Ginger was happy to find that their former rapport had returned, yet she still felt that something was off balance. Marla was almost too attentive, too eager in her interest. It seemed a little forced.

But, wanting to think the best, Ginger attributed Marla's behavior to, of all things, nervousness. She had rarely seen her friend nervous, but she thought Marla was now. Ginger assumed that Marla felt bad, perhaps even a little guilty, about the awkwardness of their last meeting and wanted to make it up.

The lunch proceeded amiably, and they discussed many things. Ginger asked about Jack Whiting, and Marla made an amusing story of their last date. It appeared things were on an even keel between them, although Ginger was still surprised at the casual way Marla joked about Jack. It seemed Marla was not taking her affair with him very seriously. Ginger hoped Jack wouldn't wind up with a broken heart; but perhaps she was misjudging both their feelings. In any case, it was none of her business.

The lunch had been so enjoyable, they decided to throw caution to the winds and order desserts. The restaurant specialized in home-made pies, and Ginger had deprived herself for weeks. As she was sinking her fork into her mouth-watering blueberry pie, she noticed Marla looking out the window in the direction of her real estate office across the street.

"Do you have to get back to work already?" Ginger asked.

Marla's eyes darted back. "No. No, not yet," she said, hurriedly glancing at her watch.

Ginger began talking about a recipe for apple cake she had seen in the newspaper when Marla's anxious gaze again flew to the window. This time Ginger turned and leaned closer to the pane of glass so she could look back at the real estate office. Her heart stopped as she glimpsed Devin coming from the building. He was stepping into the street and waving at Marla.

The fork fell from Ginger's fingers and clattered onto the table, startling her. She looked at Marla. "Did you know he was coming?"

"No—well, not this early. He said he would be by this afternoon. He must have left work sooner than he thought he would." Marla seemed flustered, and she avoided Ginger's eyes.

Ginger was surprised and hurt that Marla apparently had known she would be seeing him and hadn't even mentioned it.

In the next moment the restaurant door opened and Devin walked in. "I saw your Out to Lunch sign," he said to Marla as he approached the table. Ginger's back was to the door, and she was hidden by the high back of the booth's seat. As Devin came up to the table, the smile on his face vanished.

"Ginger!" he said, obviously shaken to find her there. Marla looked very uneasy.

"Sorry if I'm in the way," Ginger said, her voice sounding tense.

"No, of course not!" Devin said. "I—just came to see Marla about the house. You're not in the way at all."

Oh, sure! You've both got guilt written all over your faces. Do you think I'm stupid, she thought. Ginger's eyes fell to the tabletop, and she stared without seeing at her piece of pie. Don't make a fool of yourself, Ginger! Don't overreact! Maybe you're misjudging the situation. Maybe they're not—

"Well, sit down, Devin!" Marla said as she moved over to make room for him. "Join us!"

Marla's uneasiness had seemingly disappeared. Ginger looked up at her in surprise, hurt and suspicion still in her eyes. Marla smiled sweetly at her, then glanced at Devin, who had rather cautiously taken the seat next to her. "I'm glad you saw us through the window."

What do you mean us? He saw you, Marla, and you know it, Ginger thought with rage. How dare they? Didn't they have any respect for her feelings at all?

Suddenly she sat absolutely still as she heard her own thoughts. What was the matter with her? She was reacting as if . . .

With trembling fingers she opened her purse and began to take money out of her wallet to pay her check. She'd better leave before she made an even bigger fool of herself. There was nothing to verify that anything more than business had gone on between Devin and Marla. Even if he had taken her to dinner. Who cared, anyway? If they wanted to have an affair, let them! It was no concern of hers.

She put the money on the table. In as calm a voice as she could muster she said, "I have to get back to the shop." Without a further glance at them, she slid out of her seat and went to the door. She heard them murmur something in response, but she paid no attention. In minutes she was back in her shop, alone in the sanctuary of her small back office.

Over the next couple of hours she tried to analyze her own reaction and speculate on what was actually developing between Devin and Marla. But it was all such a muddle in her head, she soon gave up, telling herself it didn't matter anyway.

Yet her thoughts would not leave her alone. The image of them sitting together across from her kept playing on her mind. They made a handsome couple. Marla had the svelte sophistication and quick wit she imagined Devin would want. And Marla had already made it clear that she found Devin attractive. Suddenly Ginger felt like crying.

With determination she got up from her desk and walked into the main room of her store. Needing to distract herself, she picked up a cloth and began dusting. It was a slow afternoon. Only one customer had come in to look around briefly and then left without buying anything.

She was replacing some brass candlesticks she had been polishing when Devin walked in. She tensed, and resentment filled her. What was he doing here?

"Ginger?" he said as he approached.

"Hello," she replied quietly and coldly.

He came within a few feet of her and stopped. "You didn't have to run off so fast."

She did not reply to that. "How are things going with your house?" she asked. Her voice sounded waspish even to her own ear.

"Fine. With Marla's help, the seller and I have agreed on an amount. She's even arranged the financing. That's why I came down—to discuss it with her and sign some papers."

"It took all afternoon to settle that with Marla?" Immediately she wished she hadn't said it. What was the matter with her!

Devin casually leaned his elbow on the display shelf they were standing near. There was gentle humor in his voice. "You know, Ginger, you seem a little jealous."

She flashed a hostile glance at him and walked away.

He followed. "Are you?"

"I wouldn't jump to conclusions!" she said coolly. In her heart she was finding it difficult to deny that she was indeed jealous.

"It's hard not to, especially as it's something I'd like to believe. I like Marla, but it's strictly business between us. You have no cause to—"

"You had dinner with her," she said in as cool a voice as she could manage.

"She told you?" he said with some surprise.

"Yes. We *are* old friends," Ginger said, looking at him squarely. "It's not the first time we've had entanglements with the same man." She knew her statement tended to exaggerate the truth, but she didn't care. She didn't want Devin to think he could play Marla and her against one another to suit his own objectives.

Devin's eyes darkened as he looked at her. But his voice was gentle as he said, "I asked *you* to dinner first. Remember?"

Ginger looked down and did not reply.

"You refused, and I didn't feel like eating alone," he explained. "What I'd like to know is why you're so upset about it."

"I'm not!"

"Ginger," he said in an amused, chiding voice, "don't forget how well I know you. I think you're jealous." She turned away from him, but he caught her elbow and kept her near. "And if you are, then it means you still have some feelings for me."

His words provoked her. "What egos you men have!" She turned and glared at him. "Yes, I have feelings for you, Devin: resentment, bitterness—sheer rage at your audacity to come back here and try

64

to worm your way into my life!" She could see from his wincing expression that her words were hurting him. "You don't know me so well anymore. I was naive enough once to be blind to your lack of integrity, your fickleness, your—your weakness for easy women! I'm a little smarter than that now—or at least wise enough to know I shouldn't go near you with a ten-foot pole!"

Her angry barrage of words had left her breathless. Both stood for a moment saying nothing, recovering.

"So you hate me," Devin said at last. "I—expected you to, and I understand. You may be surprised to know that in a way I'm glad you hate me. It was your indifference I feared."

Ginger's brows drew together and she looked at him in astonishment.

"But you aren't indifferent," he went on. "I still matter to you somehow, even if it's in a negative way. There's a thin line between love and hate, you know. A love that's been betrayed naturally turns to hate. But perhaps—is it still capable of becoming jealous?"

A stinging glaze of tears made her eyes glassy. He was so incisive; he could think on his feet so well. He was as quick and instinctive as Marla. How could she match wits with him? It would take her half a day of contemplation to analyze her emotions and find a good reply to his argument.

"All right, maybe it's true," she said, blinking hard. "It's hard for anyone to forget an old relationship completely. But that doesn't mean a person should nurture whatever remnant of feeling is left. I don't know what you're looking for from me, Devin, but I don't want anything from you. Not friendship, not love, not anything!"

Devin's expression was crestfallen, but he stood where he was, showing no trace of inclination to leave. He was looking a little pale, as though he didn't feel well. She turned away from him and walked toward the cash register. Absently she toyed with a pen that was lying on the counter. After a few moments she heard footsteps, and soon Devin's voice was near her ear.

"Ginger, have dinner with me tonight."

She turned abruptly. "Haven't you heard anything I've said?" she asked with astonishment.

"I heard. I don't agree."

She could see a stubbornness in his countenance now. "I don't care whether you agree or not!" she said.

"I think the way you're dealing with me is very unfair."

65

"Unfair!"

"Yes. Years ago I wronged you; I've never denied it. Can't you allow me some chance to make restitution?"

"I don't want restitution!"

"Can't I at least be allowed the chance to make some sort of peace between us? Is it healthy for us to go through the rest of our lives this way—you with your bitterness, me with my guilt?"

"Guilt?" she repeated dubiously.

"Of course. I told you back then how terrible I felt about what I did to you. That hasn't changed."

"You apparently didn't stop to think about what you were doing to me when you took up with that woman!" she shot back. "I'm afraid I can't sympathize with your guilt feelings now."

"How do you know what I thought about?" he said, a tremor of anger in his tone. He paused, blinking quickly as if to quell his emotion. "Ginger," he began again in a more subdued, intellectualized tone, "years ago English law dictated that a person who couldn't pay his debts had to be sent to debtors' prison. That always seemed to me a very unfair punishment. If a person was locked in jail, how could he ever earn the money to pay his debt? He would remain in prison forever, without hope. You always had a sense of justice, Ginger. If you shut me out, if you won't even have dinner with me, how can I ever have any way of making up for what I did?"

Did she really want him even to try to make it up to her? Ginger closed her eyes. She was frankly too worn out to argue any more with him. He was almost succeeding in making *her* feel guilty. Maybe if she just had dinner with him, he'd go away and leave her alone. "All right," she said in a grudging whisper, "I'll have dinner with you!"

Ginger closed the shop early. It was a slow afternoon, anyway. And she wanted to get this dinner over with.

"Where will we go?" she asked resignedly as Devin led her to his car, which was parked on Second Street.

"Since you have such an elegant dress on, how about someplace nice?"

She smiled slightly at the compliment. As he opened the car door for her, she realized she was getting into a Mercedes.

"It's a beautiful car," she acknowledged rather coolly when he had gotten behind the wheel. "Did you buy it in Chicago?"

"Yes. I drove it all the way out here. It was kind of a lonely trip."

They passed her house as they took the road out of town, but she thought it unnecessary to point it out. "Why did you leave Chicago?" she asked.

He hesitated quite awhile before answering. "I was beginning to feel like a lost soul there. I like Chicago, but it never felt like home to me. Coupeville isn't the right place for me anymore, either. I've grown accustomed to a big-city atmosphere. I thought maybe Seattle would be a compromise between the two. It's near Whidbey Island where my roots are, and being a large city, it has many of the advantages Chicago has."

"Why are you buying the house on Double Bluff Beach then?"

He glanced at her and smiled. "Trying to fulfill another old dream, I suppose. My former fantasies about living happily in Chicago never quite came true. Contentment has always—eluded me somehow. I thought by spending weekends at Double Bluff Beach I might be able to find the balance, or whatever it is I need. You're happy in Langley?"

She replied that she was, and they discussed the town and her shop as they drove northward on the main road up the island, passing farmland and patches of thick evergreen forest.

She had assumed he was driving to Oak Harbor. Being the largest town on the island, it had most of the better restaurants. She was surprised when he turned down the road that led to Coupeville, passing near where the MacPherson farm was located.

"We aren't eating in Coupeville, are we?" she asked. She was alarmed that someone in her family or some old acquaintance would see them together, a possibility that would cause her no end of commotion with her relatives.

"No, just driving through," he said.

She was wondering if he was taking a scenic route or if he just wanted to get another look at Coupeville on his way to Oak Harbor. When he turned onto a tree-lined, narrow road called Madrona Way, however, a new possibility arose in her mind. Oh, no, she thought. He wouldn't dare!

"Where are we going, Devin?" she asked with quickly escalating anxiety.

He didn't answer.

"Devin!" She watched in near-horror as he turned down the tiny road that led to the Captain Whidbey Inn.

The inn, named for the sea captain who discovered the island, was a picturesque old resort, built in 1907 of madrona logs. It was also the place where almost eight years ago Ginger and Devin's wedding dinner had been held.

He drove up to the aged, compactly built two-story structure. The dark gray-brown weathered logs of which it was constructed gave it a rather stark, haunted quality. Ginger bristled at the sight of it.

"Are you out of your mind, Devin? You're not taking me in there!"

"Ginger—"

"I mean it! Are you trying to be cruel? How can you even think of—"

"Ginger! Shhh. Don't get upset," he said quietly. "We won't go in if you don't want to."

"I don't!" she practically spat at him. "I can't believe the nerve you have even bringing me here!"

"Yes—yes, I have a lot of nerve," he softly agreed. "But, Ginger, we're going to run into the past almost everywhere on this island. Why not get the worst hurdle over with first, and the rest will be easier?"

"W-what do you mean, the rest?" she said. "I just agreed to go to dinner with you tonight because somehow you managed to twist my arm. I'm not planning any future outings with you!"

He swallowed and hesitated. "It's going to take some time—more than one dinner together—to—to try to wipe the slate clean and find some basis for a new friendship."

"I don't want to be friends!"

"Well, I do!" he argued gently. "I thought we just settled all this awhile ago at your shop. Your sense of justice told you that you owe me the chance to atone for the way I hurt you, remember? It's not good for either of us to live with these unfortunate memories. We have to be able to face the past, look it in the eye, before we can make peace with ourselves and each other."

He sounds like either a clergyman or a con artist, she thought. Why didn't I sent him out of my shop the minute he walked in? She said nothing aloud, but she could see he was studying her silence.

"I don't think having dinner here will be so traumatic," he went on. "It's just a place, built of wood and mortar. It's the memory that makes it uncomfortable; it's the memory we have to deal with."

Ginger had heard enough. He could probably go on like this all night. She took hold of the door handle and jerked it open, got out

68

of the car, then slammed the door shut. She walked around the parked vehicle and up the wood steps of the inn, leaving Devin hurrying to catch up with her.

They walked into the small lobby, which was dominated by a large stone fireplace. Over the fireplace hung a portrait of a very serious little girl dressed in old-fashioned clothes. There was a huge, low round table in front of the fireplace, loaded with magazines and surrounded by an assortment of big easy chairs. They walked through to the entrance to the dining room.

As Ginger looked in she felt a shudder go through her. The room hadn't changed much. The walls were wood paneled, decorated with large paintings and shelves arranged with antique plates. It was a rectangular room, set with neat rows of wood tables and antique chairs. On the left were large windows that looked out on Penn Cove and the inn's private dock.

Tonight the atmosphere was different, however, from when she had last seen it the afternoon after the wedding ceremony had taken place. The tables had been arranged differently for their large party, and the room had been filled with the laughter and anticipation of friends and relatives. It had been a long-awaited, joyful day for all the Cowans and MacPhersons.

Since it was still early for dinner, the dining room was quiet now and not at all crowded. Voices were soft in private conversations, and the ambience was calm and comfortably impersonal.

The hostess seated them at a table near one of the windows and gave them menus. Both chose to have baby coho salmon, a specialty of the area. When the waitress came to take their order, Ginger was surprised when Devin asked for cottage cheese instead of a salad.

"Didn't you used to hate cottage cheese?" she asked when the waitress had gone.

"I've learned to like it," he said. "It's not so bad being here, is it?"

She glanced wistfully about her. "I'd rather not answer that," she replied, trying to sound flippant.

"All right," he said with a little smile. "I appreciate your coming, Ginger. Thank you."

She felt uncomfortable and did not reply, turning her head to look out at the calm waters of the cove. On the other side of the water was flat, peaceful-looking farmland.

A movement caught her eye, and she glanced back at Devin to

find him putting a piece of white candy into his mouth. He put a small aluminum-wrapped roll back in his pocket.

"Candy before dinner, Devin? Aren't you going to offer me a piece?"

He looked like he didn't know quite what to say. "It's an—antacid tablet. If you like the taste of chalky mint, I'll give you one."

"No thanks." She hesitated but couldn't keep herself from asking, "You're not feeling well?"

"I'm okay."

Her brows drew together. "You eat them for fun?"

He smiled self-consciously. "No, my stomach often bothers me. A lot of accountants have the problem—you know, worrying about deadlines and pleasing clients."

"Is that part of the reason you left Chicago—to get away from the pressure?"

"Well, with the company I work for, the pressure's bad anywhere."

"Oh." She felt herself wanting to ask him more about what seemed to be a chronic ailment for him, but she forced herself to appear disinterested. She didn't want him thinking she was concerned about his health.

The waitress came to pour their wine. Ginger had half-expected him to raise his glass of Chablis and make some toast to peace and friendship, but he didn't. In fact, as the meal progressed, she noticed he drank no wine at all.

They talked about a number of things—her family, his family, Coupeville, Langley—with Devin initiating and keeping up the conversation most of the time, as Ginger was not inclined to talk. At one point he asked her about Jack Whiting.

"Have you known him long?"

"A few years," she said.

"Have you gone out with him a lot?"

"Regularly," she replied, deciding he could read into that whatever he chose.

"Is there—something serious between you?"

He had asked the question with casual straightforwardness. She thought a minute before answering. Something urged her to say, "At the moment he's having an affair with Marla."

He stopped toying with the food on his plate and stared at her. At first something like relief passed over his face, but in the next instant his eyes were darkening and honing in on her. It was easy to read him: He was wondering if Ginger had had a similar relationship with Jack. With a Mona Lisa smile she calmly lowered her eyes from his questioning gaze and finished the last bite of salmon on her plate.

Devin said nothing for a while, and they finished their meal in silence. When Devin had put down his fork for the last time, however, Ginger's eyes fell on his full glass of wine. She remembered once hearing something about alcohol being irritating to a stomach ulcer.

"Devin, you don't have an ulcer, do you?" Her voice sounded small, like a little girl's, though she had hoped to sound casual.

His eyes rose quickly to hers, and his look was guarded. "No, I don't think so."

"Do you always order wine and then not drink it?"

"I—didn't like this particular wine much."

How could he know? He hadn't even tried it. She remembered when the waitress had poured a little in his glass first for him to taste, he had asked that Ginger taste it, a gesture that she had simply thought part of his efforts to be especially gracious toward her. His glass was still untouched.

"Have you seen a doctor about your stomach problem?"

"No. It's nothing."

A shade of worry clouded her light brown eyes. She wished he didn't look like he needed taking care of. "Maybe you should," she said, sounding more solicitous that she wanted to.

He smiled slightly. "Want some dessert?"

"No, thanks."

"Shall we walk around the grounds a little?"

They spent some time walking near the water and looking at the overnight accommodations, new and old, that the inn provided. When it was completely dark they drove back to Langley. Ginger directed him to her house, and he pulled his car into the driveway. He walked with her to her back door entrance. She supposed he wouldn't mind coming in, but she wasn't about to invite him.

"Looks like a nice place," he said under the pale porch light.

"Yes, it is," she replied coolly. "Well, thank you for dinner, Devin." She extended her hand. He took it and kept it, and she speedily realized she had made a bad move. The nerves along her

71

spine prickled at the warmth and feel of the large, once-familiar hand encompassing hers.

"It wasn't so awful, was it?"

"I guess not," she admitted. If she didn't argue with him, maybe he would leave more quickly. He was moving closer, and her hand was now clasped and being fondled by both of his. She tried to pull away, but he wouldn't let her. "I'm going in now, Devin," she told him in a no-nonsense way.

"Not quite yet."

Panic gripped her as she saw the look in his eye, but she had no time to escape. In the next instant she was in his arms, enfolded by his warmth and masculine strength. Her soft bosom was forced against his vest, and his muscular thighs came against hers. When she opened her mouth to protest, her cry was smothered. She struggled against the hard insistence of his kiss, but it was useless. His lips moved possessively over hers in a heated, sensual back-and-forth movement. In a mere few moments he had overwhelmed her both physically and mentally.

She felt lost and weak. His mouth devoured hers as his hands moved with caressing sureness over her back to her small waist and rounded hips. Part of her was horrified to feel long-lost sensations of desire curling within her. But another part of her craved them, hungered for their promise of fulfillment. She sought to stifle the heady inclinations growing within her, and she pressed her hands against him in a renewed effort to fight him.

He kept her against him with ease. His kiss increased in intimacy, and the feel of his warm, strong hands through her thin dress began to mesmerize her senses. Gradually she gave up and grew pliable in his embrace.

"Devin," she protested in a limp whisper when he finally took his mouth from hers.

"I want to see you tomorrow." He spoke in a soft, sure tone that said he was ready to argue if necessary.

"No," she whispered. It sounded almost like a sob.

"Yes! I'll come by about ten and pick you up."

"My shop—I have to work—"

"Your shop is closed Saturdays. It was when I came by two weeks ago."

"I was visiting my family," she said, pushing away, trying to clear her head.

72

"Then you can close it to be with me." He drew her against his broad chest again, kissing her mouth feverishly, then trailing his lips urgently down her throat, which quivered with her uneven breaths.

"Don't . . . you have no right!"

"Maybe I don't, but I'm taking it!" he said as he held her close, his warm, moist breath hovering over her lips.

He kissed her hard on the mouth once more, and then he was walking away in the darkness.

CHAPTER FIVE

Shortly before ten o'clock Devin pulled into the driveway where Ginger lived. So far his stomach was better this morning, and he hoped it would stay that way. He loathed the idea of Ginger thinking he was sickly, although the fact that she had seemed concerned had encouraged him. She still had some feelings for him, he was sure.

He got out of the car and looked up at the attic windows. He hoped he hadn't come on too strong last night, but he hadn't been able to hold himself back. She was so beautiful to him. He had longed to touch her again from the day he first walked into her shop. And he had to be forceful; it looked unlikely that she would move toward him or make it easy for him in any way, for that matter.

The sun was reflecting off the windows, and he couldn't see inside. He began walking around to the back porch, where he had left her last night. As he neared the corner of the house, he almost ran into a small, gray-haired woman who was coming from the other direction.

"Oh!" she said, startled. "I thought I heard a car pull up."

Apparently she was Ginger's landlady. Devin noticed she was wearing gardening gloves and guessed she had been at the back of the house working. "Excuse me," he apologized. "I'm here to see Ginger."

"Ginger?" the lady replied, eyeing him oddly. "She left about an hour ago. She's usually at her shop on Saturdays—you know, Ginger's Spice over on First?"

"Oh. Yes, I know. Thanks." It had occurred to him that Ginger might do that. He should have expected it. He nodded to the landlady and walked back to his car. So he would have to go through another debate with Ginger. Well, if she could stand it, so could he. She must have known he'd come after her.

He paused at the car door as the thought occurred to him that she might not have gone to the shop. He sighed wearily, and his hand went to his abdomen. If she was bent on avoiding him, she might have gone to her family in Coupeville for the day. He shook his head slightly as he reached for his roll of antacid tablets. He didn't think he had the stomach to face the Cowans just yet.

Ginger nervously looked at her watch. It was ten o'clock. He was probably finding out at that moment that she had purposely broken his date arrangement. It served him right. He had no business insisting she spend the day with him, even telling her to close her shop! She had to support herself, after all. Why hadn't she told him that last night?

A vivid memory of the sensual strength she had felt while she was in his arms swept over her, and she knew why she had objected so weakly. His kisses had been more overpowering than she had ever remembered from their courting days. Her mother was right: He was dangerous.

She had to be strong, she told herself as she unpacked some cutlery sets that had been delivered the day before and absently arranged them on a shelf. She couldn't let him use her lifelong weakness for him to undermine her.

But he was right—even if she hated him, she somehow still cared for him. The realization frightened her. She couldn't allow herself to chance trusting him again. She must—

"Hello, Ginger."

She whirled. He was standing not far from her. She hadn't heard him come in through the shop's open front door.

"You don't have to scare me like that!"

"Sorry. I'm glad to find you here."

"Where else would I be?" she replied irritably.

"Out in the woods somewhere, hiding from me."

"Maybe that's what I should have done," she said, acting busy as she continued her unpacking. Yet it hadn't escaped her how handsome he looked in tan pants, an open-collar shirt, and a casual tweed jacket.

"Why didn't you?"

"What?" she asked with annoyance, not understanding.

"Nothing," he said quietly. He hesitated only a moment, then said, "Marla gave me the key to the house. I told her I wanted to

75

go out and look at it, see what kind of furniture I'll need to buy and so on."

"Is that proper? You don't legally own it yet."

"Not exactly," Devin admitted. "Since the present owner is on the East Coast, Marla figured he'd never know the difference. She's going to see if she can make an arrangement so I can rent it until the closing date, when I take legal possession. That way I can begin to use it sooner."

"How nice of Marla," Ginger said. She didn't mean to sound catty, but she knew she did.

She heard a soft laugh, and suddenly his arms were around her, pulling her to him. "What are you doing?" she said, trying to twist away.

"Hugging you."

"I don't want you to!"

"Too bad," he said as his lips grazed her cheek. "Come out to the house with me! I want you to see it."

"No," she said, still trying to get out of his grasp.

"We had a date."

"I didn't agree to it!"

"You can change your mind," his soft, coaxing voice whispered in her ear. It sent a little quiver through her. This was terrible; he was being sweet and playful, like he had been with her years ago. It scared her to realize she was almost enjoying it.

With all her strength she broke out of his arms. "Stop it!" Quickly she moved away from him and took refuge behind the counter near the cash register.

He stood where he was for a moment, watching her flee from him. Slowly he walked up to the counter opposite where she was standing, her head bowed and her forehead crinkled in agitation.

"Are you afraid of me, Ginger?" His tone was quiet and caring.

"No. Why should I be?" she said defensively, trying to look tough.

"I don't know, but I think you are. You never used to be." There was a vulnerable edge to his voice, and she could sense it weakening her own resistance.

She had never known if he was aware of it, but she had always been acutely sensitive to his voice. It could mesmerize her with its low gentleness, and he was capable, whether he knew it or not, of using it to infuse her with some of his own emotion. It was why, long

76

ago, he had usually been able to calm her with a few words when she was upset. She could feel his sorrow now because her trust in him was gone, and that in turn made her feel bad. Keeping her gaze on the counter, she said nothing.

"You're afraid if you let yourself like me again, I'll do something that hurts you again, aren't you?" he said, his voice a little uneven. "I wouldn't, Ginger. It's the last thing I want. I know it's hard for you to have any faith in me now, but I wish you would try. I still—care for you a great deal."

His words had the effect of a strong wind sweeping her off balance. Tears filled her eyes, and her stoic facial expression weakened. She turned away from him slightly, hoping he wouldn't see. But he came around the counter to stand behind her, and soon his arms were enveloping her. Her back was pressing snugly against his chest, and his head was next to hers, his lips near her ear.

"Please, spend the day with me," he softly urged.

She swallowed and could hardly speak. "I should work today."

"It's a beautiful spring day. Why spend it inside?" His arms were over hers, and he gently took hold of one of her small wrists and shook it as he said the words, like one might coax a small child.

It made her want to laugh, yet she wasn't through with her tears. She felt slightly hysterical inside. "I have to pay the rent," she said, trying to keep an adult state of mind. "I can't make money if I close the shop."

"I saw your books. You're not doing so badly."

"Because I stay open on Saturdays and make extra money," she said. It was a good reply, she congratulated herself, one with which she didn't think he could argue. She tried to smother the tiny, yearning voice within her that hoped he could.

"All right," he said, "let's see what we can do." Abruptly he took his arms from around her and moved away. She felt bereft.

He walked around the shop for a few minutes, then picked up a tray on which was placed an expensive English bone china tea set. It consisted of four cups and saucers, a teapot, a hot-water pot, a sugar bowl, and a creamer all in the same graceful pattern of violets and twined stems against a white background. It was one of her favorites. He brought it to the counter and set it near the cash register.

"I would like to purchase this," he said, getting out his wallet.

77

"What would you do with an English tea set?" she said in suspicious astonishment.

"Well, you see, Madame Proprietress, I'm buying a house and I need to stock it. How much?"

"You saw the price tag—two hundred and seventy-five dollars."

"Fine. You take Mastercharge or Visa, I presume?"

"Devin, you're just doing this so I'll—I won't sell it to you!"

"Won't sell it!" he said with quiet indignance. "You won't do business with me?"

"No!"

"You discriminate against certain of your customers in this shop, Mrs.—Miss Cowan? I'm afraid I'll have to report this to the government authorities!"

In consternation, she wanted to cry and laugh at the same time. "Oh, Devin!" she said with acute annoyance as she jerked the credit card from his fingers.

"Thank you," he said. "And I'd like that properly wrapped!"

A few hours later Devin was holding Ginger's hand as they walked slowly along the beach. The tide was out, making the sandy beach look endless as it stretched out to the point where it met the ocean's edge. A long single row of houses of varying style made a shallow crescent at the inner edge of the sand beach. In front of them was another, much more haphazard crescent of large, white-gray logs that had washed up on shore over the years.

Awhile ago they had just finished a light lunch sitting on one such log in front of the house Devin was to buy. Before leaving Langley they had stopped at the quiche-and-sandwich shop and gotten sandwiches and soft drinks to take with them. Devin had shown her the lower floor of the house, a wood frame home that was modern and at the same time quaint in its design.

It was fresh and clean both outside and inside, as though it had just been built, though Devin said it was four years old. Inside, the wall-to-wall carpeting looked brand new and the kitchen appeared to have scarcely been used. Apparently the previous owner had not had a chance to use the house much.

Ginger glanced back at it now and then as they walked along. She liked the house and she liked the location. She thought it must be nice to look out the large front windows and gaze at the bay and at Double Bluff, a high, rounded cliff off to the right that gave the place its name.

"This beach will be great for running or jogging," Devin said, letting go of her hand to put his arm around her.

Ginger did not object. She was enjoying herself and had given up fighting him, at least for the time being. When she felt Devin's large hand at her waist through the thin fabric of her deep blue blouse, she could almost hear her mother lecturing her that she was in for trouble. She suppressed the warning voice. Her mother was always too emotional and excitable, anyway. Ginger could see no harm in walking down a beach with her former husband on such a glorious, sunny day.

"Do you jog?" Devin asked.

"What? Oh. No, I don't, but I should. As you can see, I've gained some extra pounds," she said ruefully.

Devin smiled. "I noticed." He pointedly adjusted his glasses with thumb and forefinger as he gazed over the curves that filled out her blouse and gave shape to her beige pants. "I wouldn't call them *extra*, though. They look like they're all in the right places."

"Devin!" she said, laughing a little with embarrassment. But for the first time she almost felt proud of her figure. She also noticed that she didn't really mind him admiring her, either. Vaguely she wondered why her attitude had changed but felt uneasy with the question and let it go.

"In fact, the more I think about it, I'd love to watch you jogging along this beach!" Devin said wickedly.

She gasped, her mind quickly envisioning the picture of her bobbing bosom he must be imagining. She pushed him playfully, broke away and began running toward the wet sand further out that had been left by the receding bay water. There were a few low areas that had large, shallow puddles of seawater, and she was intent on getting him a little wet.

She ran to one, bent and dipped her hands into the salty water. When she straightened and turned around, he was upon her. She flicked some drops into his face, which splattered his glasses and hair. The newly moistened neatness of his fine-boned, square-jawed countenance and glasses made her laugh.

"Very funny!" he said, grinning as he grabbed one of her hands and pushed the wet palm into her own face.

"No!" she squealed, trying to back away from him. He caught her off balance, so that she had to cling to him to remain upright in the soft sand. In the next moment he was kissing her.

Their little water fight was immediately forgotten in an embrace that soon became consuming and urgent. Ginger's hands rose to his shoulders, then twined around his neck. She realized she had been waiting, wishing for him to kiss her for hours.

His arms were tight around her, clasping her to him, crushing the soft, rounded thrust of her breasts against his broad chest. The feel and force of the pressure between their clinging bodies excited her, making her pulse begin to race. She felt reckless as she returned each hard kiss. Her eyes closed dreamily as her warm and willing lips opened under the sensual onslaught of his mouth.

As their kiss deepened, his hands at her back moved restlessly over the smooth silken material of her blouse, down to her petite waist, then glided firmly over her derriere. Gradually his hands rose again to the sides of her waist, then moved up her small ribcage to the sides of her breasts. The palms of his hands pressed and caressed her rounded contours, making her quiver slightly in a sensual frisson.

She remembered years ago, stolen private moments away from watchful relatives, when Devin would gently unbutton her blouse and fondle her uncovered breasts. Young and inexperienced, she had felt embarrassed and uneasy at first, but soon grew to want his intimate touch. She wanted it now.

"Oh, Ginger," Devin whispered with feeling when he finally drew his mouth away. She weakly pressed her forehead against the base of his neck, and he bowed his head over hers, resting his cheek in her hair. His arms slipped around her again in a warm embrace. "I've missed you so much," he murmured. "I tried all these years to forget you, but I couldn't."

All Ginger's eager, positive feelings toward Devin disintegrated with the nightmarish memories his words brought back to her. Her eyes became glassy and her expression hopelessly troubled as she began to recoil within his arms.

"Ginger?"

"Why did you ever leave, then? Why did you have to go to Chicago? Why did you take that woman to bed when you knew you would be marrying *me* soon and could have had *me* to make love with?" she said in a burst of emotion. "Was two or three weeks so long to wait after all the years we'd been going together? Or was she so much prettier than me?"

"Ginger—"

"Don't try to calm me down! You come back now, wheedling me and kissing me as if I'm supposed to forget all that. Well, I won't—I can't! So you missed me—isn't that too bad! *I* nearly killed myself when you left!"

She glimpsed the horror in Devin's face before she wrenched herself out of his arms and began to run away down the beach. "Ginger!" she heard him calling after her, but she wouldn't stop. In a moment, however, she was forcefully halted by his strong arms.

"That's something we need to talk about!" he said as he firmly gripped her upper arms and made her face him.

"I don't want to talk, I want to forget it!" she said, trying not to break down completely.

"But you said you can't forget it. Neither can I. If we talk about it, maybe we can put it behind us somehow." She was crying now, and he put her head on his shoulder. "Let me try to explain. Why don't we go back to the house?"

Ginger fought hard to control her unruly emotions. She had to get hold of herself! She wanted to have some dignity left. Besides, when she allowed her emotions to run rampant, it only left her more vulnerable to Devin's strong arms and comforting voice. That she mustn't allow. She wanted to see him for what he was, not for what he could make her think he was.

She dried her eyes with her hands and drew away from him. "All right," she said in a firm, almost challenging tone. "I'd like to hear your explanation. You never gave me one that made any sense eight years ago!"

"I know," he said quietly. Taking her hand, he led her to the house.

When they got back inside and glanced about the empty rooms, Ginger was the first to state the obvious. "There's no place to sit."

Devin's face brightened. "Yes there is! You haven't seen the upstairs bedroom yet."

They climbed the staircase to the upper level, to a large, empty room papered with an antique floral pattern. The floor was covered with a luxurious, spotless white rug. A large recessed window overlooked the beach. Below the window was a built-in window seat

81

covered with a cushion that matched the yellow of the window's café curtains.

"It looks like a doll house," Ginger rather reluctantly commented. Such a pretty setting seemed incongruous to the unpleasant subject they had come up to discuss.

"I hoped you would like it," Devin said. They walked to the wide window seat and sat at opposite ends, each leaning for back support against a recessed wall.

"Well?" she said after several moments of silence.

"It's hard to know how to begin," Devin said softly. He took off his glasses and set them down, then rubbed his eyes. He looked a little careworn and tired now. "You remember, Ginger, how well I did at school—winning those scholarships and so on?"

"Of course. We were all proud of you."

"I know, but it was around that time that the idea of my own brilliance began to impress *me* as well as everyone else. Everyone had such high expectations for me: my family, my teachers—everyone. I began to set high goals for myself; I felt I was obligated not to disappoint anyone." He paused a moment. "That's not fair; I shouldn't blame it on others. I wanted success for myself, too. But it made me nervous. Here I was a farm kid who had attended a small high school and lived all his life on a rather obscure island. How could I compete at a big university and make it in the business world?

"But, of course, I was successful and even graduated college with honors, as you know. My professors encouraged me to aim for the best. Lo and behold, I got a job with one of the country's top public accounting firms. Even they said, when I was hired, that they had high hopes for me. Part of me began to believe it all; and it was true, I did have the ability. But I always worried, underneath, that I didn't have the sophistication, the big-city savvy that I figured others I'd be competing with would have just because they grew up in a metropolitan area. So in one way I had grown rather conceited about myself, but I also had a lot of insecurity. Meanwhile, like a prize glittering ahead of me, was my goal of becoming a top executive, with a big salary and a lot of clout."

"Where was I supposed to fit into all that?" Ginger asked.

Devin shrugged and leaned forward, resting his elbows on his knees. "I always saw you there with me. It began to worry me when you didn't seem to want to move from the island, but I—I guess I figured you'd follow me anywhere. You used to be pretty dependent on me in a lot of ways—emotionally, intellectually. You were very young. You didn't seem capable of standing on your own two feet."

"Why did you want me, then?" Ginger asked, a little disgusted with his description of her youthful self, though she knew it was fairly accurate.

He looked up at her, his green eyes translucent as they reflected the light pouring through the window. "I loved you. I always loved you. Even when we were grade-school kids, I had a special feeling for you. I don't know why." He smiled slightly. "You were three years younger than me, a skinny little thing who cried a lot. But you always seemed to trust me and look to me for guidance when we were playing with other kids. You were kind of afraid of the others, maybe because you were so frail, and I found myself wanting to protect you. And as you grew older, you grew more beautiful—always feminine and changeable. I remember every adolescent stage you went through: shy, then silly and giggly, then aloof. I tried to ignore you for a time and work up an interest in girls my own age, but I never could get away from my attachment to you. So when you got old enough and your mother permitted it, I started going with you, and—you remember how close we grew over the years . . ."

His eyes were shimmering now as he looked at her, and Ginger had to turn her gaze from his. She tried to swallow away the tightness forming in her throat as tears threatened to rise in her eyes.

"What was between us is too complicated, too—tender a subject for me even to begin to try to analyze it. I just loved you. You were part of me. Even with my growing insecurities when I was at college and when I started working, I knew that whenever I was with you I could just be myself again and not worry whether you would accept me. Just as you clung to me, in a way I also clung to you."

Ginger sniffed a little before speaking. "You never mentioned your insecurities."

"No," Devin admitted, lowering his gaze. "I was facing a lot of pressures, Ginger. Not only about achieving career goals, but about becoming a husband and supporting you properly. We were so young! I didn't say anything because I didn't want you to think I couldn't handle it. You had always looked to me for guidance; I didn't want you to think I might fail you then, when we were planning to marry."

"I see," Ginger said softly. She looked up. "So what happened in Chicago?"

Devin sighed, as though he was hesitant to tackle the main issue. "I'm still not exactly sure how or why . . ." He left off and began again. "I was going to the company's training classes. I fell in love with Chicago—the tall buildings, the challenging business atmosphere, the pace of the city. Downtown Chicago is really quite attractive. I still think you would like it if you went there."

Ginger lowered her eyes defensively.

"It also has a well-entrenched, influential business community, and I decided it would be better for me to make a start there than in Seattle. Of course, when I called you, you—refused to live there. Well . . ."

He sighed again, rather more tensely this time. "As you know, I met the—the local Chicago girl who was also attending the classes. She was my age, very attractive and poised, and—what shall I say? Not exactly an innocent. We got acquainted between classes. I was upset at the time about your attitude. Somehow, I think, she began to embody to me everything I wanted then. She was from Chicago and knew her way around. She was bright and sophisticated. And I could tell she was attracted to me. In fact, she made it obvious she was. That alone blew my mind. What could she see in me, I thought, an inexperienced farm kid all dressed up in a three-piece suit trying to look like I belonged there? Her attention went to my head, at the same time that you were rocking the boat as far as my future plans went. I felt at that moment like the world was opening before me. But you were holding me back and—she was beckoning. I was too impressionable and immature then to handle it all; I got spun around and lost my direction.

"She—invited me to her apartment for dinner one night. I suppose I was a little naive; I thought there wouldn't be any harm if I went. Maybe I lied to myself; I don't know. I went to her place. I don't really think you want to hear the details."

Ginger tensely looked down at her hands lying limply in her lap. "How long did you go on seeing her?"

"A few times, until—that day I called you, when I asked you to postpone the wedding because I was mixed up about everything. You got so terribly upset, I felt sick. I had been so involved with my own ego, it was the first time I began to have some idea of what I had actually done to you, to our future. I thought about it and decided if I didn't tell you everything, maybe we could just go on as planned. Perhaps I didn't want to tell you, because if I did I would also have to admit to myself what I had done. Sweeping it under the rug was easier. But that didn't work, did it?" His eyes were liquid, and his voice was thickened by emotion now as he spoke.

"No, it didn't," Ginger said, keeping the lid tight on her own tears. "You never saw her again?"

"No."

"Why didn't you ever explain all this to me before?"

"I didn't know how, Ginger. Back then I couldn't analyze it all the way I can now after eight years of reflection. Besides, after you found out about the affair, we had trouble even speaking to each other."

Ginger nodded, recalling the deeply strained atmosphere between them after the revelations their wedding night had brought.

Both were silent for a long while. At last Ginger's voice broke the stillness. "So why have you come back? What do you want from me now?"

"Whatever you're willing to give," he said. "All these years I haven't really been happy. When we first got divorced and I went back to Chicago, I thought, well, I'll just have to start a new life. Maybe she and I weren't suited for each other after all. Maybe what happened was for the best. I still didn't want to face my own guilt and passed it off like that. But losing you was like a great wound constantly bleeding. I kept assuring myself I was young, I'd get over it." He paused. "But I never got over it."

Ginger was about to speak, but he rushed on.

"Year after year passed. I progressed in my career. I dated an assortment of women. Nothing—no one—could ever fill the void left when I lost you. I knew it was you that I needed, but I assumed you either hated me or had forgotten me. I knew through my family that you had never remarried, but I didn't place much hope in that. I figured you wouldn't want me in any case.

"Then I had to come back for my mother's funeral. I was astonished to see you there. You didn't talk to me; I could understand why. Seeing you after all that time, the true value of just how much I had lost finally hit me. I decided there was nothing left but to move back here and try to—to see if there was anything of what we had that could be salvaged. I knew it might be more painful than leaving things as they were and going on without you, but I had to try. Life didn't seem worth bothering with anymore. It took time and a lot of arguing with my superiors to get disentangled from the Chicago business scene, but I did it. So now here I am, throwing a wrench into your life," he said, smiling apologetically.

Ginger returned the same pale smile. She didn't know what to say.

"What do you think, Ginger? What are my chances?"

She pondered the question, her face sad. "I don't know, Devin," she said at last. "Even though a lot of time has passed, it's still difficult for me to overlook the fact that you were untrue to me. I understand better now what led you to it. Maybe it was even partly my fault. But the fact that you actually—" She stopped, for her voice and words failed her for a moment. "When we were so close, I don't see how you could have been so—intimate with a—a woman you hardly knew. I couldn't have done that, Devin. Even now I couldn't—sleep with someone I just met."

Devin made a small, hopeless smile. "Men are sexually aroused much more quickly than women. A man's ego is involved to a great extent, too. And I was so young. But I don't think I can give you any answer that would satisfy you. I have no good excuse. All I can do is admit my mistake."

She sat still, looking down at her hands with a disappointed expression. After a few moments he moved to sit beside her and put his hand over hers. "I know it will be hard to forget what happened, Ginger. Couldn't we try to put it aside for now and start fresh? We had so much together once. I think the potential is still there—at least for me it is. I still think you're beautiful. You still fascinate me—even more, now that we're both more mature."

His eyes dropped to scan her curves again. Her gaze caught him, and he smiled self-consciously. Something made her smile back a little. She couldn't deny even to herself that she was happy he wanted her.

"Maybe I'm deluding myself, but I think you still find me somewhat attractive, too. Do you?" he asked.

His voice fell softly over her while his hand made a comforting back and forth movement over her lower arm. An old feeling crept upon her, like she had been captured in a warm, intimate veil he had magically thrown about them, enveloping them and protecting them from the outside world.

She had felt that way often when she was with him, during her late teens. She used to imagine that it was what being married to him would be like: There would be just the two of them, together experiencing a continuous warmth and intimacy as if they were secluded in a tent in a thick forest on a rainy, foggy night. A tear slipped down her cheek as she felt herself recapturing the feeling now.

He was more than attractive to her. She couldn't even begin to express what he was to her. She mutely nodded her head to his question.

He drew her closer and gently wiped away the tear with his thumb. Lowering his face toward hers, he lightly kissed her eyes and cheeks, and then her lips. "Let's try, Ginger," he said, his voice uneven. "We have a lot of catching up to do. Will you see me—spend time with me so we can get to know each other again?"

"All right," she whispered, nestling her head under his chin.

He put his arm around her. "You won't try to avoid me, like this morning?"

"No."

"Promise?"

She made a tearful little laugh. His asking for a promise reminded her of when they were children. "Yes!"

"Okay." He sounded satisfied. She felt him kiss the top of her head while his hand came up to toy with her hair and tug at her ear. He ran his fingertips down her cheek to her chin, then lifted her face to his. His eyes moved over the contours of her face, lovingly examining their feminine sweetness.

Ginger looked up into Devin's green eyes, their color intensified by his dark lashes. She studied the tiny lines that fanned out from the outer corners of his eyes and the faint vertical smile lines in his cheeks that gave him a look of maturity he had not had years ago. His narrow nose and high cheekbones remained the same, giving him the look of refinement his mother had had. Her eyes focused on his mouth, the warm, masculine lips that were not thin or too full but smoothly shaped.

Those lips moved toward her now, meeting hers with gentle insistence. The arm around her shoulders gathered her to him while his other hand moved to her waist. Her heart rate began to rise as their kiss intensified. Her hands moved tentatively to his chest, going under the open lapels of his coat to the blue shirt beneath. Her hands trembled slightly at the body warmth she felt through the thin material. While his lips moved more and more urgently over hers, her hand rose to his open collar, moving beneath it to feel the smooth, heated skin at the base of his neck.

His own hands went to the lapels of his coat. He took his mouth from hers for a moment to smile and say, "The temperature seems to be rising!" After slipping off the tweed coat, he placed it on the seat next to him, near his glasses.

A comfortable sigh came from his throat as he put his arms around her again. Her hands encircled the back of his neck as their lips drew together. Ginger's eyes closed as he probed the softness of her mouth and his strong arms pressed her yielding curves firmly against him. She felt a heady force coming to life within her, the same as she had felt awhile ago when he kissed her on the beach. It was a positive, reinforcing feeling that made her know it was good to be alive and to be with Devin.

She was aware her family would be appalled if they knew she was with him now, but that didn't matter. Every instinct told her there was no harm in this. The past couldn't be changed, but she understood it a little better now. The future couldn't be guessed. There was only now, and all she knew was that it felt wonderful to be in his embrace. There was a bond between them that had remained through all the years of alienation. She understood now that Devin was right: She ought to nurture the remnants of her feelings for him, perhaps even let them bloom again. What they had had together years ago was very special, and if he had gone to such lengths to recapture it, then she ought to make the effort, too, oughtn't she?

Her family might never understand, but they didn't matter. *Devin* mattered. She trembled a little at the thought as her fingers curled into his hair and her senses heightened to the masculine feel of him. Yes, her hazy conscience whispered, it was just as it had been years ago; Devin mattered to her more than anyone.

Devin's moist, feverish mouth left her lips to move down her chin to the sensitive skin of her throat. A little sigh of pleasure escaped her. Then, as she felt his warm hand move slowly and exploratively over her breast, her heart began to race in anticipation. Her bosom rose and fell with her ragged breaths as his fingers moved to the row of buttons on her blouse and began to undo them. Her lashes fluttering in sensual eagerness, she glanced down and saw that his hands were trembling. But his strong fingers made quick work of

88

the buttons, then moved beneath the silken material to the cream-color lace bra beneath.

His fingertips glided over the softly rounded flesh above the confining lace. His lips soon followed, while his fingers deftly undid the front clasp of her delicate undergarment. In a moment her warm, voluptuous breasts were totally uncovered, her rosy nipples tilting up toward him, innocent and inviting.

Feeling embarrassed suddenly, Ginger bowed her head in confusion, but she soon was warmed and reassured by his husky whisper.

"You're lovely, Ginger—more beautiful than I ever imagined. Oh, my love!" he breathed. He pushed the blouse and bra off of her shoulders and down her arms until they were completely off her. While one arm went around her naked back to bring her near, his other hand reverently caressed her breasts, feeling their softness, gently fondling each nipple.

Ginger's eyes closed dreamily in pleasure as she rested her head against his shoulder. It had been eight years since she had experienced the intimate joy of his touch. She realized how badly she craved it.

In the first years after their divorce, she had allowed a few of the men she had dated briefly to touch her like this, vainly hoping she could forget Devin by finding another man. But it had never been the same. She had always finished by pushing them away, disappointed and even disgusted. Eventually she had grown to feel a distaste for physical contact with the men she met, and as a result most of them had quickly lost interest. Only Jack had made any effort to keep her friendship after she had rebuffed his advances.

But now she felt faint with the excitement of Devin's caresses. She wanted more. Her fingers began to unbutton his shirt, then pushed the material aside to expose his virile chest, which was rising and falling with his own quickening response. With a feline movement she glided her breasts against his bared skin, feeling the tingling roughness of the thick patch of dark hair that formed a V toward his belt.

He pressed her to him urgently, crushing her breasts, squeezing the air from her lungs. But she clung to him just as ferociously, meeting his lips with equal passion. He seemed newly energized and kissed her with a hard fierceness that thrilled her.

After an endless minute that left her blissfully numb, he took his mouth away. In the next moment he was kneeling in front of her,

89

his lips moving hotly over the white softness of her breasts, his face partly buried in her firm, warm flesh. She smiled in intense pleasure and pressed his head to her as his mouth took her nipple. Under the stimulation of his moist tongue she could feel the pink tip contracting and growing erect while awakening electric sensations that coursed along her nerves.

While she was lost in her joyous sensuality, she didn't realize that he had clasped her about the waist and was pulling her forward. In another moment she found herself lying on top of him, chest to chest, on the white carpet.

"Devin!" she said, laughing a little as she realized what he had done.

With the back of his head cradled comfortably in the plush rug, he looked up at her face just above his. His eyes were bright and afire with passion. His lips melted into a smile for a moment while his eyes adored her, then his hand at the back of her head urged her mouth toward his.

It was a long, deep, sensual kiss. While his tongue moved in harmonious circles with hers, his hands stroked her back and the sides of her breasts. They moved down to her hips, pressing her more firmly against his hard body as he arched his own hips and thighs upward. She stiffened involuntarily, not knowing why. She tried to ignore the feeling of alarm and pressed her fingertips more tightly into his shoulders.

Holding her against him, he turned them onto their sides, then rolled over completely so that he was on top of her. Suddenly she felt his total weight pressing down on her chest, stomach, and thighs, and again she grew rigid. The harrowing vision of their wedding night rose before her eyes. The humiliating memory of Devin lying on top of her in the hotel bed, lovelessly using her body, made her feel ill. She couldn't allow him to do that to her again.

"Devin!" she cried, forcefully pushing her hands against his muscular shoulders.

He rose away from her and saw her pained expression. "What's wrong, darling?"

She couldn't respond but scrambled away from him to sit by herself on the carpet by the window seat. She covered her naked bosom with her arms.

Sitting up in front of her now, he reached to touch her forearm, but she backed away. Her eyes were focused tensely on the carpet in front of her.

"I'm sorry if I went too fast. I didn't intend to, but—you were so responsive. I thought you wanted it, too," he said gently.

She knew he was studying her, hoping for some feedback from her as to what was wrong, but she couldn't say anything. Part of her thought with resentment that he ought to know; he ought to remember their wedding night as well as she. It was the callous, insensitive way he had touched her that night that had led her to ask him if he had had an affair. Didn't he remember that? Why should she have to speak of it? Why was he behaving as if he thought she was merely afraid of becoming intimate with him so soon? Didn't he know he had destroyed her fantasy of what it would be like to make love with him?

He moved slowly toward her, and she flinched as he reached in back of her. In the next second he was dropping her blue blouse into her lap. "Maybe you ought to put this on again," he said softly.

Tears came to her eyes as she clutched the blouse. Devin rose to his feet and reached for his jacket and glasses. As he rebuttoned his shirt he moved a little way away. Ginger dressed herself while his back was turned, her shaking hands fumbling with the material of her blouse.

She got up then and left the room, holding the rail tightly as her weak legs took her down the steps.

"Ginger, wait!" She heard his voice and hurried footsteps behind her. Suddenly his hand grabbed her wrist. Her fingers tightened grimly on the rail. "I love you!"

She became still and wooden. "Don't say that," she whispered, afraid to turn around and see his eyes.

"Why not? It's true. I love you more than ever!"

His voice was so certain and declarative. It made a person want to believe him. She had believed him once, and he had broken her trust. And when he had come back to marry her, fresh from the arms of another, he had taken her to bed in a way that showed little affection. He hadn't been rough, hadn't hurt her physically; but he had been uncaring, totally involved in his own raw passion, almost as though she were just a female body put there for his convenience. She had felt used and in a way degraded. Their lovemaking had erased all her expectations for fulfillment in his arms.

No, there was certainly no love in the way he had touched her that night. It seemed ludicrous that after bringing back such a memory so clearly to her mind, he would now insist that he loved her. *Love*—what did he mean by the word?

"How can you know what you feel?" she asked, staring down at the bottom of the steps. "It's been only a short time since you came back. It's too soon to—"

"I *love* you, Ginger!" She felt the hand at her wrist move up to grip her arm tightly. "The truth is, I've never been able to stop loving you. You've spoiled me for any other woman. Now, being near you again, I know I'll never be happy without you."

His insistent tone disturbed her. She took a step down, hoping to get away from him, but he kept hold of her arm and moved down a step himself so that he was still directly behind her.

"I don't know what happened upstairs," he went on. "I'm sorry if—if somehow I offended you. I just wanted you so much, I—" He seemed to catch himself as Ginger's body grew taut. He paused a moment and then said in a reassuring voice, "I'd never push you to do anything you didn't want to do. We'll try to keep things platonic between us for a while—"

"I don't want to see you anymore!" she said, her voice rising emotionally. She tried to pull her arm from his grasp. She had to fight him! Her family was right; it was dangerous for her to be seeing him. What power he must have over her if she had allowed things to go as far as they had today!

"You don't mean that!" His voice behind her sounded wounded and a little desperate. She didn't dare turn to look at him, knowing how he could play on her feelings and manipulate her. Listening to his voice was difficult enough.

"I mean it!" She would have said his name for emphasis, but found she couldn't. "I don't want to see you. I want you to leave me alone!"

"You owe it to me—"

"I don't owe you anything!"

"But you promised!"

"Promised?" she said in angry confusion, almost turning around. "What do you mean?"

"Awhile ago, upstairs, you promised to spend time with me. Remember? You always kept your promises, Ginger."

"We're not children anymore!"

He stepped down between her and the railing and made her turn to face him. His eyes were firm and intense as he looked at her, but his face was pale. "No, we're adults! All the more reason why promises should be kept!"

"You tricked me into saying that," she objected weakly.

He pushed the hair back from the side of her face and stroked her cheek. His gentle touch made her want to cry. "I didn't trick you. You may not have taken it seriously when I made you promise, but *I* was serious. I know you well, Ginger. You've always wanted to bolt from uncertainties. You haven't changed much in that respect. You go through life a little scared and ready to panic. That's why you used to need me. I was your rock. Now you don't have me for a mainstay anymore, and maybe that's good. You should be able to look to yourself for strength. Something I did upstairs scared you, and you want to run away again. Why don't you try facing it— facing me! Why don't you try being mature enough to hold to your promise, to move through this situation with me and see where we arrive? I expect you to keep your word, Ginger."

Ginger listened with a rebellious mind, but his remark about her maturity stung. "For how long?" she said bitterly.

"As long as it takes."

"Until what? You've seduced me?" Her tone was caustic.

He looked at her with some hesitation. "Until Christmas."

"That's too long! One month."

"Till the end of summer," he countered.

"One month!" she said angrily.

"Two!"

"One month!" She ripped her arm out of his grasp. "And remember—you said it would be platonic! I'm holding *you* to that!"

Devin looked back at the island as the ferry sped to the mainland in the misty twilight. She had been cold toward him for the rest of the afternoon, and between that and his stomach, he was feeling wretched. He leaned against the ship's railing, feeling almost dizzy for a moment. He sat down on one of the benches along the side of the vessel.

At least he had gotten her to keep her word about seeing him, he thought, taking off his glasses to rub his eyes. He was glad he had had the foresight to make her promise. What had gone wrong? She had been responding to him much more than he had dared to hope. She had kissed him back eagerly, had undone his shirt to touch him,

93

had laughed when he pulled her down on top of him. Her caresses had put him near delirium! And then she had suddenly frozen in fear. Why?

An image from the past came unbidden to his mind—their wedding night at Lake Louise. He crowded the troubling vision from his thoughts and hurried to replace it with other memories—memories of Ginger warm and responsive in his arms before their marriage.

The remembrances made him smile now, in spite of the miserable way he felt physically. She had always been sweet and affectionate with him, and yet had managed to make him wait all those years! And she had been right—they were both too young. It wouldn't have been wise. But it showed she could be strong when she needed to be. She had been ready to follow him in every other way, but she was always firm about that—that and moving to Chicago! Maybe she had been afraid, both of leaving home and—sex. Was she still afraid of sex? Was that the problem? But she was twenty-eight. And there was Jack Whiting.

Forget Whiting, Devin told himself, shifting uneasily on the bench. No, there was no reason to assume that she was afraid of sex or that she had ever been. He had never thought she feared him physically when they were young; it was the possible consequences of premarital sex she had feared. And on their wedding night she had been warm and willing.

Oh, God! he thought, burying his face in his hands. That *was* the problem, wasn't it? There was no escaping it. Naturally she would remember, though he had pushed it to the furthest recesses of his conscience ever since.

To try to make her forget that night seemed impossible. He could remember so clearly now her recoiling from him, her silent tears, the heartbreaking look of disillusionment and humiliation on her face. And then she had asked him the question he had hoped never to have to answer. He had been surprised at her insight, her perceptiveness. He thought he had convinced her that there had been only a temporary attraction between him and the girl in Chicago that had never amounted to anything. After being in bed with him, Ginger had instinctively guessed his lie.

He sat for a long while, his elbows on his knees and his face in his hands, rubbing his eyes and forehead. His mental state was at one with his physical pain.

When the ferry neared the mainland dock, he slowly got up to go to his car below. He glanced back at the dark outline of the distant island on the horizon. He could picture Ginger, angry and brooding in her attic apartment, wishing she would never have to see him again. Well, she *would* see him again, he told himself, his eyes glowing with strengthening determination. He *would* erase that bad memory from her mind. There was only one way to do it.

CHAPTER SIX

Several days later Ginger was working in her store when the phone rang. "Hello, Ginger's Spice," she answered.

"Ginger, it's Devin."

"Oh." Her voice showed a distinct lack of enthusiasm.

"I know, you're so glad to hear from me," he joked, but he sounded halfhearted. "I'm afraid I can't see you this weekend as we'd planned. Something's come up."

She was surprised and puzzled, having assumed he would take every opportunity to see her over the month she'd promised. But she said, "That's fine with me."

"I know it's fine with you," he replied, his voice dropping with resignation. "How about next Wednesday? By then I should be—I think I'll be able to take part of the afternoon off. We could go to Meerkerk Garden. The rhododendrons should be in bloom by now. That would be nice, wouldn't it?"

"Why do you assume *I* can take off from work?" she asked snappishly.

"It would just be from three o'clock or so on. That's not so much. Come on, Ginger," he coaxed.

"I suppose you'll remind me of my promise if I don't agree."

"I might."

"What if I said I don't care what promise you made me give, I don't want to see you?" she said with rising temper.

"Ginger . . ." he began, and then there was a long silence. She assumed he was thinking up some new line of argument to use on her. It took her off guard when at last he said, "Be nice to me, Ginger? At least for the duration of this phone call? Just—say you'll see me Wednesday. You can argue with me then. I'll buy a set of bread boards to make up for the revenue you'll lose from closing early."

96

His tone was so odd, she felt at a loss. She sensed that something was wrong, that he was under some difficulty, but didn't want to ask because he might think she was concerned.

"Bread boards don't come in sets," she said, not wanting to lose her argumentative stance.

"Well, some flatware or mugs then—I'll find something I need for the house, I'm sure. So how about Wednesday, about three?"

She hesitated. "I suppose so," was her curt reply.

"Good. Take care of yourself meanwhile," he said earnestly.

"I will." She was taken a little off guard by the admonition; she wasn't sick.

"I love you."

Her hand stiffened on the receiver. "G-good-bye, Devin," she said, and hurriedly hung up.

The next morning Marla called to ask about having lunch together. Ginger was reluctant, but Marla asked so nicely that she agreed. After so recently experiencing Devin's ardent pursuit, she had lost her jealousy of Marla. She had good reason now to believe Devin when he told her their dinner together had been businesslike—as, indeed, Marla had told her.

Her hesitance to lunch with Marla was due more to the fact that their friendship had lost its former easiness and trust. She felt she didn't understand Marla anymore; her friend's motivations seemed hidden and her behavior inconsistent.

But, Ginger decided, they had known each other a long while; she ought to give their friendship another chance. She found herself laughing a little. It seemed Devin's logic had insinuated its way into her own thought processes: Her *sense of justice* forbade that she should be *unfair* to anyone!

"It's been a little while since I've seen you," Marla said when they were seated in their usual restaurant booth. "How are things going between you and Devin?"

Ginger was surprised at the question. Marla had been reticent about discussing Devin the last two times they had met. She was unsure how open she should be with Marla.

"We've agreed to see one another for a while."

"There's a chance you might get back together, then?" Marla asked in a hopeful tone.

"I wouldn't say that," Ginger replied.

"He wants to, though?"

"Yes," Ginger said, wondering at the fact that Marla was asking personal questions as though there had never been any rift in their friendship.

"So you're the one who's not sure."

"Yes—more than not sure. I would rather not have to deal with him at all, but he got me to agree to see him for a month," Ginger found herself admitting. Marla seemed so interested, and Ginger had missed their intimate conversations about men and life in general. She had no one else to confide in about Devin.

"Got you to agree," Marla repeated sardonically. "He wouldn't have had any trouble getting *me* to agree!"

Marla's bluntness made Ginger smile. It was odd to hear her sounding envious. It was more typical for Ginger to be envying Marla her self-confidence and tall, slender figure.

"He was never untrue to *you*," Ginger reminded her.

"Maybe he's sorry and regrets what he did years ago," Marla suggested.

"Yes, he says he is."

"You don't believe him?"

"I . . ." Ginger was lost for words. She had never asked herself that question. "I suppose I believe him."

"He must really love you!"

Ginger nodded. "He says that, too."

"Well, he must, Ginger! He left his position in Chicago and moved all the way back here, hoping to win you back in spite of the fact that you have every reason to hate him. That took a lot of guts—and a lot of love for you, to make him do all that."

"How do you know he did it all just for me?" Ginger asked curiously.

"It's obvious!"

"Maybe he just got tired of Chicago. Now that he's here, maybe he's interested in me because he figures I'll be an easy target."

"Target for what?"

"Sex."

Marla stared at her a little blankly. "You really think that's all he's after?"

"I don't know. It's possible. He's already tried to . . ." Ginger left off, feeling it unnecessary to finish the sentence.

"But Ginger, if he loves you, it's only natural for him to want that, too."

"I don't think a man needs to be in love to want sex from the most convenient place he can get it. Devin slept with that woman in Chicago, and he wasn't in love with her."

"Maybe *she* was the one who was looking for convenient sex," Marla suggested.

Ginger eyed Marla accusingly. "You certainly are a good advocate for Devin! He's clearly made a glowing impression on you—but then Devin has always had a talent for that. Why do you defend him? Has he unburdened his heart about how unfeeling I am or something?"

"No!" Marla said immediately, her eyes showing a slight alarm. "I said long ago that I thought you still loved him, and it seems obvious that he cares for you. I just think you ought to give him a chance. No, when I see Devin, he just—discusses the house, signs the papers I give him, and—chews his antacid tablets." Marla's voice held a nuance of anger on the last phrase.

"Well, I'm giving him a chance," Ginger muttered defensively.

"If you don't, Ginger, there are plenty of women who would be only too willing to change places with you! You might be sorry if you lost *your* chance."

Marla's warning annoyed Ginger, and she concentrated on finishing her club sandwich. After some silence Marla made an effort to continue the conversation on other subjects. Later they parted amicably, Ginger having swallowed her irritation. It seemed now they were back where they had been when Ginger was still fretting over Devin's impending return. But at least their friendship was more like it used to be.

Late that day Jack unexpectedly stopped by Ginger's shop. It had been awhile since she had seen him, and she was glad he had come. After the usual preliminary greetings, he asked if she would like to have dinner.

"Fine!" she replied. "Is Marla busy tonight?" she asked with an impish smile.

He smiled back a little sheepishly. "I guess you know we've been seeing each other a lot. Yes, she had to meet with one of her clients tonight—someone in the hospital, I guess."

"Oh?" Ginger said.

"I suppose she has to get some business buttoned down with them. Real-estate agents have to work constantly, it seems."

They went out to eat, and over dessert Jack happened to mention that Marla had been out to dinner last week with a client who was buying a house on Double Bluff Beach.

Ginger put down her coffee cup and stared at him. "It must have been Devin. He's buying a house there, and Marla's his agent. I doubt she would have two clients buying in that same small area."

"MacPherson? Your former husband?"

"Yes."

"I see!" Jack said, apparently not liking the news. "Did you know they were out together?"

"No, not last week. I knew they had dinner together two or three weeks ago, though."

"This is getting better all the time!" Jack said with growing discomfort.

"Maybe she didn't realize you had met him and that's why she didn't mention his name," Ginger said.

"Maybe . . . Or perhaps she didn't want to have to make any explanations about why she was out with a good-looking, successful businessman who happens to be unattached. He is single, isn't he?"

"Yes," Ginger said, growing a little uncomfortable herself.

"Well, I don't own her, I guess. She's not the type of woman any man can totally possess. I suppose that's why she fascinates me so," Jack said, his tone becoming rather despondent.

She looked at his lowered eyes and drooping blond mustache and felt sorry for him. He *was* in love with Marla. She couldn't reassure him that Marla returned his feelings, but she was certain about another point. "Devin has been seeing me," she told Jack. "In fact, he—says he loves me, and he wants us to get back together."

"Oh!" Jack said, sounding as though that threw a whole new light on the issue.

"Yes." She smiled at his instant relief. "It bothered me a little when Marla told me he had taken her out to dinner that first time. But it was just because they were working together on the house. I imagine their being out together last week was the same sort of thing. Although neither of them mentioned it to me . . ." Her voice trailed off quietly as a trace of doubt surfaced. She stifled it. Perhaps neither had mentioned it because they knew it might upset her again. The dinner was probably just another extension of one of

100

their business meetings, she assured herself, as innocuous as her being out with Jack tonight.

"That puts me at ease a bit," Jack said, taking relish in his Black Forest cake again. "When I met Devin that day I thought there was still something between you two. So you and he are together again?"

"Hardly," Ginger said. "We're just seeing each other on a trial basis."

"Well, that sounds good. I liked Devin. I mean . . . I don't want him hanging around Marla, but—now that I know you're the center of his interest, I think he's a damned nice fellow!" Jack said with a broad smile.

That Sunday Ginger visited her family in Coupeville. She had decided against going up on Saturday and making it one of her full weekend visits. Knowing honesty would require her to tell them she had been seeing Devin, she wanted to spend as little time with them as duty required, anticipating what their reaction would be. She was not wrong.

"Well?" her mother asked when the midday dinner after church was over and the women were alone for the first time, cleaning up in Val's kitchen. "Have you heard anything of Devin, Virginia?"

Ginger had known from her mother's look and manner the whole morning that she had been waiting nervously to ask her that question.

"He came to visit me at the shop," Ginger said, finding no way to avoid answering such a direct question. The only thing she had ever tried to hide from her family was that she had once contemplated swallowing a bottle of sleeping pills. And that Val had guessed. It was no use trying to keep any secrets.

"Oh, I knew it! Didn't I tell you?" Martha said, immediately upset and almost dropping the wet rag she was wiping the counter with.

Val appeared concerned, but she said in a calm voice, "What did he say?"

"He asked me out to dinner," Ginger said, summarizing events.

"You didn't go!" her mother exclaimed, as though she was astonished at Devin's audacity.

Ginger wet her lips and carefully set down the plate she was rinsing at the sink. She turned off the running water and faced them both. "Yes, I went."

Her mother gasped, a stricken expression on her face.

"Why?" Val asked, her calmness belying her concern.

"He feels we should try to bury the past and—and at least become friends again. I—agreed with him." She realized she was stretching the truth, even portraying herself as siding with Devin. In defending her own actions, she found it necessary to defend him as well.

"You agreed!" Martha said, her voice rising in what sounded like all-consuming panic. "How could you be so foolish? I warned you he would try to get around you!"

"Don't get so excited!" Ginger retorted. "There's nothing the matter with forgiving someone for a past wrong! That's what the sermon was all about this morning. Didn't you listen?"

That effectively silenced her mother for the moment, as Martha had unwavering respect for their church's minister. Ginger was glad she had come early enough to attend the service with them.

"But," Val interrupted, "what did he mean by 'at least' becoming friends again?"

Ginger hesitated, not knowing what she should say. At last she replied, her voice oddly weak, "He says he still loves me."

She had told that to people so often lately, its meaning and import were finally beginning to sink in. Before she had passed the statement off, too upset with him to consider it. Perhaps she had been afraid to consider it. But at this moment a warmth and excitement began to stir in her. *Devin had said he still loved her.*

Val lowered her eyes, her face now expressing her serious concern. Martha Cowan came back to life again.

"Of course he would tell you that! He's moved back here, he's alone, and he wants a woman to play with! Naturally he would work on your old feelings for him. You should know better than any of us what type of man he is, Virginia! I'm ashamed to learn how naive and foolish you are at your age! You'll be the death of me yet!"

Mrs. Cowan's words still hung about Ginger the following Wednesday in her shop as mid-afternoon approached. Her mother's ideas validated her own suspicions, the suspicions she had conveyed to Marla. She didn't know what to believe. Perhaps she had doubts only because her mother had put them there.

Part of her trusted Devin, believed that he deeply regretted the past and did still love her, and that that was why he was pursuing her now. After all, he was attractive enough; he could go after any

102

woman he wanted and easily avoid all the trouble she was giving him. He could have Marla, for example, according to Marla's own admission, but he wanted Ginger.

And yet her mother's very vocal and constant warnings kept making Ginger nervously think twice. How difficult it was to get past the influence of one's parents! She had inherited her mother's emotional makeup, and exposing herself to her mother's hysterics made it hard for Ginger to stay within the adult, rational part of her mind.

But even if she felt no trace of doubt that Devin meant his words of love, there was still the memory of their wedding night to make her turn from him. No matter how hard she tried rationally to overcome those painful hours, it was as if the night had been indelibly burned into her memory, in a place where no rational thoughts could reach. That memory would always shade any declarations of affection he might utter.

As Ginger's mind mulled over these thoughts, Devin was pulling up in his car in front of her shop. After work he had stopped at home quickly to change into a sweater and casual pants. With nervous anticipation he got out of his car and walked to the door of Ginger's Spice.

She looked up as he came in. He couldn't read her expression, but she didn't look overjoyed to see him. He wondered if she ever would.

"Hi!" he said, putting on his broadest smile.

"Hello, Devin."

"You look beautiful today," he said, eyeing her navy blue pants and lacy white blouse that draped demurely over her curves. Reckless thoughts came to his mind but he quelled them. He walked up to the shelf where she was arranging some items and lightly kissed her near the mouth. He was glad she didn't back away, though she didn't respond, either. "I missed you," he murmured.

She smiled slightly and bowed her head. He wished he knew how to read her. She was so quiet—neither welcoming nor discouraging.

"Ready to go to Meerkerk Garden?"

"I think it may be closed on weekdays," she said, glancing up at him.

He paused. Was she merely stating a fact, or was this another tactic to avoid going out with him? "Marla thought it would be open," he said. "If it isn't, we can go somewhere else—Fort Ebey State Park or Cranberry Lake."

103

Her brown eyes lowered from his, but she nodded in agreement.

Devin marveled at it. She was always so changeable—steadfast in some ways, yet mysterious in others. Years ago he used to like to think he could predict her moods, but she had often surprised him. How could a man fathom the feminine mind? He still couldn't; not quite. But he supposed he really wouldn't prefer to have it any other way.

A quarter of an hour later they were well on their way, driving north up the island, and he was still having difficulty getting her to say much.

"So you worked on Saturday," he said, summarizing the few sentences he had cajoled from her. "What about Sunday?"

He noticed her long, silent sigh before she spoke. "I visited my family in Coupeville."

"Oh," he said, wishing he hadn't asked. He was quiet a moment and then decided it was no use ignoring the problem. "You told them you were seeing me?"

"Yes."

"How did they react?"

"How do you think?" she shot back.

At least he had gotten a rise out of her, he thought. "They weren't too happy, I suppose—especially your mother?"

"Right."

"Ginger, your mother was always extremely high-strung."

"I know."

"Why pay any attention to her? What about Val? Val and your father were always pretty levelheaded."

"She didn't say much. I think she's reserving judgment."

He was disappointed at her ambiguous reply. He was hoping for support from Val; he might need it.

Devin turned down a one-lane gravel road that led to a small parking area. There was no other car there, but the gate had been left open, and he pulled in and parked.

"I guess we can go in," he said. "There's no one to stop us."

They got out of the car and walked down a path that led into a wooded area in which many and various-color rhododendrons were blooming. The area had once been private property, and the owners, the Meerkerks, had started a garden of many types and hybrids of rhododendrons and other species of plants. It was a beautiful, quiet place with huge clusters of blossoms surrounding them on all sides.

Small brown and gray birds flitted from branch to branch and seemed to follow them as they moved slowly along the winding paths.

Devin took her hand in his as they silently walked, and she did not object. She looked away, however, as if she did not want to chance meeting his eyes. He didn't know if she was still angry, or if she was afraid of him, or if she just didn't feel like talking. Making progress with her, he could see, was going to be slow work. Well, he had gotten this far; he had patience. But how he wished he knew what to do or say to make her affectionate and responsive to him again! Looking at her but not really being able to touch her was torture.

From the restless way she was gazing at the blossoms and trees about them and the tenseness of her small hand in his, he sensed that she was growing uneasy or nervous. Suddenly, as if needing to break the silence which enclosed them in the woods, she said, "So how are you feeling?"

He said nothing for a moment. Her tone had been coldly irritable, and he didn't like the question. "Fine!" he said, his casualness sounding false even to his own ears. It wasn't that he was lying; he did feel good today.

"No more antacid tablets?"

"Uh—no." He wished she would get off the subject, but she was looking up at him curiously now. "I wonder what kind of birds those are?" he said, pointing to one on a branch above them.

"Did you ever see a doctor, Devin?"

She must have a sixth sense, he thought. "Yes, I did. He put me on a diet and gave me a prescription. I'm fine now."

"What did he say was the matter?"

He might as well admit it, he told himself. As they spent time together, she'd probably find out anyway. "An ulcer," he said.

"Oh." She sounded sad. Maybe he'd get some sympathy, at least. He would hate her to get the idea he wasn't strong physically or emotionally, though. She used to rely on him so much years ago. He somehow felt that if he appeared weak now in any way, she wouldn't have any reason left to want him. A man who got dizzy spells whenever his ulcer started acting up wouldn't seem like much of a pillar to lean on.

"The doctor was sure it was an ulcer? Did you have tests?" she asked, sounding very concerned.

105

"Yes."

"In a hospital?" Her tone changed slightly.

"Yes."

"What day were you in?"

"The day I called you." He had nearly passed out at work that morning. One of his co-workers had insisted on taking him to a doctor, who had immediately admitted him to the hospital. But he wasn't going to tell her any of that.

"For how long?"

"A few days."

She was silent now. Something had changed. She took her hand from his.

"What's wrong?"

She hesitated, and he was afraid she wouldn't answer. Finally she said, "Did anyone visit you in the hospital?"

Oh, no, he thought. *Doesn't Marla know when to keep quiet?* "Marla came by," he said casually. "She had tried calling me at work—something about the house—and they told her I was in the hospital. So she came to see me later. I thought it was nice of her."

"Yes, Marla is—nice."

He put his arm around her and pulled her to him. She felt soft and warm, and his heart started beating faster. "I would rather have been visited by you," he said in a low voice, smiling down into her doubtful brown eyes.

"You didn't tell *me* you were in the hospital."

"I didn't tell anyone. I don't look very good with tubes running up my nose!" Damn! He had meant to be amusing, but he shouldn't have let that slip. She looked alarmed.

"Tubes? Why would they . . .? Were you that seriously ill?"

"No, no. My ulcer was bleeding a little and that's how they stop—"

"Oh, no, Devin!" She looked like she was going to cry. Her hands were clutching the material of his sweater.

"It's all right, Ginger. They stopped the bleeding easily. I'm following my diet and I'm fine now. Really!" She still seemed upset, and he held her closer. "I'm glad you're so concerned," he said with humor as he kissed the top of her head.

She grew stiff in his arms. It seemed he had said the wrong thing. He sighed to himself. Here he was, all alone with Ginger in a lovely

106

garden on a bright spring afternoon—and he and his ulcer were getting nowhere.

Over the next few weeks Devin came by regularly, taking Ginger to dinner on weekdays and to various places on weekends. They visited Double Bluff Beach again, and Cranberry Lake where they had often gone swimming in their youth. It was a small lake at the northern tip of the island. Traditionally a favorite island swimming spot, its waters were much warmer than the frigid salt waters of Puget Sound.

The day they spent there among a new crop of young people, the age they had once been, brought back many memories and reminded her vividly how close she and Devin used to be. Ginger found herself longing to bring back that time, and it weakened her resistence to Devin, who was always eager to please her. He had kept things fairly platonic, as he had promised, kissing her often but never letting his passion get out of hand. She was beginning to feel at ease with him, and she found herself looking forward to the days she would see him.

Another element that had insinuated itself into her feelings for him was his health. She had been truly upset when she had first learned he had a serious ulcer. Years ago she had never known him to be ill, except for a minor cold now and then. He had always seemed strong and indestructible. To be made so aware that he was mortal and imperfect made her prone to worry about him as she never had in the past.

It also made her angry. Why did he have to be sick, she would think. Didn't he know how to play fair? She didn't want to feel that he needed someone to look after him. It undermined her resolve to be careful about getting involved with him again. And it played havoc with her determination to be aloof, knowing that whenever she said anything to hurt him it might also make his ulcer worse. Indeed, she often wondered guiltily if he had gotten it because of her.

Toward the end of the month she had promised to spend with him, they were driving one Saturday to the northern tip of the island. She thought perhaps he was going to Cranberry Lake again, but he passed the road that led to the lake and went the short distance further to the bridge at Deception Pass. When she saw him pull off the road into the small parking area before the bridge, she

107

felt apprehension descend on her. It was where he had proposed to her when she was seventeen. As he came around to open the car door for her, she thought of objecting, but in the end didn't.

Deception Pass had originally been charted as a river mouth. In 1792, however, Captain Whidbey noticed that the flow of water was going in the wrong direction to be a river. He took a small boat through it and discovered that the narrow, treacherous waterway was actually a tidal passage, thus proving that the landmass to the south was an island. Because of the passage's deceptive appearance it was known ever since as Deception Pass. The lofty bridge over it connected the island with the mainland.

Devin held her hand as they walked out onto the steel bridge. They paused to lean against the protective railing and looked down at the fast-flowing water rushing far below and one of the island's wide beaches off to the left. From the other side of the bridge the view was of broad waterways and the forested mainland. Snow-capped mountain peaks were just visible in the distance.

"This always was an unusually pretty spot," Devin said nostalgically as he looked about.

"Yes," she murmured, watching a fisherman trying his luck on the beach below. She remembered she had been gazing in that direction many years ago when Devin had taken hold of her shoulders and turned her toward him to say: "Ginger, when I'm through with college and have a job, I want you to marry me. Will you? You know how I love you." Thrilled to tears, she had thrown her arms about his neck and said, "Yes!"

"You know," his chuckling voice interrupted her memories, "Marla told me once that she's never been to Deception Pass, even though she's lived on the island for five years."

"Since it's a state park, there probably aren't any houses for her to sell here," Ginger said tartly. She saw him glance at her in half-concealed amusement and knew it was because of the waspishness in her tone. She couldn't help it. He had a habit of mentioning Marla at the oddest times. They must do an awful lot of chitchatting along with their business, she thought.

"When do you move into your house?" Ginger asked coolly.

"In a couple of weeks I'll start using it on weekends as I had planned. Marla's made the arrangements for me to rent it until I take legal possession. I'm considering moving in permanently, though, and getting rid of my condominium in Seattle."

"Then you'd have to commute to work."

"Yes, I'd have to commute," he agreed, staring at her in a way that was at once hesitant and intense. It made Ginger look up at him. "We've been getting along pretty well over the past few weeks, don't you think? I know I've enjoyed it—every minute," he said.

Ginger looked away. His allotted month was almost up, and he was no doubt hoping for an extension of the deadline. She wasn't sure what she wanted. But, on a moment's reflection, she realized she could no longer envision herself telling him she never wanted to see him again.

He took hold of her arms with both hands. "I love you, Ginger. And I think you still care for me, too. At least every once in a while I see a small sign that gives me hope. Ginger, I'd—like you to marry me again. We could live together at the house, the way I always said we would when we were young. It's not so far from your shop—"

His words were sinking in. "Marry you!" she said in a hushed whisper as she paled.

"Yes!" His grip on her arms grew firmer. "We should never have been divorced, Ginger. It's my fault; I didn't know what to say to you, how to handle things after—after you found out what I had done. I let you drift away. You seemed to despise me so. I thought it was best just to walk out of your life. I made one last attempt when I asked you to come to Chicago with me, but you refused. I've been angry with myself ever since that I gave up so easily. You're the only one I could ever picture as my wife."

"Oh, Devin . . ." she said, slowly shaking her head. She had never anticipated this!

"Now don't say no yet," he rushed to tell her. "You ought to at least think it over for a while. If you find some objections to the idea, then tell me what they are. I'm sure we can work them out."

She was silent for quite awhile. The tone in his voice had been so earnest and hopeful, she found it difficult to say anything to disappoint him. But she had to. Maybe she did still care for him, even love him in a way, but the memory of their wedding night and of his infidelity made it impossible for her ever to think of marrying him again. He might as well know now.

"Devin . . ." she began. How difficult it was to say. "Our wedding night—the way you—"

His sensitive green eyes read hers, and he dropped his hands from her shoulders. Turning toward the railing for a moment, he looked out over the water. "I know, darling. How can I . . . what can I say? You still didn't know then that I had been untrue. But I knew what I had done. Can you even imagine how hard it was for me to look you in the eye?"

He shook his head, as if the memory was still painful for him. "In a perverse sort of way, feeling guilty made me angry at you. I still had a hard time blaming myself. It was our wedding night and I was supposed to pretend that everything was perfect. I don't know how else to explain this but to put it bluntly: The only way I could perform sexually was to disconnect from you mentally. If I started thinking of you, I—it just didn't work. My guilt got in the way, so I tried not to think of you at all."

He turned and looked at her again, his eyes reflecting the bright sunlight through a sheath of shimmering tears welling in them. "I think I know how cold I must have seemed to you that night. In the next few weeks I tried to show you that that wasn't the way I wanted to make love to you, but you never let me come near you again." His voice was quiet and filled with regret. He took her hands in his. "I promise you, Ginger, I wouldn't be that way with you now. I want you so, I'd smother you with love if you'd let me. I might have shown you that day at the house, but you got frightened. It was because of that memory, wasn't it?"

She nodded silently.

"Darling, I really think that that's something we can work out. And I don't think it would be difficult, either," he added in a tone that edged toward amusement.

Her eyes flashed at him. How could he joke about something that was so distasteful to her? "I don't see that it would be so easy!"

The tiny grin faded from his face. "I suppose not." He sighed and leaned thoughtfully against the railing of the bridge. After a while he said, "I have an idea. Why don't we take a long weekend together and go to Lake Louise?"

Her eyes opened wide in near-revulsion. "Are you insane? I don't ever want to see that place again!"

"I understand how you feel. It's a bad memory for both of us. That's why we ought to go back and replace it with a good one," he said calmly.

"And how would we do that? By you trying to get me in bed with you at the earliest opportunity?" she taunted.

"Ginger, I told you once and I promise you now, I'd never press you to do anything you didn't want to do."

She glared at him in angry consternation. "I didn't want to have dinner at the Captain Whidbey Inn, I didn't want to go to your house that day, I didn't even want to see you in the beginning, and yet I've somehow wound up doing all those things!"

"Because you can't resist my logic and friendly persuasion," he said, leaning forward to kiss her cheek.

She backed away. "I'm serious! You're not going to persuade me to go to Lake Louise!"

He took hold of her shoulders. "*I'm* serious about wanting to marry you!" he said with sudden gravity. "What happened at Lake Louise is an obstacle between us and we've got to clear it up. If you refuse to go, you might as well also say you'll never marry me. And if that's the case," he said, looking at her with granitelike resolve, "then—we might as well never see each other again."

As he read the fear she couldn't keep from her eyes, he took a breath. In a softer but no less earnest tone he said, "It's all or nothing for me. The past month has been very nice, but I want something permanent between us. I want to live with you. I couldn't tolerate just being friends; we were always much more than that to each other. Would you prefer to stop seeing me altogether, Ginger?" he asked. His voice was suddenly vulnerable.

Ginger bowed her head and felt tears spring to her eyes. She was silent for a while, feeling his strong hands on her shoulders, knowing he was waiting and sensing his acute anxiety.

"No," she whispered at last. She wasn't sure what she felt for him, but she didn't want to stop seeing him. The very thought made her feel empty and lost.

She felt his relief in the relaxing pressure of his hands on her shoulders and could hear the suppressed joy in his voice. "Lake Louise is beautiful, Ginger. We'll see it with new eyes this time. We could take the train from Vancouver—that would be fun!" On their honeymoon they had flown to Calgary, Canada, and then driven to Lake Louise.

"I suppose you'd want us to share a room at the hotel."

"It would be more economical. It's pretty expensive," he pointed out.

"And so much cozier that way," Ginger said resentfully.

"Ginger, I promise I won't so much as touch you if you aren't

111

willing. I already have a few major black marks against me; it certainly wouldn't be in my interest to try for another."

Ginger glanced downward in thought. It was a good point. For once his logic was working in her favor.

"We'll just go and try to enjoy ourselves and see how things work out," he said. "We can look upon it as an experiment. Okay?"

CHAPTER SEVEN

"So—here we are," Ginger muttered softly as she approached the large window that had been left slightly open. Even as she gazed out at the magnificent panorama of Lake Louise and the snowcapped mountains arrayed behind it, she couldn't help shuddering. Here she was again with Devin where the worst episode of her life had taken place.

"Beautiful, isn't it?" Devin said. He had come up behind her and lightly put a hand on her shoulder. She flinched and moved away from him. Suddenly the whole trip seemed a miserable idea and she wished to God she had never come.

Until about five minutes ago, when the bellhop had brought them to their room at Chateau Lake Louise, she had rather enjoyed herself. They had boarded the Canadian Pacific train in Vancouver about nine thirty the night before and had slept in the bunk beds already made up in their compartment. Devin had been the perfect gentleman, even leaving the room for a few minutes while she changed and got into the top bunk. The next day they had enjoyed a leisurely breakfast and, later, lunch together in the dining car. Between times they had stayed in their compartment and read and talked, all the while glancing out the wide window at the wilderness of forests, hills, and mountains through which their train was passing.

Very late in the afternoon they had arrived at the Lake Louise station, where a shuttle bus took them the short distance to the chateau. And now she found herself in a room very similar to the one in which she had spent her wedding night eight years ago. The decor was slightly different from what she remembered; the view from the window was the same.

She remembered looking out at the lake early the morning after and wondering how, in what at that moment seemed an ugly world, anything could look so majestic and serene. Her new young husband she had discovered to be unfaithful, abruptly sullying her lifelong relationship with the one man she had ever loved. Even sex had been a monumental disappointment. All her dreams and illusions had been shattered. The pristine beauty of the lake and mountains had only made her cry.

"Ginger," Devin said now, following her as she turned restlessly from the window, "I'm sorry. I know it's difficult to be here again. It is for me, too. But we'll get used to it. Things will seem better in a little while, I promise."

"How can you promise that?" she asked coldly.

"I just know, that's all. Now why don't we unpack and then go down for dinner?"

"Okay," she agreed with a sigh. She could do without his optimism. The prospect of staying in this room for two nights was bad enough without having to put up with insistent cheerfulness, too. Or was he so hopeful because he thought they'd be sharing one of the two double beds in the long room, she wondered as she snapped open her suitcase. If that was what he thought, he was in for a rude disappointment.

Dinner in the spacious dining room with its high ceilings and huge, magnificently draped windows seemed to take the edge off her resentful disposition. The food was good and the wine helped numb her a little. Devin was patient, answering his own questions when her responses were lacking.

After dinner he coaxed her into walking down to the lake with him. It was a beautiful, clear evening and the atmosphere was still as they took the paved meandering path down the incline from the chateau, passing immaculately manicured lawns and gardens until they reached the broader path along the lake's edge.

The graceful three-hundred-room chateau, built in the early part of the century, was located on one end of Lake Louise, a fingerlike glacial lake. Across the small body of water and opposite the hotel was snowcapped Mt. Victoria and the Victoria Glacier, whose melt-water filled the lake. Bordering the two long sides of Lake Louise were dark, tree-lined slopes of other mountains. The trees thinned out toward the upper altitudes to give way to the lighter-hued rock cliffs of the rugged alpine zone. It was a stunning sight by anyone's standards, and the two people so tentatively holding hands at the lake's edge were lost for a few minutes in their own thoughts.

114

The wide path followed along the lakeshore to the right, and they began to walk along it. It was growing dark, and stars were beginning to appear. The whiteness of the snows of Mt. Victoria made a contrast with the darkening rocks, sky, and trees and was reflected in the gently rippling water.

The path led them among the shoreline trees when they had gotten a little distance from the small groups of other visitors near the hotel. Even so it was a busy path at that time of evening, with other strollers and joggers occasionally passing them.

"Want to jog off our dinner?" Devin asked with a grin.

"Not when I'm wearing a dress and high heels!" she replied. She shivered. With the increasing darkness it was growing chilly.

"You should have worn a sweater," Devin said. He let go of her hand and put his arm about her for warmth. "Here's a bench," he said, indicating a wooden seat a little ahead of them. They sat down and he drew her against him, both arms snug around her. Lightly he kissed her cheek.

Ginger felt compelled to say something to interrupt his sudden attentiveness. "Did we walk along this path the last time we were here?"

"I don't remember."

"I can't either. It's odd, isn't it?"

Devin didn't reply. She sensed he didn't like her choice of subject, but something within her insisted on pursuing it. "I didn't remember what the dining room looked like either."

"Ginger, the only thing you'll remember about our last visit is what we're here to put behind us. Don't think about last time; think about now."

"That's rather difficult," she said in a clipped tone.

"I know. But the past can never be changed. We have only the present—and the future," he said.

His soft, reassuring voice whispered through her mind and scattered the rational arguments she was trying to pull together. His mouth was moving close to hers now, and she knew he was going to kiss her. She didn't try to stop him.

As his warm mouth gently fixed on hers, he drew her even nearer. It was a loving kiss, nurturing and protective, but without the driving passion that had almost become uncontrolled that day six weeks ago at Devin's house. Still, she was growing nervous about going back to their room with him tonight. Was it Devin she worried about keeping under control—or her own response to his gentle lovemaking?

But as his bodily warmth permeated her clothing, she stopped shivering and began to relax against him, sensing that he wanted to give her affection and cared deeply about her feelings, her needs, and her fears. She slipped her arms around him beneath his tweed jacket and allowed herself to enjoy his tenderness. Just when she was beginning to return some of the warmth he was giving her, however, he broke their kiss and pulled away a little.

Smiling quickly, he said, "We'd better go in. It's too cold out here for you without a sweater." Before she could say a word, he had gotten to his feet and was pulling her gently by the hand. A little confused, she followed alongside, holding his hand. She would have wished to stay in his arms awhile longer. It wasn't like him to retreat from her affection.

By the time they got back to their room, however, everything seemed typical of the way they had been getting on together for the last few weeks. He immediately claimed the bed by the window, purposely creating an amusing argument as to who would wake up to the beautiful view. In the end he gave way and let her have the windowside bed.

Later, when she self-consciously came out of the bathroom wearing a long robe over her thin nylon nightgown, she found him in pajamas and a robe, sitting on the edge of his bed. He was reading a Lake Louise guidebook he had bought at the gift shop on their way back to their room. As she rather warily passed by, he said, "I think tomorrow we should get up early and take the trail up to Lake Agnes. It's supposed to be the most popular hike in the Canadian Rockies."

"Where's Lake Agnes?" she asked. While he leafed to a previous page in his book, she hurriedly slipped off her robe and got under the covers, pulling them up to her chin.

"It's in the mountains high above Lake Louise. The trail is . . . let's see here . . . three point five kilometers long. It's supposed to take about four hours round-trip."

"Four hours?" she said dubiously. But she relaxed a little now that she was safely hidden under the bedcovers and Devin seemed engrossed in plans for the next day.

"We'd be back by lunch." He looked up and grinned.

"Is it all uphill?"

"No. On the way back it'd be all downhill."

She laughed a little. "I don't know if I'm ready for that. I don't get much exercise."

"About time you did, then! I've worked out at health clubs two or three times a week for the past five years."

"Good for you!" she said with good-natured sarcasm. "You can carry me!"

"Okay!" He put the book on the nightstand and walked over to her bed. When she saw him approach she tensed, her fingers tightening on the edge of the blanket near her chin.

"Don't worry," he said, bending over her. "Just a good-night kiss."

His kiss on the mouth lasted a long second. Again, just as she was drawing to the warm moistness of his mouth, he pulled away. "Sleep well, darling," he said softly, running his thumb gently along her cheek. "It'll be a good day tomorrow."

Her eyes followed him as he moved back to his bed, took off his robe, and got under the covers. He put out the light, and she turned her eyes toward the window then. In the dim light of the moon she could see the gray outline of one of the mountains overlooking the lake. She felt content—even hopeful, somehow.

Ginger awoke rather late, as it turned out. She had had difficulty sleeping with the movement of the train the night before and had made up for it now. Devin was already dressed in brown jeans and a shirt and watching her from where he stood at the window. She started to smile at him until she looked down and realized the bed covers had slipped to her waist. Her low-V-necked, sleeveless nightgown was askew, revealing a good deal of creamy bosom. Immediately she began to adjust the thin white garment, wondering how long he had been staring at her like that. But Devin came to her rescue, reaching to hand her her robe.

"It's about time you woke up," he said, humor in his voice. "We should have been halfway to Lake Agnes by now!"

"You could have woke me," she grumbled.

Since he still intended to hike, she put on the only old clothes she had brought, a pair of jeans and a T-shirt her sister had given her. The T-shirt had a line of cats cartooned across the front and back, and it fit tighter than she would have liked. She wished now that

117

she had remembered to buy herself some new casual clothes while she had shopped for her new dressier garments.

After breakfast in the dining room, they found the trail head for Lake Agnes a short distance to the west of the hotel. Ginger had suspected the trail would be fairly steep, but she had thought it would be easy at least at the beginning. She was wrong. After only fifteen minutes she was already huffing and puffing as the trail wound continuously upward.

"Can we stop and rest a minute?" she asked, leaning against a pine tree by the dirt path. They were in the midst of thick forest.

Devin was breathing normally, as if he had just walked half a block on a level sidewalk. "You must be out of shape, Ginger!" he teased as he smiled down at her. Wearing sneakers made her even shorter next to him. He eyed her T-shirt. "Not that you look out of shape," he added in a softer tone.

She didn't know how to react to that. She wanted to smile, and then again she didn't. Moving away from the tree, she said, "We'd better move on." He caught her hand and they continued the climb.

The trail became even more rigorous, moving up through dense forest, until the trees began to thin and panoramic views of the surrounding mountains began to make the hike worthwhile. Even so, Ginger asked as she leaned her exhausted body against a high rock, "Devin, why are we doing this?"

He was breathing hard himself now. "To get to the top," he quipped between breaths.

She gave a look of exasperation, then stood and playfully pushed her palms hard against his chest, hoping to rock him off balance. She failed, of course. Laughing, they fell into each other's arms, and he hugged her warmly. He tried to kiss her, but the kiss couldn't last long as both were too out of breath. They broke apart, laughing at themselves.

As they continued, the shared physical rigors of the climb seemed to unite them, obliterating at least temporarily the problems and obstacles that lay unresolved between them. The real world and the troubled past were forgotten for a while. There was only the two of them, the relentless trail to conquer, and the grandeur of the Canadian Rockies surrounding them like the setting of a fairy tale.

After making the final steep climb to the lake, passing Bridal Veil Falls directly below it, they were greeted by the sight of a small teahouse built of logs overlooking Lake Agnes. There they gratefully sat down and relaxed for a long while, enjoying a pot of herb tea and apricot-nut bread served by several young women who lived and worked there for the season.

Lake Agnes was small and picturesque, hidden as it was in its niche in the mountains, and since it was still early in the Canadian spring, it was partly covered yet with ice.

Two hours later, after the somewhat easier task of making their way back down to Lake Louise and the chateau, they stopped for a late lunch in the coffeeshop. Afterward Ginger suggested they rent a canoe from the boathouse to the left of the hotel. A young woman outfitted them with two life jackets, paddles, and an aluminum canoe called *Misty River*. They spent the next couple of hours half-sitting, half-kneeling in the wobbly little boat, dipping their paddles into the cold, gently rippling, blue-green waters of the lake and sometimes just drifting along. The water was curiously opaque, due to flourlike silt from the glacial meltwater, and the paddles seemed to disappear as they dipped beneath the surface.

As late afternoon approached, both Ginger and Devin grew tired from the day's exertions. When they got back to their room, Ginger threw herself across her bed. "I'm exhausted!" She was too tired even to flinch when Devin sat down next to her, casually throwing his arm across her waist.

"Me, too," he said, comfortably nestling his head against her shoulder.

It seemed to her, as her mind slowly drifted into sleep, that they were like a couple who had been married a long while. She felt content, happy, and secure, as though their old relationship had never been interrupted, as though they had been together like this all their lives.

In a couple of hours they showered and changed and went down to the dining room for dinner. They sat next to one another at a small table near one of the huge arched windows that looked onto the lake. While they were waiting for their waiter to bring dessert, she looked at Devin with a little concern and asked, "Have you been feeling all right? Are you still taking that prescription the doctor gave you?"

He nodded his head. "I feel great!"

"I'm glad. The mountain air must agree with you."

He shook his head slightly as he steadily gazed at her. "I feel good because I'm happy being with you."

119

As she lowered her eyes, he caught her hand in his and leaned over to kiss her. She returned the brief kiss and found herself whispering, *"I'm* happy being with you."

His eyes turned liquid. He bowed his head and self-consciously adjusted his glasses. Tears came to Ginger's eyes as well.

After a moment, to lighten the emotion, she asked, "Don't you wear contact lenses anymore?"

"I lost the ones I had about four months ago and never bothered replacing them. I decided I had outgrown my need to impress people with my good looks," he said with self-deprecating humor.

She remembered he hadn't been wearing glasses the first time he came into her shop. Smiling to herself, she wondered if he had purposely taken them off before he walked in, hoping he would be more attractive to her. "With or without glasses, you're a very handsome man, Devin," she told him, meaning every word.

He looked at her and smiled a little wistfully. "You think so?"

After dinner they walked outside and again strolled down the path along the lakeside. They walked a good distance before turning around to come back as the sun began to set. They sat down on the same bench again, and Devin put his arm around her. She had remembered to bring a sweater tonight, but he behaved as if he were keeping her from the cold anyway. Ginger didn't mind. They sat in easy silence, perfectly comfortable with one another as they watched pink and gray clouds slowly drift behind the chateau.

As the sunset colors faded, a few stars began to appear, then more and more. Lights from the chateau and boathouse came on and reflected in wavering beams across the water. The lake gradually took on a silvery-white appearance, and the trees grew black and feathery against the sky. As the lights from the chateau grew brighter and brighter, the building itself began to fade into the darkness. It was a fantasy world.

The quietness about them had its own subtle excitement. Only soft ripples from the water and faint voices from the distant hotel could be heard, along with a few mysterious little forest noises. The trail they were sitting near grew dim and slightly spooky. Unconsciously Ginger huddled even closer to Devin. He responded by nuzzling his nose against her cheek, then leaning forward to kiss her.

Again his kiss was warm and comforting. She put her arms around his neck to keep him close as she responded with wholehearted affection. Their lips mingled, and the moist warmth increased until it flowed into a luxurious heightening of the senses. He made no move to end the kiss this time but instead seemed to focus himself into it, gently but insistently moving his lips over hers as their breaths co-mingled.

His lips parted, and she responded in kind. Immediately their intimacy deepened as he explored the honey sweetness of her mouth. As she grew aware that her breathing was softly quickening, as was his, she felt his hands moving restlessly over her back, then coming forward to feel the full curve of her breasts through her dress beneath her partly buttoned sweater. She quivered in response, eager for more of his touch, and yet growing uneasy, for she was aware where this sensual exploration might be leading. His purely affectionate manner was fading quickly. She could feel his hands beginning to tremble.

He ended the kiss and said breathlessly against her cheek, "It's getting very dark. We should go in."

Hesitantly she nodded in response. They walked close together through the darkness in silence, and her nerves seemed to swirl in increasing turmoil. There was a certain hardness in his arm about her as he moved purposefully toward the hotel, as if his mind was set. His platonic, affectionate manner toward her had slipped away, and she was almost certain what would happen when they reached their room.

In a way she wished to give him the intimacy he wanted, and a daring little voice within told her she wanted it, too. But another part of her was growing frightened, afraid of a repeat of the past, of shattering a newfound happiness, just as her dreams had been crushed so long ago in the same way with the same man. She didn't know if she was ready for that final test of their reestablished relationship. But what would happen if she refused? She didn't want to disappoint him; he had been patient and understanding all these weeks. She ought to try. Maybe everything would be all right.

The bright light of the lobby appeared suddenly, and she hesitated momentarily as he ushered her through the door. She gazed longingly at the comfortable chairs in the large, stately room, wishing for a chance to think. But he urged her into an open elevator and asked the operator for the seventh floor.

He unlocked the door of their room and turned on the light when they walked in. She had not long to wait. In less than a moment she was enveloped in his arms again, his heated lips now burning her mouth with passion, as if his own fires had kindled on the way back while hers were wavering in apprehension.

"Let me make love to you," he said in an urging voice, his hot breath on her cheek.

She tried to push away a little and lowered her face from his. "I—I'm not sure, Devin. Let me think about it a little."

"This is no time to think," he whispered as his searing lips moved down her throat. His questing mouth quickened the nerves along her tender skin. She felt his hand unbuttoning her sweater. The anticipating response of her own senses made her quake. She made a little sound in her throat when his hand firmly closed over her soft breast, massaging and caressing through the thin dress until she leaned against him for support. When his mouth took hers again hotly and possessively, her knees were growing weak. In a moment she was lifted into his strong arms, and he carried her to the nearest of the two beds.

Quickly he slipped off his jacket and glasses, then pulled off his tie before lying down next to her. She lay still and looked up at the ceiling as she felt him pushing aside her sweater, then undoing the front buttons of her dress. Feeling her body being exposed, she tensed and held her breath, afraid she was going to panic. Then suddenly her bra was unfastened and she released her breath in a near-swoon as she felt his warm hands fondle the exquisite softness of her bared breasts and sensitive nipples.

His mouth took one nipple, and the moist friction of his tongue teased it erect. The sensation caused her to inhale deeply, making her breast rise more firmly against his mouth. She felt scintillating gooseflesh rise all over her.

Putting one arm beneath her, he lifted her up a little, then carefully tugged at her dress until it was completely off. Obviously relishing his task, he did the same with her half-slip and pantyhose until only her bikini panties were left.

As her supple body lay rather helplessly before him on the bed, his eyes devoured her, moving from one voluptuous curve to the next, from her smooth, soft thighs to the graceful hourglass line of her round hips and small waist, over the downy, tender skin of her stomach and abdomen to the mounds of her full breasts.

"Oh, Ginger, you're so beautiful," he whispered. His words were barely coherent. He was breathing heavily, much like he had that afternoon climbing the steep trail. But there was an urgent, tremorous intensity in his labored breaths now that reminded her . . .

She had a sudden sense of déjà vu. It was the way he had made love that night eight years ago. In those long minutes when he had laid heavily on top of her, moving against her, using her body solely for his own pleasure as if he had forgotten who she was, he'd robbed her of the fulfillment she had so wanted from him. She grew panic-stricken. If she let him continue, would it be the same bitter disillusionment? The driving inner light issuing from his green eyes as he looked at her unnerved her.

She watched in a state of fascinated fright as he tore off his shirt and tossed it aside. It was the first time in eight years that she had seen his shoulders and chest completely uncovered. His shoulders had grown even broader and his chest deeper than she had imagined. He looked huge to her, and she saw the tough muscles rippling in his shoulders and arms as he moved toward her. As his body loomed over hers it blocked the light from the lamp on the bedstand, throwing him into a shadow that to her seemed almost sinister. Very clearly came the memory of how she had felt when he was upon her that night eight years ago and again only six weeks ago at his house when he had rolled on top of her. She grew cold inside. Putting up her hands, she tried to push him away as his big frame moved onto hers.

"No, Devin!" she cried. She slid to one side and he came down on one arm next to her. "Please, no!"

He stopped and looked at her, stunned. "What, darling? What's wrong?" He reached to touch her arm, but she pushed his hand away.

"I don't want to!"

"But—why? You were responding—"

"No!"

"Yes, you were. I wouldn't have undressed you if—"

"Yes, you would have! All you think about is your own need! I'm just a body to you—I could be any woman! You could have me tonight and another woman tomorrow and it'd all be the same to you! Just as you went from that slut in Chicago to me on our wedding night! You're just the same!" The accusing words tumbled out of her hysterically.

"Ginger, you don't know how I'd be with you tonight. We hardly

123

got started! You build things up in your mind so much. We have to try to forget the past."

"I can't forget!"

"Then there's no future for us!" he said hoarsely.

A tense silence followed his painful statement. His words and tone shook her, grounding her frantic mental state to reality. No future with Devin meant emptiness.

She sat up on the edge of the bed and brushed the hair from her forehead with a shaking hand. "I—I'm just not ready to go to bed with you yet, that's all," she said a little less emotionally, trying to sound and be rational. "I need more time to think."

"You think too much! You refine things until they take on monumental proportions. We got along wonderfully all day, Ginger. What happened? What did I do in the last ten minutes to bring this on?" he asked in genuine bewilderment.

It took her a moment to control a new tide of emotion before she could speak. "The—the way you looked at me. The way you touched me," she said with anger. "Pretty soon you'd be all over me like on our wedding night, with only your own pleasure in mind."

He glanced rather helplessly about the room. "Do you really believe that? You aroused me and I wanted to make you happy too. I can't help it if I seem aggressive," he said, gesturing with his hands in the air. His voice grew sarcastic. "Does Jack Whiting do it without looking at you, touching you?"

She turned in astonishment. "Jack! What do you mean?" Devin's darkened eyes reminded her of what she had once led him to believe. She shook her head. "No. Jack and I never . . . We're just friends. You're the only one I've ever slept with. The memory of *that* occasion made me disinclined to experiment with anyone else," she said bitterly. "*Imagining* what sex could be like is more rewarding!"

The brief light that sparked in his gaze at the knowledge that there had been no other man faded again with her final remark. He looked at her now with new eyes. "You're practically still a virgin, then. I—didn't realize. I assumed—"

"That I'd have affairs like you've had?" she taunted.

His eyes lowered from her accusing look. "I'm not proud of the way my life has turned out. But if it helps—there haven't been many women. And the few there were disappointed me—because they weren't you."

124

She narrowed her eyes and looked away, not wanting at that moment to believe him, not wanting to let herself be softened by his words.

"Ginger," he said all at once, "is it because we're not married anymore that you're upset about making love? I'll wait and marry you first, if you like. Would you feel better about it then?"

"No!" she hurried to reply. The last thing she wanted to think about at that moment was marrying him. "No . . . it's not that." It seemed odd to her—a gallant offer to wait until marriage when a few minutes ago all she had thought he had in mind was his own physical desire. Maybe her perceptions about him were wrong. She felt deeply confused.

"What is it, then?" he asked patiently.

"It's . . . I feel that you don't care about me. It's like you're a hungry dog and I'm a piece of meat," she said in an injured tone.

She looked up and saw the despair and perplexity in his eyes. "Don't *care* about you? I love you! Did I do anything to hurt you? Wasn't I gentle?"

"No, you didn't hurt me," she admitted. "But you were involved only in your own passion, like on our wedding night. You were starting to make love to me the same way as you did then. And I didn't like it then!"

He stared at her thoughtfully. "Maybe I'm beginning to understand. Darling, to me there's a world of difference between now and eight years ago," he said earnestly. "On our wedding night I didn't think about pleasing you. I couldn't because I was so guilt-ridden. But tonight, Ginger, is light-years away. We've both grown up. All I can think of is you. All I want to do is show you how I care for you, to love you—physically, mentally, even spiritually. Instead of blocking you out, I want to be part of you in every way. It won't be the same at all."

She looked at him rather distrustfully. With a gentle smile he took her hand in his. "It will be the same for you as for me, you wanting fulfillment as much as I want it." He chuckled lovingly. "You'll be as eager with the anticipation of our passion as I was."

Ginger turned a little away from him. Instead of encouraging her, his words had created doubt in her. The prospect of giving in to her deepest desire, unleashing all her passion with him, unsettled her. She had arranged her life in a calm and orderly fashion, to keep command of herself and her emotions. Maybe she could understand

125

how he might be different with her tonight than on their wedding night, but what he was promising now seemed almost more than she had ever hoped for. She didn't think she *could* respond as he expected she would after all that had come between them. Suddenly she felt alienated, as if she and he were worlds apart.

She stiffened when she felt him stroke her bare breast. "Ginger, let's try again. I must have moved too fast a little while ago. I'm sorry. I didn't realize you were still—so hurt. We'll take it slower."

"No," she said, getting up hastily and moving to the other bed. She pulled aside the covers and quickly got under them, covering her nakedness with the thick blanket. "No, Devin," she said, looking at him uneasily across the space that divided the beds. "I—I'm not ready yet. Except for what just happened, it's been a beautiful day for us. Let's leave it that way."

He swallowed, and his face darkened. "When will you be ready?"

"I don't know."

"How long do you think I can wait, Ginger? Do you know how hard it is to be in this room with you, to see you lying in bed all soft and warm and not try to touch you? Last night was miserable!"

"You were the one who wanted one room," she reminded him.

"Because the purpose of this trip was for us to get together!"

"That's not what you said. You said you wouldn't push me to do anything I didn't want to do. Well, I don't want to!"

He glared at her, apparently out of arguments. His rumpled, discarded shirt was lying near him. In a silent explosion of frustration, he picked it up and threw it against the wall. He rose then, wrenched his pajamas out of his suitcase and stalked into the bathroom. Ginger jumped when she heard the door slam shut. Never had she seen him so angry.

The shower ran for quite awhile. She lay tensely under the covers, pretending to be asleep when she heard him come out. In a second the lights went off and she heard him getting into the other bed.

There was silence then. She looked across and in the moonlight could see the jutting outline of his broad shoulder as he lay on his side with his back to her. After such closeness and the happy feeling of rapport with him during the day, now she was aware only of the gulf that had come between them—all because she had refused him sex.

Maybe she was wrong not to have let him sleep with her, but after his first attempt tonight, her nerves were on edge and she didn't feel she could cope with it. She wasn't the type who could just go headlong into things. She needed to prepare herself. If he knew her as well as he claimed, he should be able to understand that!

No, she wasn't wrong, she decided. She wasn't going to be forced into anything!

She heard the muffled sound of a door closing and then heard soft voices coming from the room next to them. The people had certainly been out late, she thought idly.

Looking across at Devin again, she wondered if she would ever understand men. Their minds were such a strange mixture of rational thinking, congeniality, and sex. For example, all the while Devin had been carefully explaining to her over tea at Lake Agnes how glaciers had formed the lake, he was at the same time subtly eyeing her T-shirt and, she had sensed, mentally undressing her. And her own reaction confused her, too. Somehow it offended her; yet at the same time she knew it also pleased her, somehow.

It was all too much to comprehend, and her mind was too muddled now to think. She closed her eyes, hoping to sleep.

Awhile later she was just dozing off when she awoke again with a start. An odd little sound caught her ear, and she wondered if that was what had disturbed her. She heard it again, louder this time. It sounded like a woman softly moaning. Was someone ill in the room next door?

It continued and grew more fervent. Soon there was another, lower voice making similar noises. A wave of cold alarm swept over Ginger. She knew what she was hearing. The R-rated movies she had seen were education enough to recognize the noises of lovemaking. Ginger wondered if Devin was asleep or if he heard it, too.

Her heart beat faster, and her wits were jangled. It was terribly unnerving! She wished they would stop, but they continued on and on. The woman in particular was growing increasingly overwrought, her acute little cries testifying to the intense sexual thrill she must be feeling. Remembering the disappointment of her own one-time experience, Ginger wondered if she was as capable of enjoying sex as this woman was. Clearly the woman's lover wasn't thinking only of himself, Ginger thought with a sense of jealousy. He couldn't be and still bring such a profound response from his partner. Why hadn't her wedding night so long ago resembled what this couple was sharing? Devin's betrayal and his guilt feelings had cheated her of it.

127

Suddenly in the dim light she saw Devin throw aside his blanket and get out of bed. With quick, fitful movements he picked up his pants and shirt from where they had been tossed and changed into them. She clutched her bedcovers as she saw him angrily shrug on his tweed jacket.

"Devin . . ." she called softly.

"I'm going for a walk!" he said in a rage, then slammed out the door.

A few minutes after he had gone, the final climactic cries of passion penetrated the wall from the next room. After that there was a little laughter, as if of delight. Then peaceful silence. Ginger listened to it all as cold, wet tears streamed down her face. Had she given in to Devin tonight, would he have given *her* the same joy?

CHAPTER EIGHT

Devin looked up from his book again and glanced past Ginger out the window of the observation car. He hadn't really been reading. He couldn't keep his mind on it. The sky was still cloudy, as it had been when they had boarded at Lake Louise early in the afternoon. Trees and mountains moved past them as the train followed a river most of the time. It would probably be his last look at Canada for a while, but it didn't make him want to concentrate on the spectacular scenery any more conscientiously.

He twisted in his seat uncomfortably. His ulcer was acting up again. If he hadn't had something to take for it, he would be feeling wretched right now, he was sure. As it was, the discomfort could at least be tolerated. They would be eating dinner soon, and that would further alleviate the gnawing, burning feeling in his stomach. The porter had just come to take their dining car reservation.

He glanced covertly at Ginger, so quietly reading in the seat next to the window. She hadn't said much all day, but then neither had he. That morning after breakfast they had even spent a few hours apart. Ginger had said she wanted to look in the hotel's gift shops when he had indicated he was going for a walk. There wasn't anger or coldness between them; it was just that there seemed to be nothing to say and it was more comfortable to be apart.

The Lake Louise weekend had been a fiasco. There was much more of a problem lying between them than he had anticipated. He hadn't realized she had been so emotionally scarred. He had thought her hesitance to sleep with him was due to her memory of his infidelity and its association in her mind with their wedding night. He hadn't known that his insensitivity toward her that night had had such a profound and lasting effect, even keeping her from other men—not that it would have made any difference to him, but he couldn't say that he was sorry about that part of it.

129

And how had he behaved last night? With anger and resentment! Well, he couldn't blame himself too bitterly. He had been horribly frustrated. It had been building all day, ever since he had seen her with the covers off in bed that morning. The day before he had managed to hold himself in check. But seeing her in that flimsy nightgown and then watching her climb the trail in that snug little T-shirt, her beautiful bosom rising and falling when she was out of breath, was too much. When she had responded to his kisses on the bench at the lake last night, he had thought everything would fall into place naturally. They had gotten along so well that he had thought the lovemaking was merely the appropriate finish and would come easily. How he had yearned for it!

It was only natural for him to become angry when she wouldn't . . . No; it was wrong of him. It wasn't her fault. He had gone about it badly, assuming too much and then moving too fast. Poor thing. He probably had done her even more damage now. And then there had been the sounds of the couple in the next room—the final, monstrous irony that had made him ready to climb the walls. He wondered what Ginger had thought.

My darling Ginger, he thought with pain. How one thoughtless, stupid, adolescent mistake on my part has scarred both our lives—perhaps permanently. If he had never been unfaithful, had their first time together not been jinxed because of it, he would have spared himself all those years of loneliness; he would have spent them with Ginger, and she might never have come to fear sex with him.

He had only himself to blame.

He's been so silent, Ginger thought, looking out into the darkness from the dome of windows in the observation car where they had gone again after dinner. He seemed to be far away from her now, lost in himself, brooding as he sat beside her, his head resting against the high back of the chair. They hadn't spoken much over dinner, and since then he hadn't even tried to make conversation. Was he giving up? Had he had enough of her high-strung emotions? Was he thinking she wasn't worth the trouble after all?

She felt tears starting in her eyes and she blinked them back. Why did she have to panic last night, she asked herself. When would she learn how to keep her emotions from escalating so quickly? If she was going to keep Devin this time—and she knew now that was what she wanted most in all the world—she would have to learn to

130

trust him again. She would have to open up to him, to respond to him. Ginger didn't think he would stay with her otherwise. If only she could give him what she had wanted to share with him so many years before, to reach ecstasy in his arms.

She glanced again at his morose profile, then looked down at her hands twisting in her lap. She could do it, she told herself. If she could just keep herself from panicking, then maybe everything would be all right between them. She would be making him happy, and that was what she wanted now—for them to be happy together so they could recapture fully the strong, warm, close relationship they had shared years ago. She had never found anyone to replace Devin, and she couldn't bear to lose him now.

Slowly and tensely she straightened in her seat, her hands gripping the ends of the armrests. "I think I'll go back to our compartment, Devin. I'm—sleepy. Are you coming?" she said, sliding to the edge of her seat and turning toward him.

Her voice seemed to break into his brooding thoughts. "No, I think I'll stay here for a while. You go ahead." He pushed himself back into his seat, making room for her to pass into the aisle.

"Oh," she said, disappointed.

"You can find it by yourself, can't you?" he asked, studying her worried face in the low light of the car.

"Yes," she softly agreed. Immediately she realized she should have said no. She bit her lip. Why couldn't she think faster! "You're sure you don't want to come?"

"In a little while," Devin said with a faint smile.

He was being patient with her now. She could tell. There seemed nothing she could do but leave as she had announced she would.

When she opened the door to their compartment, she found the porter had been there in their absence. The window shade had been drawn. The two chairs that had been there earlier were gone, apparently collapsed under the lower bunk bed, which had somehow been pulled down from the wall and ceiling along with the upper bunk.

Not knowing how long Devin would remain in the observation car and wanting to be ready when he returned, she changed quickly into her white nightgown. It was long, graceful, and rather demure even though it plunged between her breasts. It was only because it had gotten askew while she slept that it had been revealing. Ginger had never been inclined to buy herself sexy little nighties. Even this

131

one had been given to her as a Christmas present from her sister. Usually preferring one of her old pairs of pajamas, she had brought this along because it was new and pretty, in case Devin should see her in it. Now she almost wished it were a little more alluring. She needed all the confidence she could get after last night.

She brushed her teeth at the small sink on the wall opposite the beds, standing in the narrow floor space that remained now that the room had been changed to a sleeper. After combing her hair she scrutinized herself in the three-way mirror above the sink. Instead of looking warm and appealing, she appeared nervous, anxious, and pale. Oh, what could she do? Would he even want her after everything she had put him through?

She climbed the carpet-covered steps of the metal ladder to the upper bunk. Both bunks were the same, but the upper one seemed a bit more roomy with the train's high ceiling. Pulling the blanket and sheet up to her waist, she leaned back against the two soft pillows at one end. She switched on the reading lamp on the wall behind her and picked up the paperback she had been trying to read earlier.

Ginger's eyes moved from word to word in her book with little comprehension while the train clamored on at a good steady clip. There was a continuous rocking movement, with constant squeaks and rattles. She had ceased to notice it during the day, but now, waiting for Devin, it began to be all she was aware of.

An hour slid slowly by, then two. It was after midnight now, and still Devin had not returned. Ginger was desperately trying to restrain tears and chewing her nails. Had he fallen asleep in the observation car? Or had he chosen to spend the night there rather than chance another emotional encounter with her? Was it all over? Would he leave her? Did he loathe her?

She was trying to tell herself that she was getting carried away again when the sudden turning of the compartment door handle made her jump. Fumbling, she picked up the book from her lap, opened it, and pretended to be reading.

"Still up? I thought you were sleepy." Suddenly Devin was standing next to her bunk, looking up at her. The top of her mattress was at his chin level. As she looked down at him she thought she saw a touch of annoyance in his green eyes, as though he would have preferred her to be asleep.

"I—got started reading. Couldn't put it down." Her heart

132

thumped as she lied. She tried to smile, hoping to look calm and relaxed.

"The train gets into Vancouver at seven A.M. You'd better get some sleep," he said in a parental way.

"So had you. Why were you gone so long?"

"Oh, I don't know," he said with a tired shrug. With his back to her, he began unbuttoning his shirt.

His evasive answer wounded her. He was shutting himself off from her. She watched in silence as he peeled off his shirt. Because her bunk was so high, she couldn't see all of him directly. But the mirror allowed her easy glimpses of his broad, naked back, which narrowed with masculine grace to a slim waist and hips. She began to tremble slightly, the manliness of his upper body fascinating as well as frightening her. He always looked so proper and well behaved in his tailored clothes. Uncovered, he appeared quite different.

As he put his shirt on a hook on the wall, he glanced back at her and found her staring at the mirror. After looking toward the mirror himself he said, "My pants come next, Ginger. Unless you want an eyeful, you'd better read your book or go to sleep." He took off his glasses then and put them in his shirt pocket.

His warning tone was rather brotherly, as if he wanted to spare her alarm. But she also sensed a touch of impatience.

She swallowed hard. "M-maybe I want an eyeful."

He turned around at that, facing her and squinting slightly in his nearsightedness. "After the way you reacted last night, you—"

"I'm sorry about last night," she apologized in a rush. Tears filled her eyes, and she put shaking fingers to her mouth to try to quell a sudden tide of emotion.

"It's all right, darling." He moved to the head of her bed and looked up at her, putting a gentle hand on her arm. "I'm sorry, too. Don't cry."

"I'm not crying," she quickly assured him, taking her hand from her lips and shaking her head. As she looked down at his concerned face through telltale moist eyelashes, she was glad they had finally spoken of last night. "W-what should we do?" she asked, her heart beginning to pound again.

"Do?" His brows drew together slightly. "Don't worry about it all now, sweetheart," he said softly. "It's late. Just go to sleep." He squeezed her arm lightly in reassurance, then let go as he began to

133

move away. She caught his big hand in hers. He turned to her again, his green eyes questioning.

She felt so breathless she could barely speak. "Devin—p-please—s-stay up here with me tonight."

His eyes widened, then grew incandescent as he stared at her in astonishment. "Are you saying . . .?"

She nodded her head, suddenly feeling too weak to speak.

"Here? Now? Don't you think it might be better to wait awhile after last night?"

"No," she said in a whisper that was almost inaudible over the noise of the train. "I want to make things right with you now. I want us to be happy." She spoke with intensity, unconsciously gripping his hand tightly. When she realized what she was doing she self-consciously loosened her hold.

He slowly pulled his hand from hers then and, turning away, grasped the metal edge of her bed. He bowed his head. She wasn't sure what it meant. Was he rejecting her? Tremorously her finger-tips reached out to him, running lightly over his shoulder to his nape, then upward to lose themselves in the soft edges of his hair. She felt a slight reaction in his body to her touch. As her hand went to the back of his head, he turned to her again. His eyes were clear and bright with inner intensity, wondrous and frightening. She saw there all the hope and despair and longing he must have been hiding throughout the long day.

"Ginger, last night was hard enough," he said in a husky, strained voice. "Don't say you're ready unless you really are."

"I am." She leaned forward to kiss him and felt him trembling as his lips eagerly fastened onto hers. Putting his hands on each side of her face, he drew away a little.

"You're absolutely sure?"

"Yes," she told him, though she didn't feel nearly as certain inside. All she knew was she couldn't lose him.

"All right, my darling," he said with another little kiss. He moved away then and began undoing his belt. In a few moments he was completely undressed. Ginger's eyes widened with awe as she glimpsed in the mirror his strong, muscular legs and thighs and tight, firm buttocks. Suddenly feeling small and helpless, she slid down under the covers as if for protection.

Devin turned off the ceiling light so that her reading light was the only illumination in the darkened room. She watched his lean muscles ripple as he climbed the ladder. All at once he was on the upper bunk with her. Sliding alongside her against the wall, he gently pulled the covers aside, then got under them with her. She grew tense and apprehensive as she felt his large frame lying close to her, his thighs coming against one of hers through her thin nightgown. He leaned on one hip and elbow and looked down at her. Touching her face with his hand, he said, "You're getting nervous again, aren't you?"

"N-no."

"Yes, you are. Am I so frightening?"

"You look so strong and big," she tried to explain with embarrassment.

"I won't hurt you."

"I know. I'm sorry—"

He put his finger to her lips. "Don't apologize for what you feel. It's all right. We'll take it slowly, Ginger. Try to relax."

His fingertips moved over her lips and down her cheek, then his large hand cupped the side of her head over her ear, turning her face toward him as he leaned in to kiss her. She closed her eyes as his warm lips touched hers, her mind drifting comfortably for a moment with the languid sweetness of his mouth. Then the remembrance of exactly what this kiss was a preparation for broke her momentary ease. Before she had even made the smallest move, however, Devin seemed to sense her renewed apprehension. He drew his mouth from hers and looked down at her. She cast her eyes away.

"Darling," he said, turning her face to his again, "this may sound strange, but try to understand what I'm saying: You aren't all alone here, facing this by yourself. I'm here, too, with you. I'm not the enemy. Everything you feel, I'm trying to feel, and I share it with you. You and I—can be one. At last."

A faint, long-forgotten echo of the minister's words at their wedding ceremony whispered its way through her mind. Something touched her deeply inside. A tear slid from the outer corner of her eye back into her hair. As he dried her face with his fingertips, she whispered with feeling, "I love you, Devin." New tears choked her voice a bit. "I always have. I always will."

A transparent wetness shimmered over his luminous green eyes. "I was afraid I would never hear you say that to me again. Oh,

135

Ginger, I've loved you forever. I want you for my own for always. Be mine, darling!"

The rich emotion between them seemed tangible. She made a little sob as he took her in his arms and pulled her to him. His kiss was passionate, his embrace so strong that she grew limp with love in his arms even as she felt a reborn life rising within her. She wanted fiercely now to make him happy, to return all the joy his sensitive, loving words had given her. She wanted to give him herself, to enjoy as he pleased. For her own self, she thought little.

With tenderness he laid her back on the pillow. As she breathed deeply, recovering from his heady kiss, his adoring gaze moved from her mouth down her white throat to the soft rise of her bosom. Using a most gentle touch, he glided his long fingers over the chiffonlike material of her nightgown from her shoulder downward over the ascending slope of one breast. The soft, prickly feeling made her smile. Devin noticed and smiled back. His face came close and he whispered in her ear, "I want to undress you."

"Yes," she said on a breath, a feeling of eagerness coming over her.

He pushed the nightgown off her shoulders and down her arms to her waist, slowly revealing the swell of her bosom until the two rosy tips suddenly peeked out from beneath the white material. He gazed at her body appreciatively, stopping for a moment to kiss and lovingly bite one nipple. A slight electric sensation went through Ginger and she longed for more. But Devin continued pushing the nightgown downward, moving the high elastic waistband over her stomach and hips, then her thighs until it was completely off and she lay naked beside him. He gazed at the length of her, the full bosom, small waist, and rounded, sensually inviting curves of her thighs and hips.

With embarrassment at his raw gaze, she bent one knee toward the other, wanting to hide herself. But the movement exaggerated the provocatively sloping curve of her hip, and Devin's eyes kindled. He ran his hand along her smooth thigh, then his lips followed, moving upward over her hip and then across her soft stomach. Her stomach muscles contracted in quivers at each touch of his heated, moist mouth.

He looked up at her face then. Ginger's eyes were wide and perplexed. She felt jittery all over, confused by the jumble of sensations in her body and feeling unsure as to what he was going to do

136

next. She was accustomed to him caressing her breasts, but she had never anticipated what he was doing now. She had never thought a man would want to kiss her stomach and thighs.

Devin seemed to sense her state of mind, for he moved forward then, lying down on one arm beside her again as he drew the covers up over their hips. "You're so sweet, Ginger," he said, spreading light kisses over her face. "All sexy innocence!"

"*I'm* sexy?"

"You don't know that?" he asked with a smile. "You've never looked at your body in the mirror?"

"I thought I was a little too—plump. I know men like busty women, but—"

"Plump?" he said, laughing. "Maybe you don't look model thin anymore with clothes on, but without clothes—you make my blood boil!"

He moved in impulsively then with a hot, heady kiss, coaxing her mouth open to explore her more completely, his arms tightening around her as his breathing quickened. Beneath the covers she could feel his growing arousal, and she began to be alarmed in spite of herself. She tried to keep her body pliant and relaxed against him so he wouldn't be aware that she was feeling tense again, but he seemed to sense it nevertheless.

He took his mouth from hers and looked down at her, his trembling fingertips on her cheek. "I'm sorry . . . I'm going too fast for you again. It's so hard to—"

"No, Devin, don't worry about me," she interrupted. She reached up to stroke his brown hair at the side of his head. "I told you, I want to make you happy. Maybe I'll be a little nervous, but I won't be like I was last night, I promise," she said, praying she could keep her word.

"I want you to enjoy it, too," he said earnestly.

She turned her eyes away. "Maybe . . . I want to. But I won't mind if it doesn't happen now." She looked at him again. "All I want is to give you pleasure. That will be enjoyment enough for me."

He studied her with concern for a moment, bowing his head as if unsure what to say. He smiled sadly to himself, then leaned forward to kiss her with infinite tenderness.

Looking at the warm mounds of her breasts then, he brought his hand down to caress them. He noticed the slight change in her expression, the glaze of softness in her eyes and the faint parting of her lips as the warmth from his gently fondling hand spread through her body, lulling her and yet insidiously exciting her at the same time.

"You like this a lot, don't you?" he said very softly, watching her face until she looked at him.

"Yes," she whispered.

He smiled, and the low, amused, masculine sound of his voice invaded her senses. "You always did. I remember so well all those stolen kisses and caresses when our parents weren't around."

She smiled, too, closing her eyes as a luxurious feeling permeated her body through his touch. The sheets seemed to have turned to satin beneath her, and she felt as if she had drunk champagne. Without considering what she was doing, she reached up to run her fingers over the matted hair on Devin's chest. She toyed with it, then glided her fingertips to his nipple to caress it as he was doing to her. When he closed his eyes and his forehead contracted slightly in a sensual wince, she smiled again.

"You like it, too," she taunted playfully. He opened his eyes, and she saw the smoldering inner light as he gazed at her. Now instead of frightening her, it made her senses reel. Her mouth softened and her eyes grew needy. "Devin, I like it when—when you kiss my breasts," she said shyly.

His eyes opened wider, and the barest knowing grin crossed his mouth. He leaned over her and kissed a circular path around one nipple, then finished by taking the nipple itself and teasing it with his lips and tongue until it contracted into a ripe, berrylike nub. She felt her breasts swelling and growing taut under his caresses. Her heart was starting to beat faster, and her hands were beginning to feel warm and tremorous with the need to touch. As Devin moved to her other breast, she began to stroke his hair, the back of his neck, and the heavy muscles on his shoulders. Her quickened breathing caused her breasts to rise and fall against his seeking lips. She pressed his head closer and could hear his breathing thickening and growing labored. It didn't matter. She felt rather delirious.

Some part of her gradually became aware that it was very quiet around them. "The train has stopped," she said, her hands pausing in their gentle kneading of his shoulders.

Devin raised his head.

"I wonder why," she said, looking about the small room, a nuance of worry in her tone.

138

Real life was coming back. It came to her where she was—in bed with Devin in a compartment on a train somewhere in the middle of the Canadian wilderness.

Devin eyed her thoughtfully, then brought his face near hers, leaning over her. "They probably stopped on a sidetrack to let another train pass. Passenger trains give way to freight trains. No need to be concerned."

"Will we be stopped long?"

Devin smiled with adoring patience. "I don't know. You always find things to concern you that nobody else does. We don't have to get out and push," he said with a little laugh. "There's no use in us worrying about it."

"I know," she said, lowering her eyes sheepishly. She paused then, listening. "Is that the train whistle?" She listened again to a distant, low monotone that sounded and then stopped, sounded and then stopped at varying intervals.

"Maybe it's some kind of signal." Devin adjusted his position next to her to make himself more comfortable, as if anticipating this little conversation might last awhile.

"It sounds so lonely."

"Aren't you glad *you* aren't?" he asked.

"What?"

"Lonely."

She smiled and relaxed against the pillow, looking up at him. "Yes, Devin. Very glad."

"So am I. Now," he said, edging closer and smiling gently, "let's get back to the business at hand. Don't let yourself be distracted, darling. Lovemaking takes place in your head as much as in your body. You've got to concentrate!" He lightly ran his fingertips along her forehead. "Try to focus your mind on what's going on between us, on what your body is telling you, and block out everything else."

She tried to smile, but she was touched inside and it hurt a little. "You're sweet, Devin, being so patient with me. But don't be distressed if—if I don't act—well, like that woman in the room next to us last night. I have a lot to learn."

"I'm a great teacher. I'll help you," he said softly. "It's my fault that you were turned off to lovemaking. But I think we can change all that. You were doing fine until you let yourself be distracted. In a little while from now you may be crying out in pleasure just as she was."

She looked at him soulfully. Somehow she wanted to believe him. "I hope so," she whispered, touching his cheek. Her expression changed. "It's so quiet now," she said, keeping her voice low. "If we did make any noise, wouldn't the people in the compartments next to us hear?"

Devin raised his eyes to the ceiling, sighing patiently. "Ginger, Ginger," he said, shaking his head. He tweaked her nose. "Who cares if anyone hears? They don't know who's in here. You think too much!"

"You just said I should concentrate!" she said as a smile twitched at the corner of her mouth.

His shoulders shook as he laughed. "On *us*, silly! Not on everything else that may or may not be happening!"

She grinned up at him, oddly enough feeling wonderful now. This was getting to be fun. After talking and laughing with Devin she felt much more relaxed about their impending intimacy, and her apprehension was even turning into curiosity. He was so entirely different with her now than he had been on their wedding night that she had already dismissed that memory. She didn't know to what extent she would be able to enjoy what was to happen, but she felt at ease now, and for that she was very thankful.

She coyly ran her fingers down the strong column of his neck to his chest. "I'll try to concentrate, Devin. Let's get back to business."

A flame lit his eyes, and his smiling lips straightened to a firm, purposeful line. His hand settled on her lovely, full breast as he moved in to kiss her. It did not take long for his insistent lips and knowing hands to bring her to the luxurious point her senses had reached before she had become distracted. Her heart was beating a heady rhythm as his lips seductively fondled her nipples once again while one hand moved down her abdomen and under the blanket. He stroked her soft, supple stomach in circular motions, then moved his hand toward that very intimate place she had earlier tried to hide.

She gasped as a sweet arrow of intense pleasure coursed through her. With another tiny movement of his fingertips it ran through her again, making her quake. Her breathing was suddenly very erratic. "Oh! Oh, Devin!" she gasped, taking hold of his shoulders.

"Does that feel good, darling?" he asked knowingly as he nuzzled her cheek with his nose.

"Yes," she breathed as an electric pulse radiated through her again, merging now into a heightening of tension in the area below her stomach.

"Years ago you used to make me stop when I did this."

"I was—embarrassed," she said between uneven breaths. "And the—the feeling—scared me."

"Does it scare you now?" he asked gently, never stopping the magic movement of his fingers.

"A little." She edged herself closer to his body, putting an arm around his broad rib cage as though seeking protection.

"But not enough to want me to stop?" he asked as if already knowing the answer.

"No!" Her small voice had taken on a pleading quality.

He smiled then and kissed her mouth, gently at first, then more forcefully as his own passion grew. She stroked his body with her hands and arched her back so that her soft breasts pressed into his chest.

"Ginger!" he said hoarsely, as if his resistance to his own desires was weakening radically, his patience suddenly disintegrating.

Sensing this as she lay against him, she held her breath for a moment, then whispered, "Do you—want me now?"

"Oh, darling, yes!"

She had thought he would come down on top of her as he had before. Instead, he guided her to turn slightly away from him, then drew her back against his chest so that she was lying half against him and half on her side on the small mattress. She felt his thighs move along the backs of hers, then he shifted her slightly until their legs tangled together deliciously. Then came the riveting yet wonderfully comforting moment when he became one with her, her special feminine place welcoming now from his sensitive caresses.

With joy she heard his groan of pleasure as their bodies melded. His arms tightened around her, one hand stroking her breast while the other roamed restlessly over the lower part of her soft stomach and her hips.

"You feel so good!" he whispered roughly. His words filled her with pride and the confidence that she could please him. He began a rocking movement of his thighs and hips against her. In a moment a new, delightful sensation began in the lower part of her body. The muscles in her thighs began to flex in unison with his, yet moving against him in a delicious friction both within and without. One part of her was a little astonished at the feeling that was rising upward

141

through her body, while the other part was lost in pure pleasure. She could go on like this forever, she thought.

"Devin?" A little smile appeared on her face as she leaned her head against his beside her on the pillow. "I like this." She sighed.

She heard a low chuckle in his throat. "Do you?"

"Don't laugh at me," she said in an amused pout.

"I'm not, angel." He gave her an extra squeeze. "You're so damned adorable! The things you say, your beautiful body . . . the way your soft skin feels when I touch you! I'm afraid I can't take this much longer, darling."

She heard the ache and note of regret in his voice and knew he was concerned about her fulfillment. She was going to tell him again that his satisfaction was enough for her. But then a swift erotic arrow seared through her and made the words fly from her mind. His fingertips had found their way again to that small, hidden place between her thighs, coaxing wild sensations that inflamed her body and made her writhe against him in a consuming need for more.

She sensed within her also a growing anxiety for—for something. She felt a straining within her as they moved more urgently together in a heightened rhythm that had taken all-powerful control.

All at once it was becoming too much. She felt she was rushing headlong toward the edge of a tremendous cliff. She was afraid to let herself go over. She wanted to wait, to try to get a grip on herself. The relentless frenzy she was feeling was intolerable, unknown, acutely frightening.

Her hand closed over his wrist. "Devin . . ." She didn't know what to say. Her voice was small and quavering.

His low, masculine tone was soothing in her ear. "It's all right. Relax. Let it happen."

"I'm scared."

He was silent for a few moments, his movements slowing. "Do you want me to stop?" There was deep pain in his voice.

He was barely moving against her now. Every cell within her soon felt the intense loss of his masculine energy. Her body screamed with demand.

"No. No! Please . . . Ohhh . . ." She was wild with relief as he resumed. But with it there was again that torturing pressure that seemed to imprison her in unbearable tension, from which she could not escape or find release. She clutched the edge of the bed, then

142

gripped Devin's arm in agitation. Her shallow, gasping breaths began to sound like faint sobs.

"Darling, try to relax. Don't fight it. Don't be afraid."

"Oh, Devin," she moaned, beginning to weep in agonizing frustration.

But his name on her lips was drowned in a sudden, riotous rush of noise from out of nowhere that came crushing in on them. As if they were being hit by a tremendous earthquake, the metal walls of their compartment vibrated and the bed shook. The roaring permeated their senses, jangling through their bodies. All thought stopped as they simply clung to each other. Ginger felt as if they would be swept away.

"It's another train passing. It's all right," Devin said, relaxing against her after his initial startled reaction. Then his body began to shake of itself—with laughter. "Of all the moments!" he said, his voice fading into the continuing din.

The rhythmic roar from outside seemed to suspend time as the long train continued to pass. The heavy vibration mixed with Ginger's already extremely heightened tension, putting her on the verge of hysteria. She didn't know whether to laugh or cry.

"Now this shouldn't ruin our concentration, darling," Devin said, nudging her rib beneath her breast playfully. "Just because the bed is shaking—"

Suddenly the farcical unlikeliness of their situation came home to her. Her sense of hysteria was released in a convulsion of laughter. As she laughed with him, she didn't think she had ever truly appreciated Devin's sense of humor before.

Still amused, Devin kissed her cheek and nibbled her ear. He started moving against her again. His hips and thighs quickly began urging them back to that heightened sensual plane from which they had momentarily been distracted. His hands and fingers once again worked their spell on her swollen breasts and tautened nipples and at that honey-moist vulnerable place between her thighs, which now after a brief respite was supersensitive to his touch.

Outside the thundering train continued to pass. Its intense and heavy vibration seemed to become part of her, moving her incessantly forward with no chance for a backward pause. To her surprise, the deadlock within her seemed to be gone now, as if it had been broken and dispersed by their laughter.

She closed her eyes. Devin's masculine frame moving against her and his sensitive, urging hands worked like hot magic on her body. She felt herself plunging forward. Yes. Yes . . . moving, climbing. Like a train ascending a rise . . . yes! So steep . . . so wonderfully high. Oh, yes! Yes!

All at once, almost quietly, she knew she had reached the top. The deep tension below her stomach suddenly melted away. She knew then in her soul that the blessed release was going to happen. It was only a moment away—a beautiful, tiny moment . . . away . . .

Her head fell back against Devin's shoulder as she instinctively arched her back and neck. She breathed in shallow, high-pitched gasps, a counterpoint to Devin's low, eager murmurs. Their bodies strained together feverishly.

And then it happened—a violent internal explosion that shook her body and spirit. Hot stars seemed to flow through her blood, as if from a volcano. She cried out, rejoicing in it, taking equal joy in Devin's thrusting culmination of his need for her.

When it was all finished, she lay against him, her limbs growing limp against his relaxing body. A dewy glaze of moisture gave a soft sheen to her skin. It was over. She had reached the edge of the cliff, and Devin had set her soaring. How curious and wonderful that in the midst of giving him so much pleasure, he had returned it and in the process given her a most precious gift: a sense of pure freedom that she knew she had always wanted.

Her cares and lifelong apprehensions seemed lifted from her and blown away. Outside the other train had passed on into the night, she didn't know exactly when. She felt now in this peaceful moment as if her former self had sped away with that train. If she never caught up with her old anxieties again, she would be content. Her new, carefree self would stay here under the warm covers with Devin, and there she would be happy forever.

How beautiful and bright and pleased with herself she looks, Devin thought with a smile as he glanced at the lovely blonde next to him. She sat near the window as they occupied one side of a breakfast table. They had been awakened that morning in one another's arms by the porter outside their door, announcing to the people in the car that the train was running two hours late and a full breakfast was available in the dining car. Wide-eyed and startled from her sleep, Ginger had lifted her head from Devin's shoulder and looked dazedly about her. He had stroked her smooth body

144

then to reassure her. Smiling softly, she had kissed him on the mouth so tenderly it brought tears to his eyes. If he could wake up to that every morning, his life would be paradise. But no need to wish. He was quite sure that would soon be the case.

How marvelous, how sweet and delightful their lovemaking had been! He had never dreamed she could be like that. Once she got past old memories and let herself go she was consumingly sensual. A little hedonist after all these years, he thought with a secret grin. No wonder she looks so pleased with herself.

"Devin," she said, turning suddenly toward him, a new sparkle in her soft brown eyes, "the sun's so radiant this morning, isn't it?" There was excitement in her voice even at that simple statement, as if the sun had come out just for her.

Devin smiled at her. "A beautiful day."

Her eyes moved over each feature of his face appreciatively, the faintest hint of mischief coming into her gaze. He looked at her curiously. What was she thinking?

"You know who you're like?" she asked. Her voice sounded like honey.

"Who I'm like? No, not a clue!" he answered, amused at her odd question.

"Clark Kent—all neat and mild-mannered. And last night you turned into Superman."

Devin blushed. Nervously he adjusted his glasses and glanced quickly at the table in back of them, hoping no one had heard her. When he looked back at Ginger, she was watching him and smiling broadly, thoroughly enjoying his discomposure.

"Now let's behave ourselves," he admonished her in a quiet voice.

"That's no fun!" she replied. "What if we had behaved last night? What we would have missed!" A soft flame of sensuality warmed her face. "Want to know what I feel like doing when we go back to our compartment?" she asked in a provocative whisper.

"No, I don't want to know. Here, have some toast," he said, noticing that the waiter had set some on their table. He took a piece off the serving dish.

She laughed softly, the sound like a clear little bell in his ear. When he leaned toward her to put the toast on her plate, she kissed his cheek. The soft, lingering touch of her mouth created a spark within him that he forced himself to ignore. He felt heat rising to

145

his face again and was glad the waiter hadn't seated anyone across from them at their table yet.

Ginger was watching the color rise in his cheeks. "You don't know what to do with me, do you?" she teased, obviously proud of herself.

"No! Who wound you up this morning?"

"You did—a few hours before dawn!"

Devin closed his eyes. He had walked right into that one. The caressing, honeyed tone in her voice did things to him. She was positively simmering! He opened his eyes and began buttering her toast for her. Why couldn't he distract her now? Suddenly she had a one-track mind! He wished the waiter would come with the rest of their breakfast.

"Devin?" she said as he spread another lump of butter on her toast. Her voice had a breathless, secretive quality now. He purposely did not reply, but that did not seem to stop her. "Do you think anyone overheard us last night? After the train passed?"

Devin glanced in back of them again and drew a deep breath. "I don't know. But if you keep talking about it, everyone will know exactly who it was if they did hear anything! What kind of jelly do you want?" He picked up a dish containing a dozen little sealed plastic containers. Each had a picture on top of the kind of fruit flavor it contained.

"Look at this one," she said. She chose one with two peanuts pictured on it. "I never saw peanut butter come in one of these."

"Good!" he said, taking it from her and opening it. "Let's put some on your toast. Maybe it'll stick your mouth shut for a while!"

As she laughed at that, he slid the peanut-buttered toast between her teeth.

A half-hour later they were back in their compartment. Devin was glad breakfast was over. A few minutes after the peanut butter episode, the waiter had seated a rather austere-looking elderly couple opposite them. Ginger had held her tongue after that, but throughout the meal she surreptitiously slipped her hand under the table to stroke his thigh, knowing she was driving him mad.

Now she was sitting on his lap, her arms around his neck as she kissed him and teased him anew. "Why did the porter have to be so efficient," she pouted, running her fingertips lightly through the chest hair beneath his unbuttoned shirt. "Why did he have to put the beds away?"

146

"That's his job. We'll be arriving in Vancouver soon," he said, lightly kissing her chin. "There wouldn't have been enough time anyway."

"Oh, Devin," she sighed, moving restlessly against him. He could see the soft ache in her eyes. "When will we make love again?"

It thrilled him to know she wanted him so much. A surge of need filled his own body. He also began to wish that the porter had left their room alone.

"In a few hours, after we drive back to Seattle, darling. We can go to my apartment," he told her, trying to keep a tight rein on his own arousal.

"Really? Promise?"

"Promise." He watched her smile, a little shyly now. He was glad to see some remnant of her usual self. One extreme to another—that was Ginger! Two days ago he would never have guessed she would be begging him to love her now. Well, he might as well enjoy it. Once they were married, she would settle down.

"Ginger . . ." he said, pushing her away from him a little. She was ardently kissing the nape of his neck while her fingers under his shirt stroked his nipple softly. He couldn't take much more. "Ginger, we have something to talk about yet. When are we going to get married? We ought to start making plans."

A startled expression crossed her face. He noticed she quickly made an effort to hide it. "I—just got used to step one, Devin," she said in a joking way. "Can't we—wait a little while before moving on to step two?"

He thought her reaction odd. He didn't think remarrying him would be monumental for her at this point, especially after last night. But she was probably right. Maybe pressing her about marriage *was* too much for her all at once. "Okay, we'll wait. But not too long!" he said, giving her a little shake.

A light came into her eyes at his gentle roughness. Her arms crept around his neck again and soon they were lost in a sumptuous kiss.

Marla eyed Ginger curiously as she sat across the table from her the next day, Monday, at lunchtime. "You look absolutely glowing, Ginger! I assume your weekend with Devin went better than you expected?" Ginger had told her her misgivings about the Lake Louise trip at lunch one day the week before.

147

"It was *wonderful*!" Ginger softly said, breathing the last word out in a slow gush.

Marla looked a bit discomfited. "Well, are you going to tell me about it?" She sounded as if she really didn't want to ask.

Ginger, spilling over with happiness, was eager to share her joy. "We had a few problems to overcome, of course," she said with a smile. "But we worked them out—on the upper bunk on the train home!" She finished with an embarrassed but contented little laugh.

"I see," Marla said, lowering her eyes and shifting in her seat. She smiled. "Well! It was—better than on your wedding night?"

"Oh, Marla, I never would have dreamed Devin could be the way he was. He was so sweet and tender and yet so—you know, masculine and strong." Ginger's voice was soft, and her eyes had a glaze as she spoke. In her mind's eye she saw herself transported back to those hours in Devin's arms. "Then yesterday morning on the drive back to Seattle we were going out of our minds, we wanted each other so much! When we finally got to his place in the afternoon, we just—went straight to bed!" She laughed at the memory of their eagerness. "We didn't do much of anything for the rest of the day except, well, enjoy each other! He drove me back to Whidbey Island early this morning. We never got much sleep, but I don't care! Even now I wish I were with him again."

Ginger brought herself back from her private world, and her eyes focused on the dark-haired woman across from her. Marla looked strange, as if she was a little shaken. "Is something wrong, Marla? Don't you feel well?"

Marla's dark eyes were unusually clear and chastened. She made a curious, self-deprecating chuckle. "I'm fine—just green with envy, that's all! You don't have to tell me every detail, Ginger."

Ginger's cheeks reddened. "Well, *you* talk about Jack."

Marla smiled ruefully. "Not like *that*, I don't. Oh, don't take me seriously. It's just that I always harbored a—a faint hope that Devin might give up on you and notice me. I was very attracted to him and curious about what was beneath that polite exterior. You shouldn't look surprised, Ginger. I warned you! That was why I was uneasy with you awhile back. You kept insisting that you didn't want him, so I did what I could without being too obvious to try to draw him my way. Later you showed signs of jealousy, so I decided to cool it. By the time he was in the hospital with an ulcer *you* had given him, I decided it was no use anyway. He was so

148

hooked on you he never even really saw me." She paused to chuckle. "I bet he couldn't even describe me if I wasn't in the same room! So, Ginger . . . I hope you don't mind my bluntness, but a small part of me still wishes I could have shared that"—she chuckled again—"that glorious weekend with him instead of you. But I'm very happy for you. Honestly. I always thought you two belonged together, remember?"

Ginger nodded. "I remember." She knew Devin was hers, in any case. Her eyes still showed confusion. "What about Jack, though?"

Marla glanced to the side. "Yes, well . . . that's another aspect to consider, another reason why I gave up on Devin. Jack . . ." She laughed slightly and shook her head, as if something were perfectly ridiculous. "Jack wants to marry me."

"Oh." Ginger looked at Marla with sudden understanding. "And you don't want to."

"I don't know. I—he—it's so—Look at me stuttering! I don't know, Ginger, he has some effect on me. He's pursuing me. In fact, he's been a little like Devin going after you. He's always there every time I turn around—I'm getting claustrophobic! I would have thought I'd have gotten rid of him by now. But I haven't; that's what baffles me."

Ginger smiled brightly. "Maybe you're in love, Marla!"

"Who, *me*?" Marla said flippantly. But Ginger noticed her face color slightly.

"I didn't think I loved Devin anymore, but I did. I only began to realize it a few weeks ago," Ginger said. "It could be the same with you."

Marla smirked. "That would be a surprise! What about you? You and Devin are going to remarry, I suppose."

Ginger's confident expression sobered. She wet her lips with her tongue. "He wants to. I don't think I do, though."

Marla seemed almost alarmed. "Why?"

"I don't see any purpose in it. I married him once; it didn't keep us together. After being alone all these years, I don't know if I want to be married anyway. You've been happy just having an affair with Jack, haven't you?"

"But Ginger," Marla said uneasily, "I'm not you."

"How am I so different?"

"Well . . . I just never pictured you as having a long-term full-fledged affair with a man. I mean . . . gee, you were a virgin when

149

you married, you've only been deeply involved with one man in your life, and you even made sure you were still in love before you slept with *him* again! You've conducted your whole life with a lot more caution and reserve than I have. You take things much more seriously than I do. By it's very nature an affair is impermanent and undependable. I would think the idea would go against your grain."

"I learned a long time ago that nothing is dependable, Marla. Remember that conversation we had once—about women being better off going it alone? You agreed with me. Just because I love Devin doesn't mean I have to forget the lessons experience has taught me."

Marla eyed her worriedly. "I doubt that Devin's going to be happy with that. Have you told him?"

Ginger lowered her eyes. "No."

"Don't you think you should?"

Ginger's lower lip twitched slightly. "I imagine he'll get used to the idea as time goes on. We both have our careers. We can see each other whenever we want, and we can spend weekends together at the house. We have each other for love, and for sexual fulfillment. It's all I want, and—I don't see what more Devin could want. A marriage license is, after all, only a piece of paper."

CHAPTER NINE

Alone in his office, Devin tried to concentrate on the papers in front of him. But his mind wandered again to Ginger and a warmth enflamed him, making him wish she were there. In the month since the Lake Louise weekend, their lovemaking had become much more proficient and even more ardent than the first time. Some days when he worked—like today—he could think of nothing but when he would see her and love her again. It played on his mind like a fever.

And on those evenings and weekends that he did see her, she was just as eager as he, or even more so. He'd pick her up at her shop in the late afternoon and they'd drive to the house. She'd put on some skimpy little nightgown she'd bought just to please him and then she'd play at seducing him—as if she needed to! She had even dieted and started exercising so that her hips and thighs had slimmed down—not that he would have cared. But she was damned sexy now, with clothes and without!

He moved restlessly in his chair. He wished he could see her tonight. But he had to have dinner with a client in Seattle, and it would be too late after that to go to Whidbey Island and the house. She didn't want him to come to her attic apartment; Mrs. Poole might not understand. Probably not. If they were married, he could be seeing her tonight—and every night. She might have even had dinner with him and the client.

His expression grew concerned. He had thought they would be making plans to marry by now. He wouldn't have thought she'd want to continue as they were this long, keeping her relationship with him secret from her family and friends. Marla was the only one she had told. Wouldn't it be easier to marry him than to have to live with a situation that she felt would embarrass or upset others? But whenever he mentioned marriage, he always found himself discuss-

151

ing something else a few minutes later, or she would begin to touch him again and . . .

He shook off the heady thought. There was something wrong, somehow. More and more lately he had had an inkling that their relationship was going askew. The house, where he wanted to live after they married, was still bare of furniture except for the double bed upstairs they had bought. She always agreed that they should shop for more furniture, but somehow they never did. Sometimes they hardly talked at all, spending most of their time together in lovemaking. It had become almost obsessive.

Suddenly a queer feeling came over him. A light went on in his head. He was just realizing now, after all this time, what was happening. And he had let it happen! She never allowed him time to think rationally around her. Whenever he brought up marriage, she always gave evasive answers, then made him forget the question two minutes later with her caresses. Why?

He didn't really want to consider why. She *was* going to marry him! Another thought came to his mind. When he had seen Marla last week, she had asked him if he was happy with Ginger. He hadn't thought anything of the question then, but perhaps Marla could see what was going on more clearly than he. He could sense it now: Marla knew Ginger was playing some sort of game with him.

Well, he would get to the bottom of it. Tomorrow night he was meeting Ginger. Things would be a little different this time.

On Whidbey Island Ginger was on the phone with Val.

"We haven't seen you for ages, Ginger! Have you disowned us?"

"Of course not!" Ginger's smooth voice was at odds with her sudden nervousness. She had been spending every weekend with Devin instead of visiting her family.

"How have you been? Is business good?"

"Great! Everything's fine."

"The reason I called is Brian's birthday's coming up, you know. He'll be five. We're having the usual family party for him Thursday evening. You're coming, aren't you?"

"Oh . . . sure!" Ginger's expression was troubled. She didn't really want to go, but she couldn't disappoint her little nephew. Well, she would get through it somehow. She would just evade any questions about Devin.

"Good! Brian will be so happy. The kids have missed you. Have you seen any more of Devin?"

Ginger's hands grew clammy. "Yes . . . some."

"Dinner dates?"

"Yes." Ginger answered too quickly and too brightly. It sounded like a lie even to her own ear.

Val was silent for a moment. "It's more than that, isn't it?"

Ginger hesitated, growing stubborn. "What's between Devin and me is none of your business, Val," she said quietly and firmly.

"I'm not trying to butt in, but I am your sister! I'm the one who took you to the hospital to have your stomach pumped when you took those sleeping pills because of him! I care about you and I want to be sure you're happy."

"I didn't take that many pills," Ginger said, not wanting to be reminded of all that.

"I know, but I bet you thought about it. Ginger, is he the reason you never come to visit us anymore?"

Ginger moistened her lips. She wished she could lie better; now she was forced to tell the truth. "Yes."

"Is it serious?"

"What is it you want to know, Val?" she asked testily. "Whether or not we're sleeping together?"

Silence. "I think I know." Val's voice dropped acquiescently. "Otherwise you wouldn't keep yourself so totally from us—not even a phone call in the past month."

Tears came to Ginger's eyes. She didn't know what to say.

"You love him that much?" Val asked gently.

"Yes," Ginger said brokenly.

"Are you going to marry him again?"

Ginger sniffed back the tears and said in a more controlled voice, "No, I'm not. I intend to stay single."

"You're not? Are you going to have some kind of long-term affair with him?"

"Lots of people do that nowadays."

"Not in Coupeville."

"I don't live in Coupeville anymore! It's my life, Val. I don't need anyone's approval for what I do."

"Yes, I know that," Val said with a sigh. "I suppose you love him so much you'll take whatever he's willing to give. I just wish things were different. Will you be all right?"

"I'm perfectly all right," Ginger assured her sister, not bothering to mention that Devin was pushing for marriage. "Devin is really very tender and sweet."

"Well, I'll try to keep this from Mom. It may be hard. You know how she asks questions."

"Just like you," Ginger said.

It was mid-afternoon on Tuesday, the next day, when Ginger found herself growing restless for the time to pass more quickly so Devin would come and they could go to the house. She hadn't seen him since the weekend and she longed for his touch. She needed him so.

How her life had changed since they had become lovers! Instead of one day being much like any other, now her life was divided into the ordinary days and the days she saw Devin. Now there was always something to look forward to; now there was a meaning and a brightness to her life.

She had changed in other ways, too. She had lost some weight and gained some muscle tone with jogging. Devin had shown her the proper way to run and the stretching exercises to do before and after. She felt she had extra energy now, and she looked better. Instead of dawdling around the shop, she now spent her time there more efficiently. The place had never been so organized and spick-and-span. All because of Devin. She yearned to please him. She wanted him to keep on wanting her the way he did. It was when she was in his arms that she felt most vibrant and alive—in his arms in their bed at the house.

She smiled as she picked off a thread that had fallen on her blouse from the woven place mats she was arranging. How odd it seemed now that she used to try to hide her well-endowed figure. Now she was glad she had curves! Sometimes she wondered how she compared to the other women from Devin's past. She hoped she had as much to offer him as they did. Sometimes lately she also began to wonder if he would have been as attracted to her now if she were still very thin, as she used to be. He had strayed then. He said that had happened for other reasons, but . . .

Well, there was no use worrying. She apparently had what it took to keep him now. At least he keeps coming back for more, she thought with a grin.

She heard footsteps at the door then and turned to greet her customer. She saw the portly figure of her mother walking in, her expression thunderstruck, followed by Val, whose face was wreathed in apology.

"Mom asked if I had talked to you about coming to Brian's party and . . ."

Ginger nodded grimly, understanding immediately that Val had not been able to keep Ginger's secret.

"She insisted I drive her to Langley to see you," Val added in a subdued voice.

"I thought I'd better talk some sense into you before the rest of the family sees you! Carrying on so shamefully with *that* man of all people! Have you lost your senses, Virginia? I'm just beside myself! I can't believe you'd behave the way you are. Didn't I bring you up better than that?" Martha Cowan's voice was growing choked with emotion.

Ginger closed her eyes. Why did she have to go through all this? She had been so happy a minute ago. And Devin would be here in an hour or so. She didn't want an argument with her mother to make her nervous and spoil her time with him.

She opened her eyes and tried to remain calm. "Let's go into my office. I don't want my customers walking in on this," she said with distaste.

"I can understand that!" her mother said, pushing past her to lead the way toward Ginger's office.

When all three had entered the small back room, Ginger closed the door, leaving it slightly ajar so she might hear any customers coming into the main room.

Ginger sat down behind her desk. "Look, Mom, I'm going to be twenty-nine in a few weeks. It's been a long time since I needed your permission for anything! If I want to have an affair with someone— anyone, even Devin—I will!"

"I can't imagine what's in your head! It's bad enough you're acting like some common harlot—but why with *him*?" Her mother was shaking now with a mixture of sorrowful tears and anger.

Ginger's face reddened at the word her mother had used. "How dare you speak that way to me! It's not like that at all. I love him and he loves me. There's nothing *common* about our relationship at all!"

"If he loved you, he'd marry you, you stupid girl!" Martha exclaimed, pointing a shaking finger at her.

155

Ginger was amazed. "I would have thought marrying him again would be the last thing you'd want!"

"If you're going to go on sleeping with him, I'd rather see you properly married! Of course he isn't the man I would choose. But you wouldn't listen to me anyway. Since you've decided to get mixed up with him again, to chance ruining your life once more, you might as well try to use some common sense! If this 'relationship,' as you so prettily call it, was legal, at least you'd be protecting yourself a little. You'd have some rights under the law. Can't you see he's just using you?"

"What you're mainly concerned about, Mother, is what your neighbors will think if they hear of it! I can take care of myself. I happen to think a woman is better off remaining single. Devin and I love each other deeply, but we don't happen to want to get married. And you'll just have to accept—"

A low voice interrupted her. "What do you mean, *we* don't want to get married?"

Ginger paled as she looked up into Devin's narrowed eyes across the room, where he stood half in and half out of the partly closed door. He stepped into the room then and shut the door behind him. "Sorry to interrupt this cozy family gathering, but as long as I'm here, I might as well join the conversation, since it concerns me, too," he said, staring steadily at Ginger.

Ginger's eyes lowered contritely. Oh, God, she had done it now, she thought. If she hadn't been so distracted with her mother she might have heard him come in. It had been hard enough avoiding the subject of marriage with him. She didn't want to confront him about it; she'd kept hoping he'd forget the idea once their lives had fallen into a pattern, but he hadn't. And now he'd caught her in a half-lie about it.

His voice made her raise her eyes again. She found him addressing her sister. "Hello, Val. It's nice to see you again," he said with a cordial grin that showed a hint of tension.

Val hesitated and then said hello. Her eyes dropped to his immaculate gray three-piece suit and silk tie, then up to his handsome, clean-shaven countenance with its innate steadfast quality. "You haven't changed much," she said in a complimentary way. Her eyes shifted briefly to Ginger, an odd light in them as if she was beginning to understand, or perhaps remember, why her sister was so profoundly attached to this man.

156

"I have and I haven't," Devin said with a small, enigmatic smile. His clear green eyes came to rest then on Martha's careworn face. Ginger noticed there were tears in her mother's eyes and that she looked away when his gaze met hers. It was as if the feisty older woman was having trouble facing him. For once she was mute.

"I happen to agree with you, Mrs. Cowan," he said in his smooth, engaging manner. "I'm sorry, but I overheard a good deal of what was said. I think you're perfectly right—she ought to marry me! It was what I wanted in the first place. In fact, I've repeatedly tried to get her to set a date for the past month. But she always—changes the subject!" He gave a telling glance at Ginger. "It's curious she didn't mention that to you."

Ginger opened her mouth but found nothing to say. Heat rose along her slender neck. She felt as though she were being made to stand in a corner like a child. She had told a lie, and Devin was intent on punishing her. The feeling of suddenly being alienated from him made her want to cry.

While Ginger stared fretfully at the top of her desk, Martha found her tongue again. "Well, Virginia?" Her quavering voice demanded an explanation.

"This is between Devin and me," Ginger said belligerently, not raising her eyes to look at anyone.

"She's right," Val said quietly. "We should go, Mom. Come on." Taking her mother's arm, she urged her toward the door. Devin stepped aside. As they passed him, Martha Cowan did something quite unexpected: Reaching out, she placed her hand on Devin's sleeve and gave his arm a squeeze. Saying nothing, not even looking up at him, she let go and walked out behind Val.

Ginger saw it all and felt a little betrayed. "She really loves you, you know," she told Devin softly when the others were gone. "She always said you were like a son to her. That was why she was so bitter when . . ."

"She had good reason," Devin said. He approached Ginger's desk and looked down at her. "Now: What did you mean by telling them that *we* don't want to get married?"

"I—didn't feel it was necessary to tell them everything about us."

"That doesn't answer my question. You know *I* want to marry you. And you've never told *me* that you didn't want the same thing."

157

Ginger bit her lip. She had no explanation. She could hear the anger rising in his voice.

"Let's make it simple: Do you intend to marry me?" he asked.

Ginger put trembling fingertips to her forehead. "Please, let's discuss it later. Seeing my mother always upsets me. Let's—go to the house?" Her eyes lifted, childlike, to his. "I'll feel better when we're alone together there."

Devin stared down at her. "You've answered my question. All this evasiveness means you *don't* want to marry me!"

She rose from her chair and rushed to him. Clutching his lapels, she said, "Don't misunderstand, Devin. I love you—more than anything! I couldn't live without you now. I love you desperately!"

"Then why not marry me?" he asked, making no move to touch her.

She looked up at him pleadingly. "Devin, we have everything now that we would have if we were married. I—I've gotten used to being single. I wouldn't know how to be a wife anymore. I like things the way they are. I don't see what's so wrong with that."

Devin looked away from her. She could see he was deeply troubled, and it pained her. He took hold of her hands and slowly lowered them from his suit coat. In a deadened voice he said, "All right, let's find someplace to have dinner and then go to the house. We'll talk some more then."

Dinner in a local sandwich shop was a solemn occasion. Neither seemed very hungry. They drove to Double Bluff Beach then in silence. Ginger kept wondering what he was thinking, how angry he was. She had to find some way to pacify him, she told herself.

When at last they reached the house, they walked in and Devin turned on the lights. He went into the living room and pensively looked about him.

"Devin?" she said, following him in. She took his arm.

"Look at this place," he said. "It isn't much different from the first time I saw it. It has a couple of folding chairs and the fireplace has been used a little, but that's all. I thought by now this would be our home, that we'd be living here together."

"It—it is like our home," Ginger said.

He glanced at her sardonically. "I don't know what your definition of *home* is, but I always thought it meant a comfortable place with furniture that you came back to every night. What this is is an empty trysting place!"

158

"W-we can buy furniture, Devin. I was too busy to—"

"You thought if we bought furniture, there was only one step left to take, and you didn't want to get that close to marriage. I don't know why I didn't realize it all sooner. Your behavior over the past month is stunningly clear to me now."

She put her arms around his waist and pressed her forehead to his shoulder. "You make it sound like I've been trying to trick you. I haven't. I just—"

"You just were never straightforward enough to tell me you didn't want to marry me! Why?"

"I was afraid you'd be angry," she said in a small voice that was muffled by his jacket.

"Angry or not, it was something we ought to have discussed!"

"I was afraid of losing you," she whispered brokenly. A tear streamed down her cheek, and she reached up to wipe it away. She looked at him through wet eyes. "I love you so much."

His face softened. "Then I don't see why you won't marry me. I'm not expecting you to play the perfect housewife or anything. You can go on as you have been, running your store. But we could live here together, see each other every day, come home to each other at night . . ."

"I—I could live with you here."

His face lightened for a fraction of a second, then his eyes narrowed. "You mean live together without being married. No, Ginger! I want a wife, not a mistress. I want something permanent and stable and legally binding. When I take you to meet clients I don't want to have to introduce you as my lady or my companion or whatever euphemism is currently used. I want to say you're my wife, damn it!"

Again Ginger had no reply.

"Why did you tell your mother you think a woman is better off staying single? I've been single all these years and I don't see anything so great about it. Are you afraid of a commitment?"

No answer. Ginger felt as if she couldn't think.

Devin's searching expression altered. "Or—are you afraid of trusting me? Are you afraid I'll be untrue again? I promise you, Ginger—"

Her bowed head came up. "No!" she rushed to say, not letting him finish. She didn't want him to think that. "No, I believe in you, Devin. Maybe it's because—when we were young everything went

159

along fine between us until we reached the point of marriage. Then it fell apart. Everything has been going fine now, and—why take a chance of spoiling it? Maybe marriage isn't right for us."

"What kind of cockeyed logic is that?" he said with heated impatience. "Besides, everything isn't fine right now!"

"Because we're discussing marriage," she retorted. "Devin, I don't see why we have to rush things. We haven't been back together that long. There's plenty of time to get married if—if we want to. Shouldn't we both be sure?"

He sighed, long and quietly. "I suppose so," he murmured grudgingly.

She relaxed a little. She had won! A smile crept into her eyes, and she ran her hands over the vest of his suit. "Let's forget it for now, darling. We have other things to do."

His eyes fixed on hers resentfully. "Make love?" he said in a voice tinged with sarcasm.

"D-don't you want to?"

"It's all you ever want to do! Isn't there some expression that says there's more to love than making love?"

She took an unsteady step back from him. Once more her expression wavered on the point of tears. "I—I thought you enjoyed—"

"Of course I enjoy it! But sometimes you behave as if that were the only reason for us being together. Sometimes you don't seem to think about anything else!"

Ginger put her hands over her face and turned away from him. His words had cut her deeply. All she had wanted was to please him, and now he was ridiculing her! How was she supposed to behave? What did he want?

"Oh, don't cry," he said with annoyance. "You always get so emotional!"

"I'm sorry I've become such a bother!" she said in wounded anger, her voice choking. "If you don't want to be with me, then leave me alone!" She turned and ran up the stairs to take refuge in the bedroom.

She was lying facedown across the bed, sobbing, when she heard his voice and felt the sinking of the mattress as he leaned over her. "I'm sorry, Ginger. I shouldn't have said those things." She felt his gentle hand stroke her hair, then move down to massage her shoulder. "Don't cry. I love you and I want to be with you."

Her sobbing faded. She pressed a wet cheek to the quilted bedspread, facing away from him, trying to steady her convulsive breathing. She felt his long fingers push her hair back from her face. His lips and warm breath touched her cheek.

"Do you want to make love, angel?" he asked softly, his voice a caress.

New tears of relief started in her eyes. Unable yet to speak, she nodded yes.

He held her quietly in his arms for a few more minutes until her intense emotions had calmed. They undressed then and got under the covers together.

When she first felt his touch on her body in the darkness, she thought everything would be fine now. But even though they were so close, she gradually sensed a distance between them. She used everything she had learned over the past month to please him, and he responded with his usual sexual ardor. But even as she held his surging body tightly in her arms, meeting his passion with every ounce of her own, still there was something missing. An ethereal, spiritual aspect she had not been aware of before was gone, and she was only aware of it now because of its absence. They had not quite become one this time, except in body. Something was missing. Something was wrong.

When it was over they instinctively drew away from each other instead of falling asleep in one another's arms as they usually did. As he turned his back and his warmth drifted away from her in the darkness, she pressed her face into her pillow. She had thought she had learned to use the enticements of her body to keep his love strong, but now she knew she was failing. Even that wasn't enough for him. Whatever it was she had lacked at the time of their marriage, she apparently still did not have. Her pillow grew damp with silent tears as she asked herself: What did he need that she couldn't give? Was she losing him again?

She was nervous early the next morning as he drove her back to Langley before returning to Seattle. When he dropped her off at Mrs. Poole's house, he took her hand and said, "I'm going to come up to the house this Thursday afternoon after work. I'll take Friday off and we can spend a long weekend at Double Bluff. We need to have a lot of time together to talk things through. Is that all right with you?"

Ginger nodded. "Of course. I'll close the shop." But she hesitated

161

as a thought came to her. "Thursday evening Val's having a birthday party for my nephew. I promised I'd go."

"That's okay. You'll be back later that night?"

"Probably about ten or eleven." She thought of adding, early enough for us to make love, but somehow it no longer seemed appropriate. There was a heavy sense of serious deliberation in his manner. It made her look ahead to the weekend with foreboding.

CHAPTER TEN

Ginger was still at the shop about five o'clock Thursday when Val phoned. "I'm afraid we have to cancel the birthday party, Ginger," she said. "Brian's been coming down with something all day. I kept hoping we could still have the party, but he's got a fever now, so there's nothing else to do but postpone it."

"That's a shame," Ginger said sincerely. "I hope it's nothing serious."

"I don't think so. I'll let you know when he's better."

Ginger closed the shop for the weekend then and went to her attic apartment. She changed into navy slacks and a white sweater. As she picked out some extra clothes to take with her for the long weekend, she wondered if Devin was on the island yet. It occurred to her that she could call, but she was hesitant to do that. The closer the time came to see him again, the more of a sense of trepidation came over her. She knew he would want to discuss their marrying again, and she didn't want to. Now more than ever she thought marrying him was a bad idea. Already he was tiring of her emotional nature. And she hadn't been able to make him forget everything but her when they were in bed last time, as she felt she always had before. She feared their relationship was beginning to fail. If she married him, wouldn't the tedium of daily life together only make things worse? Why didn't he see that? Or perhaps he did. Maybe what he wanted to discuss this weekend was whether they should go on seeing one another.

She paled. Oh, dear God, have I lost him already? Tears started in her eyes, and she forced herself to get a grip on her emotions. It couldn't be that bad yet, she told herself. She was letting her thoughts run away with her again. He still loved her. He told her so just before he made love to her two days ago. And if their lovemaking wasn't quite the same, it didn't have to mean that their relationship was over. How ridiculous she was!

Now she was annoyed with herself. She went into the kitchen and washed a few dishes she had left in the sink. She checked her refrigerator then and noticed that there was some casserole left from yesterday. She decided to have it now for supper. Devin wasn't expecting to have dinner with her, so it wouldn't matter. And she wanted the extra time to pull herself together completely before seeing him again.

By the time she was on the road leading to Double Bluff Beach it was almost seven thirty. She turned onto the small road behind the row of homes that gave access to each house. When she reached their house, she saw two cars in the driveway—Devin's Mercedes and a white Datsun. The Datsun looked familiar. Marla had a car like that. Ginger looked closer and saw the emblem of Marla's real estate agency in the back window.

That's odd, Ginger thought. Neither Marla nor Devin had mentioned that there was any further business to discuss about the house. In fact, the closing date had been almost two weeks ago, and Devin was now the legal owner. Why would Marla be seeing him? A queasy feeling came over Ginger. And why would Marla be there at the very time Devin knew Ginger was supposed to be away in Coupeville? He still mentioned Marla from time to time—Marla had said this or that, he would tell her. Ginger hadn't thought too much of it since she and Devin had become lovers. Perhaps she ought to have.

She wondered with a sick, nervous feeling if she ought to go in and face them, to find out exactly what was going on. But what if it was perfectly innocent? Then she would have made a fool of herself. And if—if it wasn't innocent? Could she face it?

She chewed her fingernail. There were no lights on in the house, but it hadn't gotten dark yet outside. She thought of peeking in through a window, but the idea made her feel even more ill. She had more pride than to stoop to that.

Perhaps she was making too much of all this. She knew it was typical of her to do that. She didn't know much about real estate; maybe there was some reason for Marla to see Devin. Or maybe she had been in the neighborhood and merely stopped in to say hello.

After a few more minutes of looking at the house and deliberating, she decided the best thing was to drive back to Langley, wait a couple of hours, and come back again. That way she wouldn't embarrass herself by walking in on them whatever the circumstances. Most likely it was all perfectly innocent and Marla would be leaving soon. If not—well, she would think about that if it happened.

After driving back to her place she watched a little TV and thumbed through some magazines for an hour, her mind on neither activity. She began to grow more and more edgy then and started walking restlessly from one small room to another. When an hour and a half had gone by and it was after nine, she decided she had let enough time elapse.

As her car wound through the darkness toward Double Bluff, her increasing nervousness gave her a floating, slightly dizzy feeling. She kept telling herself she was being ridiculous. But when at last she reached his house again, she saw that she wasn't. A clammy, sick coldness froze her as she saw Marla's car still there. From the back the whole house looked dark, including the bedroom upstairs. As she gazed at the upper side window, she remembered Marla telling her that she had wished it could have been she who had spent the weekend at Lake Louise with Devin instead of Ginger. Hot tears scalded her eyes. How clever of Marla to disarm her suspicions with all that honesty! How stupid she had been to confide in such a friend! Marla suspected there were serious problems developing between Ginger and Devin, and she knew just when to move on him. *I'm very happy for you. Honestly! I always thought you two belonged together* . . . Marla's false words burned through her brain.

And Devin was certainly not blameless. He and his promises to be faithful! He wasn't capable of it. They had both betrayed her! And now Devin was lost to her . . . unless . . . Could it be she was still mistaken, that whatever was going on in there was blameless? It seemed unlikely, but she had no proof either way. And she didn't want to walk in and find out. She felt very insecure sitting in her car out there in the darkness. What if one of them looked out and saw her? It would be best to go home again and think what she should do next.

A short while later she was sitting tensely, hunched over her small kitchen table, her hands over her eyes. Silence enveloped her. Inside she felt tied in knots. Lies. Had they both told her nothing but lies? How could they do it? She loved them both—

165

The shrill ring of her phone shook her. Immediately on edge wondering if it might be one of them, she hurried to answer it.

"Hi, Ginger, how are you? It's Jack," came the friendly voice at her anxious hello. "I was just calling to see if Marla was over visiting you tonight. Is she?"

"N-no, she's—not," Ginger replied with great hesitance, knowing where Marla was.

"Oh." He sounded disappointed and a little worried. "The other day she had said she'd probably be free tonight to see me. But she hasn't come by or even called me. I phoned her office and they said she quit about seven. There's no answer at her home number."

Ginger's lips trembled slightly. She didn't want to tell him, knowing he would be hurt. And she felt curiously ashamed, too; Devin had apparently forsaken her for another once again. But Jack ought to know, oughtn't he? "I drove out to Devin's house earlier this evening," she began. "I—saw Marla's car there. I wasn't sure what to think, so I left and went back again about a half-hour ago. Her car was—still there. Do you suppose there may have been some business reason for her to meet Devin?"

There was a long silence on the other end. "She never said a thing to me about it," Jack finally replied in a heavy voice. "But she doesn't like to tell me her comings and goings—seems to think it's none of my business," he said tightly. "How long has she been there?"

"Since seven thirty at least. I had told Devin I'd be in Coupeville tonight, but I just learned this afternoon I didn't have to go."

"Interesting. But I thought you weren't worried about her and Devin."

"I wasn't, but—that may have been foolish of me. Marla's told me several times that she found him very attractive. She used to say that if I didn't want him, she'd be happy to take him. And when I returned from a trip to Lake Louise with him, when—he and I became lovers, she said she envied me, that—she wished it could have been her." Ginger bowed her head as she spoke, her eyes growing glassy.

"That seems to make everything pretty clear, doesn't it!" Jack sounded angry, fed up. "Well, there's only one way to find out for sure what's going on!"

"W-what are you going to do?" Ginger asked.

"Drive out there! Want to come?"

166

Within ten minutes he had picked her up and they drove to Double Bluff Beach. When Ginger pointed the house out to him, he stopped the car. Eyeing Marla's Datsun, he quickly got out, slamming the door behind him. Not waiting for Ginger, he walked across the small backyard to the door and pounded on it. Ginger got out but stayed near the car, shaking.

As Jack was giving the door a second pounding, it opened. Ginger saw Devin and heard their voices.

"I want to see Marla, MacPherson!"

"Marla? Sure, she's here. Come on in," Devin said as Jack barged passed him. Devin walked away from the door, leaving it open as he followed Jack into the house. He hadn't noticed Ginger. Through the open door she could see lights on in the living room, which faced the beach. Like a nervous animal, she waited and watched for a few minutes, then couldn't stand not knowing any longer.

She reached the back door, which opened into the kitchen. As she walked in, she could see Jack and Marla arguing in the other room. Devin was watching them, his expression disturbed.

"I don't owe you any explanations!" Marla was saying. "We've just been sitting here talking and having coffee. What excuse do *you* have for pounding the door down like that?"

"I had reason to believe there was more going on between you two than just talk. I won't embarrass you with some of the things Ginger told me. I just want to make it clear I'm not going to put up with this anymore!"

Marla paled slightly but did not retreat. "I'm not going to put up with you trying to keep me on a leash! If I can't even spend an evening talking with a friend who happens to be male—"

"What were you talking about?" Jack asked, folding his arms over his chest as if daring her to make some reasonable explanation. "Interest rates?"

"We were talking about Ginger!" Marla said hotly. "Not that it's any of your business! Since I'm her best friend, Devin has often asked me for advice about some of their problems."

Jack looked at Devin. "So you just invited her over for some coffee, since Ginger was going to be away for the evening?" Jack's eyes were like red coals. "Is that how it was?"

"Marla called about seven and asked if I'd be home so she could bring over a housewarming gift from her agency—that candle centerpiece by the fireplace," Devin answered with tethered patience as he pointed toward the decorative creation of a candle and artificial flowers. Ginger could get just a glimpse of it behind Marla. It was similar to those she had once seen in a large box in Marla's home.

"When she got here,. I offered her some coffee and we got to talking. Ginger and I have been having problems, and . . ." Devin left off with a mute gesture of his hand.

Jack seemed to have quietened. "I see."

"And what prompted you to come here like this?" Marla asked angrily.

Ginger edged back behind the kitchen wall and closed her eyes. No one had seen her so far; she wished she would never have to see any of them again. Her rambunctious emotions had caused her to misjudge everything, embarrassing Marla, Jack, and Devin, not to mention herself.

She heard Jack's voice: "Ginger saw that your car's been here all evening. I happened to call asking if she knew where you were. I was stupid enough to have gotten worried about you. She told me, and together we assumed the worst. But from what you told her in the past, Marla, I'd say the assumption wasn't out of line!"

"Ginger's supposed to be in Coupeville!" Devin said.

"That was canceled or something. She's here with me, out in the car."

Some last shred of pride impelled Ginger to step forward, make her presence known, and face what was due her. As she moved back to the doorway she was almost knocked down by Devin rushing through into the kitchen, no doubt on his way outside to the car.

"Ginger!" he said, grabbing her almost savagely by the shoulders. "What the hell is the matter with you?" His voice was raw with anger.

"Devin!" Marla exclaimed, hurrying toward them. "Don't be upset with her. It was a natural conclusion. She didn't know."

Devin didn't seem to hear Marla. "How could you assume that I would do something like that? With your best friend! Don't you have even one drop of faith in me? After all these weeks am I still banging my head against the wall trying to get through to you?"

"I—I'm sorry, Devin." Ginger's voice was weakened by the strength of his arms gripping her.

"Sorry!" he shouted at her, his voice growing hoarse.

"Devin, calm down!" Marla said. She pulled at one of his arms to loosen his hold on Ginger. "This isn't going to help! You won't convince her to believe you this way!"

Devin let go but continued to glare at Ginger. "Maybe I'm tired of trying to get her to believe me, damn it!"

Marla looked exasperated. "You just spent two hours telling me how much you love her!"

Devin's furious eyes turned on Marla. "So what! I tell *her* that over and over and it doesn't seem to sink in. She's afraid to marry me, she seems to think she's got to dazzle me in bed to keep me, and now at the first slightly questionable circumstance, she immediately assumes I've been unfaithful! I know I *was* unfaithful once, when I was stupid and immature, but isn't it about time she forgot that?"

Ginger turned and leaned her forehead against the doorframe, crying into her hands.

"No woman completely forgets something like that!" Marla snapped. "She has to learn to accept and live with it, and maybe Ginger hasn't quite reached that point yet. You know her even better than I, Devin. All you need is patience."

"Maybe I haven't got any left!" Devin moved away from them into the middle of the living room.

Ginger heard the decisive tone in his resentful voice, and a deep sob wrenched through her. She had lost him, and it was no one's fault but hers!

"It'll be all right, Ginger," Marla said softly, touching her shoulder. "I'm sorry this happened. I can see why you thought . . . I know it's partly my fault. You shouldn't take me so seriously."

"Yes, it is your fault!" she heard Jack saying curtly to Marla. "I want to talk to you. Let's go. These two need to work things out for themselves."

"I'll go when I'm ready!" Marla retorted.

Ginger took her hands from her wet face, even more distressed to find that Jack and Marla were still angry with each other—all because of her.

"Jack," Ginger said, "I'm sorry. Don't—"

"That's all right," he told her. "I'm glad it happened! I've learned something tonight." He turned to Marla. "We'll go *now*!"

Marla's lips tensed and whitened slightly. "I'll talk to you later, Ginger. Don't worry, everything will work out, I'm sure," she told her friend. She followed Jack then, rather contritely, into the kitchen and out the door.

Devin was standing stiffly in the middle of the living room with his back to Ginger. Her legs weak and quivering, she moved toward him.

"I'm sorry for what I thought," she said, standing at his elbow, looking up at his rigid profile. "You know how I overreact sometimes. I'll try not to be that way anymore. I promise—I'll be better!"

"You'll never trust me, will you?" he said. His eyes were distant and bleak as he looked out the window at the black sea. "Like Marla said, you'll never be able to forget. That scar will always be with you, undermining your trust. That's why you won't marry me, isn't it? You just didn't want to admit it to me."

"No . . . I don't know, Devin. I'm upset and mixed up now. All I know is I love you. Please try not to be so angry with me. It hurts."

"Does it?" he said, his voice as empty as the room they were standing in. "I'll tell you what hurts me—making love to you when there's no commitment between us; not knowing how long you'll stay with me or when some groundless suspicion will make you turn away. I can't go on like this, Ginger. It was hard enough regaining your affection. When you said you loved me, I thought everything would be fine from then on. But I was wrong. If I can't win back your trust, you'll never marry me. What else is there for me to do? Nothing."

There was a deep hopelessness in his manner and aspect. Slowly he turned away from her and began to walk toward the kitchen.

"Devin," she said, clinging to his arm, "it's not so bad as that. Where—where are you going?"

"I'm leaving."

"No, Devin, no! Don't go!" She tried to grip his arm more tightly, but he kept moving toward the door and she was merely pulled along with him.

"Why should I stay?" he said. "There's no future for us! Why prolong what will end soon anyway? I'd rather be miserable by myself."

"Of course there's a future for us!" Ginger insisted, beginning to cry again. With all her strength she pulled back on his arm as he walked through the open back door outside. "Devin, please!"

"What future? Meeting you in this empty house weekend after weekend until you suspect I'm having an affair with some other woman? Then go through all this again? That's no life for me! All I want is to be married, live quietly with my wife, and pursue my career. The trouble is," he said as he blinked back the glaze over his reddened eyes, "you're the only one I've ever wanted to be my wife. But that's *my* problem." His expression was defeated. "You're happy being single; I guess I'll have to be, too!" He reached his car and opened the door. Ginger still clung to him. "It's best if we just stop seeing each other."

Ginger felt as if the earth were falling apart. "No, Devin!" she cried, choking on her sobs. "I can't live without you! Don't leave me again! Please stay! No. Please!"

"Let go!" he said, trying to pull away from her grasp.

"No!" When he pried her hands loose from his arm, she threw her arms about his waist. "Don't leave me! I've never loved anybody but you!" Her desperate eyes looked up at him wildly. "I'll live with you—here—or in Seattle if you like! We would be happy! I promise I won't be suspicious. I'd trust you!"

He gripped her shoulders and tried to push her away. "You're hysterical!"

She tried to calm her voice. "No, I'm not. I mean it! I—I don't want to be single, not really! I'll live with you—anywhere you want!"

"I told you I want a wife, not a mistress!"

"All right!" she cried. "I'll marry you, then. Anything you want —I'll do it! Just don't leave me!"

He stared down at her in the dim light of the moon for a moment as if wanting to believe her, but then his eyes went dark. "You're just saying that because you're upset and would tell me anything. Tomorrow you'd change your mind."

"No, I wouldn't!" Her voice begged him to believe her.

"You would. You wouldn't tell me you had, you'd just find excuses to put off setting a date!" He pried loose the grip of her arms around him, then took her upper arms again and pushed her away roughly. "Even if you did actually marry me, you'd never trust me!"

"I would! I promise I would!" She fought to cling to him, but he kept her at bay.

"It won't work, Ginger. There's no hope! I want to get out now, before I go mad running in circles with you! I've already got an ulcer. I can't put up with any more!"

With those words, flung at her in a distraught voice, he got into his car, shut the door, and locked it. Ginger seized the door handle, calling his name through the closed window in an anguished voice. He started the motor. Even as the car began backing out she ran alongside it, her fingers pulling on the handle in a death grip. "Devin, don't go!" she shrieked. "I love you!"

As the car backed sharply into the street, she was forced to let go. It zoomed away then, Devin facing forward with icy determination as if not daring to give her a glance. Ginger ran after the Mercedes until it turned onto the main road. She stopped then, feeling faint and out of breath, her heart pounding in her chest as she saw the back lights disappear into the darkness.

She put her hand to her mouth to stifle her sobs. There was silence all around. If any of the neighbors had heard, no one came out to investigate. Stumbling as she walked, she slowly made her way back to the house, feeling numb. When she reached the back door, she went in. Somehow she closed the door, for she had no feeling in her fingers. Then, with a long, heartrending sob from her throat, her legs buckled beneath her and she crumpled softly to the floor.

Some time later she lifted her head, not knowing how long she had been lying on the floor semiconscious and weeping. The wall clock read eleven. She pushed herself unsteadily to a sitting position. Her hair was disheveled, her sweater and slacks were rumpled, and her face was completely white except for her stricken, red, swollen eyes.

He's gone and he'll never come back! The words swam in a singsong in her head. Why? How? Why couldn't she keep the only man she could ever love? How could she live? She needed his love for sustenance. Without him her life was a vacuum—empty, meaningless, devoid of—

Wait! Was that a car in the driveway? Yes! She heard the motor stop on the other side of the door. Devin! He's come back! He didn't mean it!

She scrambled to her feet and opened the back door. But looking into the dark yard, she saw Marla's Datsun, not the Mercedes. And then Marla was rushing up to her.

"Ginger! You look terrible! What happened?"

Ginger began shaking violently. "Oh, Marla, he's left me! He'll never come back . . ." She fell into convulsive sobs on her friend's shoulder.

172

"Don't be silly!" Marla said soothingly, though there was a hint of alarm in her voice. "Come on, let's go inside and sit down."

Half-supported by Marla, Ginger was led back into the kitchen. Marla shut the back door and walked with her into the living room. She eased Ginger's limp body onto one of the folding chairs, then pulled up the other chair to sit near her.

"Stop crying and tell me what happened!"

Ginger choked back her tears. "He said I'll never trust him—and —and I'll never marry him—and he's had enough. He—he doesn't want to see me anymore. He got into his car and drove away—and I don't know what I'm going to do, Marla!" Her voice rose on the last sentence, a prelude to another wave of sobs.

"What you're going to do is pull yourself together. He'll come back!"

"But, Marla, he said—"

"He was angry because of what happened. He had even been upset earlier when he was telling me you wouldn't marry him. It's all we talked about for two hours—what he could do to convince you to be his wife. He couldn't understand why you didn't want to. Frankly, I can't either."

"I lost him before," Ginger said, brokenly. "I guess I knew it would happen again. I couldn't stand to go through another divorce."

"But Ginger, he told me once he never wanted your divorce."

That made Ginger pause. "Well, what else could I have done after he'd been untrue?"

"Tried to forgive him?" Marla suggested.

Ginger mutely lowered her eyes.

"Well, there's no use rehashing all that. You've got a new set of problems now. If you're going to hold onto him this time, Ginger, you'll have to marry him!"

Ginger's chin trembled. "But—when he was walking out, I told him I would! He said I was hysterical and didn't mean it." She bowed her head, pressing her hand hard over her eyes as if physically trying to stop the flow of tears. "Oh, Marla, I wish I weren't so emotional. I think that's why he's tired of me."

"He's *not* tired of you! Your emotions are getting in the way of your perception," Marla said.

"Well, what should I do?"

"Marry him!"

"But he left—"

"He'll come back! Don't think twice about it."

Ginger's eyes widened, and for the first time there was a faint gleam of hope in them. "You honestly think so?"

"Of course, Ginger. I never saw a man whose every thought revolved around a woman as much as Devin! It gets to be downright tiresome sometimes. I've never talked with him for more than two minutes on any other subject! By the way, that's"—Marla lowered her eyes—"that's why I came back. I wanted to explain to you that Devin and I have been meeting every so often, to talk about you. It started when we were working on the papers for the house. He asked about you and discovered I was your friend, so I let him pump me for information. As I told you, I had mixed feelings back then. I did it because I thought you two should be together, but I also didn't mind being available in case things didn't work out between you and him. As I said, I gave up that idea pretty quickly! What Devin told Jack about what happened tonight was exactly the truth. I wanted you to be sure of that, Ginger. I'm sorry. I've behaved rather carelessly—it's typical for me. And I guess I shouldn't have been so truthful with you that day at lunch!"

Ginger smiled palely. "It's okay. I'm sorry I dragged Jack into all this. I feel I've caused a problem between you and him."

"The problem was there. It's just come to a head."

"Is he still angry?"

"Yes," Marla said with a tired sigh. "He—wants to end our affair. He says we can still be friends, but he doesn't want to be involved with me anymore. I'm too undependable, too much of a free spirit for him."

"But he wanted to marry you," Ginger said with sorrowful eyes.

Marla's faint smile had pain in it. "Yes. The one time he brought it up, I laughed! I don't think I'll be hearing any more from him on that subject."

"I'm sorry," Ginger murmured sincerely.

Marla tilted her head to one side in a wistful manner. Her light tone was slightly at odds with her expression. "I'm not! I'm not ready for a ball and chain. And besides, I can get him back if I want to." She shifted her dark, bright gaze to Ginger. "And that's what you've got to think about Devin!"

Ginger sadly shook her head.

"Oh, Ginger! You've got all the strings! All you have to do is pull them!" Ginger looked at her as if she were speaking a foreign tongue. "All right," Marla said with a little laugh, "why don't you just try to get some sleep now? Tomorrow you'll see things more positively. Maybe you should take something to help you sleep. I have some pills at home. I'll be glad to go get—"

Ginger was suddenly sickly white. "No!" She took a breath and tried to steady an onset of dizziness. "No, I don't want any pills."

Marla looked at her with new concern. "Are you all right? Would you like me to stay the night with you?"

"No." Ginger tried to smile. "Thank you, but I'll be all right. You have to work tomorrow. You'd better get a good night's sleep at home."

After a few further assurances from Ginger, Marla left. Ginger was alone again. It was midnight. She walked aimlessly through the house, her mind still confused but slowly clearing. It was Marla's mention of the sleeping pills that had made her want to get a grip on reality.

No more hysterics, she was telling herself. No repeat of the past. For the first time she realized there was a sense of self-preservation within her. It must have been present years ago, too, for something had kept her from swallowing the remaining pills in that bottle. And somehow she had survived after that, through the divorce, through rebuilding her life and finding a career. Something within her had wanted to live and had given her the strength to cope.

She paused for a moment in her pacing to look out the window at the dark beach and ocean. She shouldn't be saying to herself that she couldn't live without Devin. It wasn't true. She had for eight years! Even if she never saw him again, she would exist somehow.

But she would just be existing, as she had been over those years without him, she thought. Restlessly she turned from the window and wandered back toward the kitchen. Just existing. A sense of despair came over her again.

She kept wandering from one room to the other for the next couple of hours, sometimes sitting down for a few moments, then getting up again. She wavered between despair, grim acceptance of life without Devin, and, sometimes, small flashes of hope.

It was during one of her times of despair when she was in the kitchen that her eyes happened to fall on a bottle on the kitchen counter. It was Devin's prescription. Her immediate concern was that he was without it and might need it for his ulcer, since he was upset. And then she thought, He might come back for it! At the least, it gave her an excuse to call him and tell him he'd left it, and perhaps . . .

She glanced at the clock. It was after one, but he might still be up, like she was. Her heart started pounding. She considered, she argued, she encouraged herself. After about fifteen minutes of intense and anxious inner deliberation, she went to the phone and dialed with icy hands. Panicking at the first ring, she forced herself to grip the phone more tightly. But it was no use. It rang ten times, and no one answered.

Now she was ridden with a new anxiety. Where was he? He had had plenty of time to get home. Was he ill? Was he somewhere in need of help? Or was he just driving around, as she was pacing from room to room?

There was nothing she could do, she told herself as she sat down tensely on a folding chair. And no reason to panic, she reminded herself. Devin was a grown man. He could take care of himself. Indeed, he could take care of her, too. Such good care . . .

Oh, was Marla right? Could she get Devin back? Did she hold the strings, whatever that meant?

Maybe she could. He had come back for her, hadn't he? He'd pursued her against all odds. Why would he give up now? Maybe he *was* just angry. And even if he didn't come back, she could seek him out. She could start pursuing him if necessary! Yes! She could do what he had done—be persistent and never take no for an answer. He never had said he didn't *love* her. He was just giving up because she didn't trust him and wouldn't marry him.

And why wouldn't she? It all boiled down to her high-strung nature: Her emotions made her suspicious, and her deep fear of being rejected by him kept her from giving the marriage a chance. Was she going to go through her whole life being afraid of what might happen? Hadn't she learned anything yet?

She had an almost physical sensation of everything coming together within her. For once she felt whole and positive and hopeful—all by herself, too, without Devin there to bring it about. Oh, she had been stupid! But maybe it wasn't too late. If—no, *when* she saw Devin again she would very calmly tell him that she did want to marry him, that she was no longer afraid of making a commitment to him. And she would say it in a quiet, adult manner, so that he would know she had thought it all through and her decision wasn't the result of hysterics.

Now she was eager to talk to him. If she could just tell him all that, everything would be all right. She could feel her heart rate accelerating. Too eager, she told herself. She oughtn't let herself go up like a kite, either. Getting him to believe her might take some time, and she needed to be prepared for that. Just keeping herself on an even keel was going to be hard work for her. But she would improve. She was determined!

Hour by hour she grew more calm and positive. By the time dawn was gradually lightening the sky outside, she had come up with a small variety of strategies, all very rational and well thought out. As she gazed out the window at the sunrise, she listed them in her head. Plan A: She would call Devin again about eight and tell him he had left his medicine. If he didn't answer, she wouldn't get upset. She would call again later. He'd have to come home eventually. If he answered but didn't want to speak to her, then—Plan B: She'd drive to Seattle and see him. She'd have to call Marla and ask her to drive her home to get her car, then—

A noise interrupted her thoughts. Someone was opening the kitchen door! Turning from the window abruptly, she looked across the room into the kitchen. Suddenly there stood Devin, tired, pale, his eyes intense as he stared back at her.

"Devin!" She smiled, a light wash of tears springing to her eyes as she ran to him. "I'm so happy to see you!"

She eagerly took hold of his hand with both of hers, but he seemed not to notice. He glared down at her, careworn yet rigid. "Did you mean it when you said you'd marry me?"

She wanted to gush, Oh, yes! Oh, yes! But she bit her lip and restrained herself. "Yes. I'll marry you. As soon as you like." In spite of her pounding heart, she sounded almost businesslike.

His reddened eyes widened slightly behind the thin-rimmed glasses. He looked baffled. "G-good! Well, then . . ." As if reestablishing his bearings, he walked pensively toward a stool at the kitchen counter and sat down.

"Are you feeling all right? Do you need to take some of this?" she asked, picking up his bottle of medicine.

He eyed it distractedly. "Yes, I do . . ." he murmured.

"Want some water with it?" she asked solicitously.

"Never mind that now! We have things to settle first. We're going

177

to get married as soon as we can—in two or three weeks!" He looked at her sternly, as if waiting for an argument.

"Fine."

"I want this house put in order. While we're waiting, I want you to set your mind on decorating it and making it livable. I'll help, but you know more about that kind of thing than I do."

"All right, Devin."

He eyed her uneasily, as if things were going too well. "The last thing is that I'm not going to sleep with you again until we're married. I don't want you going back to the idea that an affair is just as good as marriage!"

She swallowed and looked down. This wasn't so easy to accept. She felt she might need his reassurance . . . No. Hadn't she gotten over the idea that she had to have his love proven through sex?

"Okay. We'll wait," she said. "Now, Devin, my ultimatum to you is"—she held up the bottle—"you'd better take this before you say another word! I don't want our wedding postponed because you're back in the hospital!"

His hard expression melted into a smile. He took the medicine. Then he said, "Did I walk into the right house? Is this the same place I left last night?"

Ginger grinned, her face shining now. "Same house, slightly different woman."

"I thought so. Not too different, I hope," he said as he put his arm about her waist and drew her to him.

She draped her arm over his shoulders as she leaned against him. "No. I just realized I'd get through crises better if I didn't let myself panic all the time. It may take awhile, but I'll improve. Maybe you won't need that medicine anymore then," she said, blinking back wetness from her eyes.

"That's as much my fault as yours. I'm emotional, too. I just keep it inside, where it does damage."

"Where were you? I tried to call . . ."

"I drove around for a long time. I had intended to go home, but when I got to the ferry, I realized I didn't really want to leave the island. So I drove awhile and then finally I came back here. I parked in the public lot down the way and just sat on a log on the beach for the rest of the night, thinking. At daybreak I decided to go in and talk to you—give it another try."

"You mean all this time you were just a few hundred yards from here?"

He leaned up and kissed her. "How far do you think I could go from you?"

The wedding was a simple ceremony held in a judge's office in Seattle. Jack and Marla were there as witnesses. None of the Cowans or MacPhersons came—neither family had any idea the wedding was taking place. Ginger felt it would only complicate matters, and Devin agreed. He was taking no chances upsetting Ginger's equilibrium. After the morning ceremony they had celebrated with Jack and Marla at the finest restaurant in the area.

As Devin and Ginger were driving back to their house on Double Bluff Beach afterward, Devin had to admit to himself that Ginger had surprised him. She had apparently never had one moment of reconsideration. Plunging herself into the project of decorating the house, she had redone the whole place, except for the carpeting. New wallpaper, new furniture, new linens and tableware—she had meticulously coordinated them all. When he had seen the place briefly in the middle of the week, it was beginning to look like a layout in an interior decorating magazine.

But that was Ginger. She never did things halfway. Though she was calmer now than he had ever expected, he sensed her throwing herself into the decorating job was a replacement for the sex he had been denying her. She was still worried about pleasing him, he feared. Now she was trying to be the perfect wife.

She had been a trifle nervous during the ceremony that morning. But she didn't cry. She had gone through it quietly, looking a little pale at times. He, on the other hand, had had trouble repeating the vows, he had been so choked up! And Marla had gotten out her handkerchief to wipe her tears and blow her nose. Jack had looked thoughtful. But Ginger just let it all pass in front of her, it seemed. She had been unusually quiet during the brunch afterward, too. Not unhappy, just as if she didn't quite know what she was doing there. No, Devin thought, sneaking a sidelong glance at his lovely wife, there was still something not quite settled. He supposed she'd always have her little mysteries for him to solve.

Ginger laughed lightly as Devin carried her over the threshold of the house. He put her down in the kitchen and, keeping her close,

179

kissed her warmly. She allowed it briefly, then pulled away and said eagerly, "The hutch and dining room set were finally delivered yesterday. Want to see?"

Taking him by the hand, she led him to the corner of the large living room that was set aside as a dining area. The dining room set was colonial, as was the rest of the new living room furniture. The hutch displayed the tea set Devin had bought at her shop months ago, and some other items she had brought over from Ginger's Spice.

"Looks great, darling!"

"So . . . the house is finished now. I hope it'll be okay," she said nervously.

She had felt peculiar and a little lost all day. Having been single so long, she didn't quite know what, as a wife, she was supposed to do or how she was supposed to behave. All through the ceremony she was keenly aware that she was entering a whole new phase of her life, and suddenly she had felt she wasn't sure what lay ahead of her. She had had a time within herself, trying to keep from panicking. Well, she had gotten through it, and the dinner, too. But what was supposed to happen now?

"You've done a beautiful job Ginger," Devin was saying. "I'm proud of you!"

A warmth stole through her at his praise. She lowered her eyes and smiled.

He tilted her chin up with his fingertips. "How come so shy all of a sudden?" His voice lowered. "Afraid of the marriage bed, little bride?"

She felt herself blushing for some unknown reason. She tried to laugh but then turned away in confusion.

Putting his hands on her shoulders, he made her face him. "What's all this?"

"I don't know," she said, looking down in embarrassment. Really, she *was* acting silly.

"Because we haven't made love for so long, you're anxious about it?"

Worry creased her forehead. "Last time . . ."

"Last time I was upset because I was afraid you'd never marry me. It'll be different now." His hands moved caressingly to her waist. "Why don't we go upstairs and I'll show you?"

Her eyes flared with a rare light as something ignited within her—the old passion she had come to know at his touch. But they were married now. It seemed odd, somehow. He had said repeatedly that he didn't want a mistress. He had made a derogatory comment once about how she had constantly tried to dazzle him with sex to keep him. It was true; she had. But what did he want now? Should she be different?

She went with him upstairs to their newly furnished bedroom. Walking to the maple dresser, she began to take off the small, expensive pearl earrings Devin had given her as a wedding present. She was wearing a beautifully tailored off-white suit whose woven material had flecks of light brown. She had bought it especially for today, along with a Victorian-style antique white silky blouse that was trimmed with rows of wide, elegant lace running in a V pattern over her bosom to her waist. They had stopped at a photographer's briefly before the dinner for a wedding portrait, and she had worn the blouse without the suit jacket then.

As she set down the earrings, Devin came up behind her, gazing admiringly at her in the mirror. He helped her slip off the suit jacket and put it aside.

"I love this blouse, Ginger," he said as his hands came up to her shoulders. "I think it must be the sexiest thing I've seen you wear!"

Ginger was a little horrified. "My *wedding* outfit? But I'm all covered up."

"Maybe that's why. You look so feminine and soft. Classy!" His eyes took on a glimmer as his hands moved lightly downward over the lacy front. "There's something totally devastating about the way the lace drapes over you." The delicate, filigreed material covered and yet accentuated her breasts demurely, provocatively. "I had trouble keeping my hands off you at the photographer's. All through dinner, too!"

His hands were moving over her breasts, lightly ruffling through the loose, rich lace. Ginger felt his touch through the material. Her nerves began to come alive with electricity. Watching him touch her in the mirror added a tantalizing dimension to her growing excitement. His hands looked dark and masculine against the lace. A warm shiver ran up her spine.

"Devin . . ." she said softly. She turned toward him, wanting more. But as she gazed up at him, she smiled, then reached and took off his glasses and set them on the dresser.

He blinked slightly as his extraordinary green eyes refocused on

181

her. With sly amusement he said, "Are you changing Clark Kent into Superman?"

"I hope so." She had wanted to hold back and let him take the lead this time, since he had implied that she was too eager with him. But she couldn't keep herself from leaning up to kiss him. Immediately his arms swept her against him, and she was reassured of his equal passion. Her arms reached up around his neck as the lace and her breasts were crushed against his chest in his strong embrace. His warm mouth quickly grew hot as his lips moved insistently over hers. Her lips parted under the pressure, and he tasted the sweetness of her mouth.

His mouth broke away from hers then and moved heatedly along her tender jawline to her throat, kissing her at the edge of her high lace collar. "Oh, Ginger," he said roughly, out of breath, "I've had a terrible time keeping away from you these past weeks. I thought our wedding day would never come. I want you so badly, I—If you aren't in bed with me in the next few minutes, I think I'll disintegrate!"

Her moist eyes sparkled with fire as she smiled her assent. She loosened his tie and pulled it off, then began unbuttoning the vest of his light gray suit. Devin, meanwhile, with warm and eagerly tremorous fingers was searching in the thick lace for the tiny buttons that ran down the front of her blouse. When he did find them, the tight little buttonholes made it difficult to free the buttons.

"I love this blouse, Ginger, but these buttons may put me in a mental institution!" he mumbled impatiently.

She laughed and said, "Let me."

As her delicate fingers deftly undid one button after another starting at the collar, Devin watched, all the while slipping off his suit jacket, then his vest, then his shirt. He stood mesmerized in front of her then, his broad, muscular chest rising and falling with each increasingly labored breath as he watched the lace flounces pull apart, revealing Ginger's deliciously voluptuous curves. She was wearing a low-cut lace bra underneath, which was also soon revealed as her hands undid the lower buttons of her blouse.

Devin's eyes were intense, hot embers. When she finally looked up at him, her job finished, she was almost frightened. He looked like he was ready to devour her. Even the hard muscles in his upper arms and shoulders were flexing slightly. But his fearsome appearance enflamed her. The fact that she could bring this reaction from

182

him made her heady, and she had learned to enjoy her power during the weeks they were lovers. Now she reveled in it again. She wanted to provoke and intoxicate him even more—she wanted to bring him to his limit, make him mad with desire if she could. Let him accuse her of behaving like a temptress; they both liked it and he knew it!

Running her hands lightly, enticingly over her breasts, she slowly pushed aside the lacy blouse. She let it slip off her small white shoulders and with tantalizing little shrugs let it fall from her arms to the floor. With a demure smile then, as if unaware of herself, she turned her upper torso slightly to undo the side opening of her skirt with both hands, knowing that the movement of her arm across her body enhanced her cleavage.

As the skirt fell from her waist, she was suddenly grasped by masculine arms. Devin's lips seared the soft mounds of her flesh above the semitransparent bra. "Oh, Devin," she gasped with pleasure, bringing her fingers up to tangle in his thick brown hair.

"You drive me wild!" he said, lightly biting her shoulder and neck. "You damn well know it, too, don't you? You little siren!" His feverish fingers found the clasp of her bra at the back. All at once she felt the delicate material loosen from her body. Her breasts were suddenly free and it made her quiver in anticipation. Her tremulous fingertips moved up his chest, lightly running through the masculine hair. The strong hands at her back pressed her hard against him. Her sensitive nipples felt the roughness of his chest hair as her firm breasts flattened slightly against him.

"Devin!" she cried urgently, clinging to him. "You're so strong . . ." She felt like swooning, so enraptured was she with the feel of his powerful body enveloping her.

His hands moved possessively, caressingly over the smooth skin of her back and then at the sides of her breasts. "You're so soft!" he murmured almost incoherently. "I need you now, angel. I can't —"

His voice was interrupted by the ringing of the telephone by the bed. Its shrill sound startled them both. "Oh, no," she said, her voice aching. "We don't have to answer it."

"No!" he said, kissing her. But the ringing persisted. After the ninth ring Devin said, "Damn!" and after another ring, "Maybe it's someone from my office. I'll get rid of them!"

Annoyance in every movement of his manly body, he strode over to the nightstand. "Hello? Yes, this is Devin . . ."

183

Ginger didn't listen much. She felt as if her whole body were throbbing with ungratified need. Wanting to make some progress, she slipped off and stepped out of her half-slip. Next she eased off her pantyhose and then her panties.

Suddenly she realized Devin was saying something about their having gotten married that morning. His tone had grown warm and friendly. Then he said, "We'd like to see you, too, Val!" Ginger was taken aback at the mention of her sister's name. Suddenly feeling naked with her family's presence on the phone, she picked up her blouse. Meanwhile Devin was saying, "Sure, that would be fine! I'll tell Ginger. See you then!"

Devin turned to Ginger with a broad smile. "Your sister and her family want to come over and congratulate us. She got this number through Mrs. Poole. Val was very happy to hear we're married. I thought it would be nice if they shared part of the day with us. You don't mind, do you?"

"No," Ginger said, feeling as though someone had just pulled the rug from under her. "W-when?"

"In a couple of hours. I thought that would give us enough time to—finish what we started," he said with a grin.

"Oh. Two hours? I—I really ought to vacuum the rug downstairs. I didn't have time yesterday. I had to fix the hem of my skirt. And I have to straighten up up here." She looked with horror at their clothes strewn about the floor. "And there's not much to offer them in the refrigerator . . ."

Devin was standing there laughing. "You know, you sound just like a wife!"

"That's what you wanted," she said with annoyance. "You want me to keep a nice home, don't you?"

"I'm not complaining," he said as he walked over to her. He took her by the hand and led her toward the bed. "But the rug looked good enough to me, it'll only take a minute to pick up our clothes, and we can all go out to eat. There's no problem."

"But . . ." She felt confused.

"Ginger, who are you eager to impress? Your sister or me?"

"Well . . . you."

"I thought so." He smiled gently and touched her face. "When are you going to get it into your beautiful head that I love you just for you. You don't have to work at keeping me pleased or happy— or entertained. I'm not going anywhere this time, darling. I looked

184

around for eight years and I never found anyone who held a candle to you. You're stuck with me!"

Warm tears of happiness, of feeling wanted and loved came into her eyes. She sniffed softly. "I just thought I should vacuum the rug, that's all," she murmured sheepishly. She melted against him as he took her in his arms.

"First things first, angel!" he said against her blond hair, humor in his voice.

"*This* comes first?" Her eyes indicated the bed next to them.

"You better believe it!"

Okay, she thought. She could live with that. Smiling up at him, she began to take off the blouse she had loosely thrown on again.

"No," Devin said, his hands coming up to fondle her breasts through the sumptuous lace. "Leave it on. I like it."

He finished undressing himself and pulled her down with him onto the bed. Leaning over her, he gently pushed aside the lace limply covering her bosom, exposing again the delightful pink tips of her breasts. His mouth eagerly took one nipple. Ginger gasped with pleasure at the erotic sensations his hot lips and tongue teased from the sensitive rosy nub. He moved to the other breast then. Expertly using his hands and lips, he quickly brought back the urgent passion that had flamed between them a few minutes ago, before the phone call.

Soon she was arching her back, pressing her chest against him. Her hips began to move in an age-old rhythm, impatient for the delicate touch of his fingertips at her secret feminine place. "Ohhh . . ." she gasped as a hot electric sensation coursed through her veins at the first slight touch of his hand. Her restless fingers caressed him with equal sensitivity and ardor until his breathing was heavy and uneven, until he said in a husky whisper, "Ginger, I need you— now!"

Her soft thighs welcomed him eagerly. She and Devin became one—one body, one mind, one spirit. Truly one! She was deeply, joyously aware of it even at the rapturous point of consummation of their new marriage, and afterward in the sweet bliss of spent desire.

She knew now it would be that way forever.

For more information
visit: www.speakingvolumes.us

For more information
visit: www.speakingvolumes.us